ANGEL PEAK

Western Stories

Other Five Star Titles by Peter Dawson:

Dark Riders of Doom
Rattlesnake Mesa
Ghost Brand of the Wishbones

ANGEL PEAK

Western Stories

PETER DAWSON

Five Star
Unity, Maine

Further copyright information can be found on page 256.

Five Star Western
Published in conjunction with Golden West Literary Agency.

June 1999

First Edition

Five Star Standard Print Western Series.

The text of this edition is unabridged.

Set in 11 pt. Plantin by Al Chase.

Printed in the United States on permanent paper.

Library of Congress Cataloging in Publication Data

Dawson, Peter, 1907–
Angel peak : western stories / by Peter Dawson. — 1st. ed.
p. cm.
ISBN 0-7862-1572-0 (hc : alk. paper)
1. Frontier and pioneer life — West (U.S.) — Fiction.
2. Western stories. I. Title.
PS3507.A848A82 1999
813′.54—dc21 99-19830

Table of Contents

The Sweetest Draw

Jonathan Glidden published all of his fiction under the *nom de plume* Peter Dawson, a name originally given him by his agent, Marguerite E. Harper. "The Sweetest Draw" was completed in August, 1936, and it was sold to *Cowboy Stories* on November 4, 1936 for $112.50. Street & Smith had purchased *Cowboy Stories* from Clayton Publications which ceased publishing it in December, 1932. *Cowboy Stories* began publication by Street & Smith with the November, 1933 issue, and F. Orlin Tremaine, who came along from Clayton House, remained its editor through 1936. This was the fourth Western story Jon Glidden wrote, and his previous story, "Lawman of Latigo Wells," had also been sold to *Cowboy Stories*. Although Tremaine wanted more Peter Dawson stories, it was not to be. The next Western fiction by Jonathan Glidden sold to Street & Smith was bought by the more prestigious and better-paying *Western Story Magazine*. Incidentally, a gunfighter in "The Sweetest Draw" is named Cliff Farrell, a Western author who had been a regular contributor to *Cowboy Stories* when it was owned by Clayton Publications and one whom Jon Glidden admired. As with the other Western stories in this volume appearing in book form for the first time, the text that follows was prepared from Jonathan Glidden's original typescript.

I

The muffled shock of the crushing explosion beat out across the still night air and rattled every window in the town of Three Rocks. Rand Rivers, sitting beside Joan Fields on the porch of her father's house, saw through the gloom of the dimly lighted street the mushroom of dust that suddenly boiled out from the front of the bank.

He was on his feet the next instant, saying sharply: "Get your father, Joan. It's the bank!"

He jumped the porch railing and vaulted the gate. Behind him he heard Joan Fields calling to her father, and then from ahead came the staccato burst of a six-gun, lancing purple flashes out of the cobalt shadows beneath the awninged walk across from the bank. The hammering hoofbeats of hard-ridden horses echoed out from the alley, and a group of riders swung into the street, far down, and raced out of town.

Cries blended in with the other sounds. Men poured out of Thompson's Place, some stopping abruptly in the dusty street to whip shots after the fleeing riders, others mounting horses at the hitch rail to wheel and string out in pursuit. In two minutes the street was emptied of every saddled animal, and, as Rand Rivers stopped short in front of the livery stable, breathless from his running, all he could hear was the far-off hoof din as the hastily formed posse sped away into the distance.

Old Harper, the stable owner, appeared at Rivers's elbow and said: "By the time you got saddled and goin', they'd be beyond Three Mile Creek, Rand. Better go up and see what happened at the bank."

"Was the sheriff along?" Rand asked.

"Hell, no!" Jed said shortly. "His mare's still in her stall. Does he ever go along?"

Rand shrugged and turned about, heading for the crowd that was already gathering up the street. His stride was brisk for a man who has been raised to the saddle; he was shorter than many, yet his hundred and seventy pounds, well-muscled over a broad frame, made up for his lack of height. His wide face, with keen blue eyes under a thatch of sandy hair, was steely as he pushed his way through the crowd and edged past the man who had officiously kept the curious out of the bank. After he had stepped through the jagged opening in the plate-glass doors, he saw that two people were already inside—Joan Fields and her father.

Someone handed a lantern in to Tom Fields, who then walked through the litter strewn across the floor and entered the yawning cavity of the vault. The light threw an elongated shadow of his spare frame along the boards when he emerged a half minute later.

He said hollowly: "They got everything! About fifteen thousand and some negotiable bonds. They didn't have time. . . ." His words ceased abruptly as he stared at a man who had just stepped through the doors.

Sheriff John Walters was drunk as usual. Even an inexperienced eye could have told that, as he stood there by the door, swaying unsteadily, staring vacantly about. A dirty gray shirt open at the throat showed his thin, corded neck below an unshaven chin.

He cleared his throat uneasily and said: "The boys'll catch 'em, Tom. I thought I'd better hang around and. . . ."

The fury of Tom Fields's low-spoken words cut into the sheriff's drawl: "Get out, Walters! Get out before I break every bone in your mangy carcass."

The sheriff's eyes widened at this outburst. As he felt the potent menace in the words, he stumbled backward, out through the door, and lost himself in the crowd.

Joan turned to her father. The lantern light played across her regular features and made a misty radiance of her chestnut hair. "Is it serious, Dad? Is the bank . . . ?"

"We've got it insured, Joan," Fields said. "But until we get some law enforcement in this town, we won't be able to take out any more insurance. Thank heaven we're going to elect a new sheriff in two weeks."

"And a new deputy," Joan added, looking at Rand Rivers.

Tom Fields gave Rand a pointed glance and said: "Rand, if you'll do things just the opposite of John Walters, you'll be the finest lawman in Arizona."

The posse straggled in at two o'clock that morning, horses sweat-streaked and dust-covered. Three riders rode double, and, when they had dismounted to confront the crowd in front of Thompson's Place, the leader explained: "They had a couple o' rannies forted up in the rocks at Miller's Pass. Shot three of our bronc's. They got clean away. We'd have been damn' fools to ride through there with those rifles cuttin' down on us."

An angry murmur ran through the crowd. Someone spoke up: "Any idea who they were?"

"Not much," the man who had spoken first answered. "Some say it was Druro Cain and his wild bunch. I'd bet my last dollar it was Steve Bassett who killed our horses. There ain't another man I know who can sling lead that accurately in the dark."

"You've got Steve to thank for not killin' you instead o' the jugheads, then, Bill."

"Sure! That's what makes me so certain it was Steve. He's not a killer like Cain, even though he travels with him."

Rand waited around another ten minutes before he went to the livery stable, saddled, and rode out of town toward his cabin. On that five-mile ride, that took him up into Green Valley, he pondered over the night's happenings, fully aware that in two weeks he had a real job cut out for himself. Everyone knew that Jim Williams would be elected sheriff and make Rand his deputy. Then Three Rocks would need some taming. And in another two months Rand and Joan would be married. As he thought of Joan Fields's refreshing loveliness, he knew that she was what he wanted above all else.

II

Steve Bassett shifted his six-foot frame nervously in the saddle, while he let his glance run over the boulder-strewn slope ahead that climbed on up to the towering rimrock. Not a living thing showed as his gray eyes squinted into the reflected sun glare that beat down into the basin.

He turned and spoke to the man beside him: "Slim, we were damn' fools to agree to meet Cain here. For two thousand he'd try a bushwhack."

Slim, one of his long legs thrown carelessly over the saddle horn, shrugged his narrow shoulders and said easily: "You're seein' spooks, Steve. Druro Cain can't do without you. Our coverin' his getaway last night was worth the two thousand split he agreed on. He'll have savvy enough to bring it."

Slim's glance hung on Steve as he finished, noting the stiff erectness of his friend's figure. He saw, too, that Steve's right hand, ungloved, ran nervously over the holster at his thigh, as though anticipating something that would call for the use of his black-handled revolvers. A frown was written on Steve's high forehead, and the sun wrinkles at the corners of his eyes webbed deeply across his face. That face was long, with a jaw that slanted out to a strong chin. Slim knew Steve's wariness; he had come to depend on it.

"I don't get this." Steve flung his left arm outward, indicating the sheer wall of rock ahead. "There's a hundred places up there where a man might hide. I don't trust Cain."

Slim grinned. "Neither do I. . . ."

Crack!

The shot slapped out across the stillness to chop off Slim's words. The man jerked spasmodically, clutched frantically at his chest, where a small crimson spot already spread across his shirt.

Steve moved instinctively on the heel of the sound, drove steel to his gelding's flanks, and slumped down along the off side of the saddle. As his startled animal lunged, he reached out and belted Slim's horse. Steve flashed a look backward and saw Slim, clinging grimly to the saddle horn, while his chestnut shied and followed Steve's horse.

The two animals had pounded a hundred yards down the basin before Steve straightened into the saddle again. Hardly had he gained his seat once more when a crushing blow from behind took him in the left shoulder and threw him sideways. The sound of the shot cracked out the next instant. Then another.

Once more Steve looked back at Slim. His tall, rawboned friend was riding close behind the gelding's flying heels, his face drawn in pain, and an unbelieving stare fixed straight ahead. Steve's glance shuttled toward the rimrock to his left, caught the faint smudge of powder smoke that drifted out from the lip of the rim. As he watched, two more shots barked out, and a bullet whipped the air ahead of his face.

The gelding slogged up out of the draw, hit the sage-studded level sand, and swung into a racing run that soon put a full mile behind them. Only then did Steve rein in, swinging around to head off Slim's horse. He took one look at the blood smear across Slim's chest and knew the awful truth.

Slim looked briefly behind, spoke, and his words brought telltale flecks of blood to his lips: "They're boilin' down off the rim, Steve. You high-tail, and I'll hold 'em back. I'm cashin' in." He reached back for the rifle slung in a scabbard behind his leg.

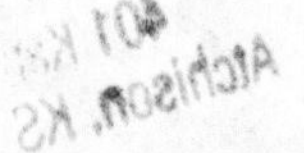

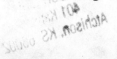

"If you stay, I stay," Steve said, his voice holding a finality.

"Damn you, Steve!" Slim blurted out, eyeing the plume of dust that now mounted up at the foot of the rim. "Two miles over there is broken country. You can make a getaway."

"So can you," Steve retorted, knowing that this was the only way of pulling Slim away from his purpose. "Hold somethin' over that hole in your guts and ride! We'll lose 'em in twenty minutes."

Slim cursed feebly, then smiled. But he could not keep the pain from showing in his eyes. "All right, hardcase. But you're wastin' time nursin' me. Better tie up your shoulder," he added, as he wheeled the chestnut and led off across the heat-shimmering sand to where broken outcroppings showed two miles ahead and to the right.

Steve followed, feeling of his shoulder for the first time. His hand came away bloody. He untied his bandanna, bound it around his shoulder as best he could. He looked back and saw that the riders behind were gaining. A sudden nausea hit him as he realized how soon he was to lose Slim. It was a bad lung wound on the left side, close to the heart. Bitterly he recalled Slim's advice against throwing in with Druro Cain two months ago, blaming himself for being such a fool as to trust the outlaw leader. Steve should have been expecting this. It was Cain's way of getting rid of a man who threatened his leadership of the wild bunch.

For two years Steve had sided Slim on the owlhoot. This patient, loyal scarecrow of a man had become like a brother to him. Steve had no notion what Slim's beginnings were, or how it was that he rode the dark trails, yet he knew him to be all man. Now he rode doggedly at Slim's side, the hot-air rush whipping his face as their horses stretched every muscle in a mad race for that taunt, broken country that stretched away to the north. He looked behind, saw that they were holding their lead over Cain's riders. Beside him Slim was making the ride of his life. A fine horseman, now he gripped the saddle horn, bending low over the withers to steady himself. The muscles along his jaw were corded. Steve could feel the terrific struggle his friend was making to ride this out. Yes, Slim was doing it for him, knowing that Steve would not leave him to die alone.

They rode into the breaks, headed up a wide arroyo that twisted back through the stretch of badlands ahead.

Steve waited until they neared the first turn before he shouted: "Go on! I'm stoppin' to hold 'em back while you ride!"

Slim answered—"Go to hell!"—and grinned.

It had been that way always with them. They had made their fights together. Slim's words served notice that he would see it that way to the end.

Later Steve climbed his gelding up the steep side of a cutbank to where he could survey the time-eroded desolation of the land that stretched away to the horizon on all sides. He knew that he was skylining himself, but for once desperation drove all thought of caution from him. Below, in the cut, Slim lay stretched out on the ground, where he had fallen from the saddle. Steve had given him a long pull at the canteen before coming up here.

He sat there for three long minutes, his keen glance prying into the light heat haze, searching for some sign that would tell him how far behind they had left Cain and his men. He and Slim had ridden miles over rock, twisted into small side cañons, so as to confuse the men who hung on their trail. After two minutes up there, he sighed with relief and rode below again.

He swung from the saddle to kneel beside Slim. One

glance told him that the end was near. The man's gaunt face was etched with lines of pain, while a deathly pallor had displaced his usual tan. He opened his eyes and looked up at Steve.

"I'm takin' harp lessons from now on, pardner," he said, his thin lips twisting into the semblance of a smile.

Steve was silent, wordless with a grief that struck him deeply, the throbbing pain of his own shoulder wound sharpening his perceptions.

Slim went on: "Hunt down that killer, Steve. When you find him, I'll be sidin' you, steadyin' your iron, helpin' you to throw your lead straight."

"He's plenty poison, Slim," Steve answered, thinking of Cain's merciless, uncanny skill with the six-gun. Time and again he had seen fast men go against the outlaw leader, only to meet death in the wizardry of that lightning draw.

"So are you," Slim answered, his voice choked and husky. His eyes hardened, deadly serious as he continued: "You've put it off long enough, Steve. You're the one man who can beat him. You're fast as hell . . . only you don't know it." He paused a moment as the blood that welled into his lungs made him gasp for breath. "I . . . I want you . . . to promise, Steve. Promise me you'll . . . kill Druro Cain."

All at once Steve sensed the bitter irony and futility of Slim's death out here in this forsaken land of weathered rock. In a way, his friend was dying for him, for these bullets had been intended for him, not for Slim. Slim was cashing in his chips. Once again Druro Cain had taken a life, once again he had asserted the cruelty and cunning that had built up a legend of terror around his name. Slim had one friend in the world, only one person who would miss his going, and he was now asking that friend to wipe out the man he hated.

"I promise," Steve said then, in the full knowledge of what

this meant. "I'll rub out his mark."

Slim's eyes closed, and for a moment Steve thought he had gone. He leaned forward, put his hand on the blood-matted shirt over Slim's heart, felt the feeble beat there.

Slim opened his eyes again, said: "Take my cutter, Steve. From now on you're wearin' double belts." His face suddenly tightened in pain, so that every muscle in it stood out. He gasped once, and lay still.

Somewhere on the unknown trail ahead would be a more fitting burial place for Slim, Steve knew. With that in mind he lifted Slim's body gently, laid him across the gelding's withers. He lashed the chestnut across the hindquarters, to watch the animal lope off down the cut. Then he climbed onto his saddle and rode on, steadying Slim's body with the hand that held the reins, gripping his aching shoulder with the other. He was alone now.

It lacked an hour of sunset when Steve topped a bald ridge and looked for the first time across a lush grass pasture spreading out over a valley floor. For two hours he had ridden hard toward the low-lying foothills that showed up out of the heat haze, and, now that he was finally in them, the quick change from the barren monotony of rock and sand to the emerald green of the scene before him was startling.

In desperation, he realized that he would soon have to find a hiding place, for the terrific heat, his thirst, and the loss of blood through his shoulder wound had weakened him until he had difficulty in sitting the saddle. Strangely enough, the first thought that occurred to him was that here was a fitting burial spot for Slim.

His searching glance picked out a cabin that stood at the edge of the cedar fringe that ran the length of the valley. This country was new to Steve, and now he debated the chances of his having eluded Cain and his men. Reason told him that he could not ride much farther, yet the full understanding of how relentlessly Cain would hunt him down was like a slow, cancerous growth at the back of his mind. He did not fear Cain—he had never feared him—yet the thought of the outlaw, finding him defenseless, was ever-present.

At last his mind was made up. He wheeled the gelding down off the ridge and out across the valley floor toward the cabin. Slim's limp form swayed loosely with the gelding's movements. Before Steve's eyes the green freshness blurred as the nausea of faintness hit him for a moment.

So it was that he rode up to the cabin, slid from the saddle to fall to his knees on the ground. To push himself erect took all his effort, yet he did it finally and staggered over to the cabin door to look inside at the one deserted room. Inside, he found a bucket of cool water and drank a dipperful. As he finished, and turned back to the door again, he saw a rider top the far ridge and take the twisting trail down into the valley. For a long moment Steve studied the horse, finally realizing that it was not from Cain's string.

An inborn wariness asserted itself. He led the gelding back into the shelter of the cedars. He took down Slim's body from ahead of his saddle and laid it against the trunk of a cedar on the side away from the cabin. Then he leaned against the tree, shielding Slim's body from view. Of a sudden, a dizziness hit him that made objects whirl before his eyes. He steeled himself and waited, wondering whether this would be friend or enemy.

The man reined in thirty feet away, sitting the saddle with an natural ease. Steve saw him to be half a head shorter than his own six feet, a trifle younger—perhaps twenty-five—and with a shock of sandy hair showing above a rugged face deeply tanned.

The stranger shot a brief glance at Steve's gelding, eyes

narrowed, but with no hint of alarm, and said slowly: "Howdy, stranger."

Steve did not answer, for all at once the pain of his shoulder throbbed so that he was afraid of crying out.

"This is my place," the stranger went on. "What can I do for you?"

"I'm wonderin' . . . ," Steve answered.

The habit of long years on the owlhoot had made his answer brief and to the point. He pushed himself away from the tree, saw the stranger's glance fall to take in Slim's body.

The man shifted in the saddle, throwing his gun side out of line of Steve's vision. Steve caught a faint hint of movement that betrayed the other's design, and stabbed his hand toward the revolver at his thigh. In one smooth down sweep he had the .45 out and lined at the rider.

The stranger's wide-eyed stare took in the miracle of that draw, then his hands slowly raised to the level of his ears. Steve saw him tense and wait for the bullet's impact.

Finally the stranger said: "It's your move!"

"Not till you've shed your hardware," Steve answered, his voice husky and weak.

The man unbuckled his belt, dropped it far out into a patch of grass, his gaze locked with Steve's. That was the last Steve knew. He tottered back on his heels; a weakness hit his knees; he sprawled his length in the dust.

The choking sting of raw whiskey jerked him back to consciousness once more. He looked up, saw the stranger bending over him. With an effort that made him wince from pain, he struggled to a sitting position and only then saw that his two six-guns were rammed through the stranger's belt. The other caught his look.

"I'll give your cutters back when you're strong enough to

lift 'em," he said, and a broad grin took the hardness out of his face. "You're in no shape to play badman."

Steve smiled, reading something in the other's straightforward look that pushed fear to the back of his mind. "I'm sure plenty harmless now," he said.

The stranger proffered the bottle of whiskey. Steve took two long swallows of the fiery liquid, feeling almost instantly the surge of new energy.

The stranger bandaged him, then leaned back and drawled: "You took that lead in the back. There's a dead man over there. Maybe I'm gettin' too curious, but it seems like you've got some talkin' to do."

The stranger waited for Steve to frame his words. Inside himself Steve felt a glowing warmth, and each second gave him added assurance that he could trust this man. At last he told him: "We were bushwhacked. I know the man who did it. He won't live long." It was not as a threat that Steve said this, but as a bluntly put, matter-of-fact statement. "Slim out there under the tree has carried two slugs in him since this mornin'. Did you ever see a man bleed his guts out in the saddle?"

The stranger shook his head.

Steve swallowed with difficulty, went on. "We didn't have a chance. I headed up here, lookin' for a hide-out and a place to bury Slim. That's all . . . only that they may come up here huntin' me." When he had finished, he raised his eyes, met the stranger's level stare, and held it without flinching.

"Who're they?" the man asked.

"Not the law," Steve told him.

The other got to his feet slowly, sensing that Steve had told him all he was going to. He looked briefly over at the still figure under the tree.

When he spoke, he voiced his thoughts: "I reckon I'm a

damn' fool to buy in on this," he said, then shrugged. "There's a spot up the hill where I could bury your friend." He paused a moment while Steve sensed the full import of his words, then went on. "If I feed and water your jughead, do you figure he'd find his way back where he came from?"

Steve frowned, then caught the other's meaning. "Sure. He'll head out o' here in a hurry."

"We'll have to leave the saddle on to make it look right."

"Give me an hour's rest, and I'll ride him out," Steve said.

The stranger shook his head soberly. "You're tough, but it'll be a week before you straddle a saddle again without fallin' off."

"The hell it will," Steve countered, and struggled to push himself erect from his sitting position. But lacking the strength, he sank back exhausted, beads of perspiration standing out on his forehead. He looked up helplessly and finally said: "Whatever you decide to do with me will be all right, stranger."

The man carried him into the cabin, put him on the single bunk that ran along the side wall. He unbuckled Steve's gun belts, laid them beside him next to the wall, then shoved the two revolvers back into their holsters, saying: "You've got the sweetest draw I ever saw, fella."

Steve did not hear him. He was asleep.

III

Two hours later the far-off hoof-drumming of hard-ridden horses echoed out from below in the valley and jerked Steve into a fevered wakefulness. One look at the stranger, who had straightened bolt upright at the sound of approaching riders, told Rand Rivers that what he had expected and prepared for was near at hand. He turned down the lamp, pushed the pan of simmering stew onto the back of the stove, and stepped outside to wait. A subtle sensation akin to fear flooded through him as he reviewed the things he had done since the wounded man had dropped off to sleep. Had he done his job well? He would know within a very few minutes.

The riders came up fast. Soon three bulky shadows moved along the trail, approaching the cabin.

"Hello! Anyone there?" The voice that came abruptly out of the darkness was gruff.

Rand answered—"Come ahead!"—and waited, standing with feet spread a little, his hand near the butt of his revolver.

The leader rode up close, shifted sideways in his saddle, and asked: "Seen anyone about?"

"Haven't seen anyone," Rand lied, spacing his words carefully. "But someone's been here. You lookin' for him?"

For several seconds there was no answer. Rand's eyes gradually adjusted themselves to the darkness, and he began to pick out details, aware of the two who hung back behind the leader. The man facing him was short and chunky, wore double belts tied low. His mount was a superb animal, thick-chested, long of leg, and showing speed in every line.

"How do you know they've been here?" the rider asked, disregarding Rand's pointless question.

"Sign," Rand answered. "But there was only one of 'em. His jughead tromped up my yard. If I read it right, he watered at the creek, fed his horse over at the wagon shed, and struck out back down the valley. I was away till near sundown."

"There was two," the man answered tersely. "We're takin' a look around." He turned in the saddle, called to the other two: "Go out to the shed and see what you can pick up." Then he faced Rand again. "You got a lantern, stranger?"

Rand stepped inside the door, picked up his lantern, and came back again. He lighted it, saying: "Better come in and feed your stomachs. I've got stew inside."

His pulse pounded wildly as he waited to see if his ruse would work. He caught the abrupt answer: "We ain't lookin' for food. Hand over that light. I'm in a hurry."

Rand handed up the lantern, followed after the rider who went out to the wagon shed. When he got there, all three were dismounted, examining the ground in front of the door. One of them kicked aside the bucket that stood in the doorway. It rang out hollowly as it hit the feed bin.

"Find anything?" Rand asked. He confidence was returning, for he was certain that he had planned this part of it well.

The leader shot him a brief glance, went on about his search without answering. Rand studied the man and got a clear picture of the rounded face with its thin gash of a mouth, light-gray eyes, and livid scar that ran down from the right temple to the square line of the jaw. Finally the man straightened, growled angrily: "We're wastin' time here. Let's light out. It was Steve's splay-foot that made these tracks."

"What do you figure he did with Slim?" one of the others asked.

The leader turned to Rand. "How do you know he went back down the valley?"

"He didn't . . . right away!" Rand told him. "He cut off up through the cedars first, came back down again, and headed out the trail. Hand me the light and I'll show you."

He took the lantern, walked over to pick out the tracks where he himself had ridden Steve's gelding up the slope through the cedars, carrying Slim's body. "Here's the sign," he said, walking in through the trees. "He went up the hill quite a piece . . . how far, I don't know. It was too dark when I got home to tell. Over here's where he came down again. Farther over's where he lighted out. If it had been lighter, I'd have tailed him. The damned polecat stole one o' my rifles."

The man with the scarred face said: "He went up the hill to bury Slim."

"If he's got a rifle, we'd better go careful. Steve can shoot mighty straight," the third man volunteered.

"Careful, hell!" the scar-faced man growled. "He can't ride far with that dose of lead poisonin'. Let's go!"

Rand saw the scar-faced man hesitate, then turn toward him. A dull, ominous foreboding told him that all his work had gone for nothing, for now the man wheeled his horse and started for the cabin, saying: "It won't hurt to take a look."

The others were watching him, Rand knew. His thoughts whirled blackly, groping for a way to stop the man who was swinging from his saddle in front of the door. Abruptly he knew it was too late—too late to save the wounded man they called Steve, who lay in there in the bunk, powerless to defend himself. Rand stiffened, ready to whirl and shoot it out with the two remaining riders as soon as the first shot cut loose from the cabin.

The scar-faced man drew his revolvers, went in through the door, and turned slowly in his examination of the interior.

Rand's tense muscles ached as he awaited the explosion he was certain would come. *Could Steve shoot first?* The quiet was louder than thunder in his ears.

Unbelieving, the next instant he saw the scar-faced man come out through the door and mount again. Before he realized it, he had ridden back and was saying: "No one there. Let's ride."

Rand was thankful for the darkness, thankful that his face was hidden; otherwise, they would have discovered his secret. The next moment they had gone, thundering off down the trail, headed for the mouth of the valley. He waited until the sound of the beating hoofs died away into the distance, then walked back into the cabin, a wild elation mounting up within him along with a curious wonderment as to how Steve had escaped discovery.

The cabin was empty. Rand's glance pried into the dark corners until he convinced himself that this amazing thing was true. The man had disappeared. He rushed outside, called out, but got no answer. He went to the wagon shed, next to the corrals, but found no sign of the wounded man. He got the lantern and started a slow circle that took him along the border of the cedars that enclosed his clearing. Here, again, he was disappointed, for he found nothing that would help him.

At last he went back to the cabin, looked at the dusty ground ahead of the door, and finally found the imprint of an unfamiliar boot sole. With the lantern furnishing him light, he followed the tracks. They led straight to the point where he had stood with the three riders as they departed. At first he thought it was the scar-faced man's sign he had followed, but then abruptly he remembered that the man had been mounted.

Behind a lone cedar that stood out away from the rest,

within ten feet of where he himself had stood with the three riders, Rand found Steve. He found him sprawled out, lying face down and unconscious, a revolver still gripped tightly in his hand. A vivid recollection of the happenings of the past ten minutes told Rand that Steve must have left the cabin while he and the others were at the wagon shed. He had been within ten feet of the men who were hunting him, and probably overheard their conversation. Admiration for this man filled Rand's being as he lifted the still form and carried it into the cabin again. Whoever he was, whatever he might be, he was an extraordinary man.

Steve moved, opened his eyes as Rand pried his fingers loose from the six-gun. For an instant a look of fierce hatred dwelt in the gray eyes, but, as soon as recognition came, the expression died.

Rand said: "It was close, Steve."

Steve gave him a long look before he answered: "So you know who I am? They told you?"

"They called you Steve."

"My name is Steve Bassett. The man with the scar is Druro Cain."

The shock of Steve's words struck Rand like a whiplash, and his memory recalled vividly the words of the man in the posse that had tailed the bank robbers out of Three Rocks. He had named Steve Bassett as the man who held the posse back at Miller's Pass, the man who had shot their horses out from under them, the one who had had the chance to kill them, yet had not. He remembered the man's very words. *He's not a killer like Cain, even though he travels with him.*

His seething thoughts settled into some semblance of order then, and Rand Rivers knew that at that instant he faced the greatest problem of his life. Here was a hunted man, a known outlaw for whom rewards were posted. He was utterly defenseless, and it was but an hour's ride to turn him over to the authorities.

He looked at Steve, sensed that the outlaw was reading his thoughts. Yet Steve made no move to defend himself, although his six-guns were within easy reach. Clearly Rand pictured what had happened, remembered Steve's blunt statement that he would some day kill Druro Cain. And suddenly Rand knew that he could not betray this man, knew that he would be forever branded as a coward in his own mind if he did.

He heard himself saying: "Any man who's got the guts to cross Druro Cain can have my help. Go to sleep."

It was the afternoon of the day following that Joan Fields waited in front of the cabin for a full half minute, while her call to Rand went unanswered. Finally she swung off the paint horse and strode across the bare yard to the door. A glance inside satisfied her that he was not there, so she walked to the corner of the cabin and looked up the valley without sighting him. She came back again and walked inside.

The click of her high-heeled boots on the rough board floor wakened Steve, and it was the sound of his stirring in the bunk that made her whirl to face him. His hand had darted up, in sudden alarm at the noise, to where his revolver hung in its holster at the head of the bunk. Sight of her checked him.

"Who are you?" she asked after a moment, her voice husky with fear. "Where is Rand?"

Steve's glance ran appraisingly over her slender figure, finally met the hazel eyes set in a finely molded face that was now a little pale.

"Rivers rode up the valley. He'll be back shortly."

"Are you a friend of his?" she asked with a bluntness that

was brought on by the fright he had given her.

"Not exactly," Steve answered. "That is . . . not yet," he ended lamely, at a loss for words that would explain his presence. The look in her eyes changed then, although the fear in them did not diminish. She flashed a quick glance sideways toward the door.

"I think I'll wait outside," she said briefly, and left the room.

She climbed hastily into the saddle and rode the startled paint a hundred yards before she pulled him in to a trot. For a moment she regretted having acted so hastily, yet, remembering the stranger's pale, unshaven face, with the sunken gray eyes that had stared at her out of the shadows, she was glad she had left the cabin.

The next instant she saw Rand. He was riding along the edge of the belt of cedars half a mile up the valley. She rode on to meet him, impatient to learn about the stranger. When she pulled up in front of him, her look must have betrayed her feelings, for Rand asked quickly: "What's the matter, Joan?"

She began—"That man up in the cabin . . . ?"—and was checked by the broad grin that crossed his face.

"You mean Steve?" he asked. "Did you walk in on him?"

"Yes. Who is he?"

"He had an accident last night and came to me for help."

She eyed him steadily as she said: "I don't like his looks."

"Steve's all right. His looks don't count."

"Why did you take him in, Rand? You should be more careful."

"He was wounded," he explained. "I couldn't turn him away."

Joan gave him a long look, feeling his reticence. "Are you going to tell me about it?"

Here was something he had been expecting. On the ride

that had taken him up the valley he had debated as to how much to tell Joan. It had come to the point where their lives were very close, to where they kept nothing from each other. So Rand had decided to tell her the whole story, and now he began with his discovery of the wounded man and ended with Druro Cain's visit to the cabin. When he had finished, he saw that she had paled slightly, was staring at him in wide-eyed surprise.

"Then why aren't you riding for the sheriff, Rand?" she asked. "He's an outlaw. He's one of the men who robbed the bank the other night."

"I know, Joan, but he's a man in trouble, and it doesn't concern the robbery. I . . . I can't just take him in."

The bewildered surprise left her face, and in its place came the flush of anger. "Rand, you can't do this! It's your duty to turn him over to the law. You're . . . you're going to be a deputy in another two weeks. And you start by protecting a criminal?"

Her anger confused him. He had never for one moment doubted that she would understand, yet now he saw clearly the reasons why she couldn't. Joan Fields, her father, her whole family and their well-ordered lives, stood for law and order. Too late he realized his mistake in telling her of Steve.

Obviously he must make a choice here. He could take Steve into Three Rocks, have him arrested, and gain the respect and admiration of everyone for his action. But deep down within him was rooted an inborn sense of fair play that made him boil up inside when he thought of betraying the wounded man. Joan did not know what kind of man he was. His thoughts conjured up the picture of Steve, lying helpless there on the ground in front of the cabin after his effort to stand up. He saw again the bright glitter to the outlaw's gray eyes that had pushed the pain into the background. He heard again those words: *Whatever you decide to do with me will be all right, stranger.*

Those words held the essence of Steve's make-up. Rand could not really explain, even to himself, the fine distinctions that made Steve more than a mere outlaw. He told her: "It was something he said last night. I could never do what you ask, Joan."

She sensed the finality in his words, half understood that here was something she could not fathom. Yet it only served to increase her anger. It flooded across her face, brightened her eyes, until Rand thought bitterly that he had never seen her so beautiful.

"Rand, for the last time, I'm asking you to do as I say. Can't you see what you're doing?"

"No, Joan. What you're asking is impossible." His words were lifeless, for already he knew what was coming. Here was the first time they had ever disagreed. It was no light matter with him.

"You're making a choice," she breathed, and he read the hurt in her eyes. "Oh, Rand, why are you doing this?"

He answered: "You'll have to trust me, Joan."

"But how can I? You're not only going against me, but against the law. What am I to . . . ?" Her words broke off as she saw the futility of them. She hung her head, and her next words were low-spoken: "I won't give you away, Rand."

She wheeled the paint around and rode slowly away. He did not attempt to follow her, but it was evident to him that what he had done could not be undone.

IV

Four days later Steve was up and moving about, still weak, sleeping a good portion of the day, and possessed of an insatiable appetite. Invariably, when he was not resting in the bunk, he sat just inside the door to the cabin, looking out across the mile-long sweep of lush grass pasture to where the trail wound down off the ridge.

It was this way that Rand found him toward sundown as he entered the cabin and set about getting the evening meal. He worked in silence, thinking that three days had passed since he had seen Joan. It had been hard to realize that the break between them was final, yet Rand knew in his heart that it was so, for seldom a day had passed that Joan did not ride out to see him, to help him make the plans for enlarging the cabin. Here they had planned to live after their marriage; already Rand had cut and notched the logs they intended using for the two new rooms. They lay up on the hillside, and for three days he had not been able to drive himself up there to continue the work.

Steve's words broke in on his thoughts: "I don't think they're comin' back after me, Rivers."

Rand did not answer, and after a while Steve got out of his chair and came to help with the meal. They were both silent, Steve sensing that Rand wished to be let alone.

Strangely enough, Rand had not once thought of blaming Steve for having caused the thing that stood between him and Joan. Although he had said nothing to the outlaw about the affair, Steve was quick to see the trouble in his eyes. The night after Joan's visit Steve had said: "I'm sorry about the girl, Rivers." That had been all. As if by mutual consent, neither of them discussed the matter further.

After their meal that night, Steve said: "I'll give you a hundred and fifty dollars for your brown mare and that saddle out in the shed, Rivers."

Rand looked up at him, suddenly aware of Steve's meaning. "You're not fit to ride yet, Steve."

"I'm leavin' tonight."

"But . . . ?"

"A hundred and fifty for the mare and saddle," Steve interrupted.

"Fifty would be too much," Rand told him. "Brownie's twelve years old and her legs are none too good. That saddle out there isn't worth a damn. I won it in a raffle . . . never used it."

"I don't plan to use it for ropin'."

"Fifty dollars! At that I'm robbin' you," Rand insisted. "But you can't ride out until you're well again."

"A hundred and fifty or nothin'," Steve repeated.

"You'll walk out, then. I won't take that much."

Steve shrugged indifferently. "All right, I'll walk."

"The hell you will," Rand said. "See here, Steve, you can hardly stand on your pins. . . ."

"A hundred and fifty," Steve cut in. "Look," he said, unbuttoning his shirt and pulling a money belt from around his waist. He opened one of the bulging pockets and poured out onto the table a handful of gold coins. "That's only part of my stake. I won't miss a hundred and fifty."

Rand looked at the money and said: "Fifty, or you walk."

Steve gave him a long look, finally grinned. "You win. You've got the makin's of a lawman, Rivers, and I'm not tryin' to insult you when I say it. Here's the money."

He left that night, deaf to Rand's entreaties that he stay another day. There was a new moon that afforded a little light and, as Rand helped him to saddle, Steve was silent, stirred by the desire to thank the man who had saved his life, but helpless as he found that words could not frame his feelings. He swung stiffly into the saddle, double holsters tied at his thighs, his tall frame outlined by the moonlight at his back. He held out his hand, saying: "You've done a lot, Rivers. Thanks."

Rand gripped his hand. There was a short silence that was more meaningful than words, and then Steve hastily rode away with a careless wave of his arm.

For a long time Rand stood there, until the pounding of the mare's hoofs edged out into the utter silence. He turned and walked slowly back to the cabin. The first thing that met his eyes was a neatly stacked pile of gold coins on the table. Steve had made a horse trade.

It was five weeks before Steve stumbled across Druro Cain's trail. Those five weeks had hardened him, put the steel back into his flat muscles, driven out the pallor from his scar-featured face until it was again sun-blackened and no longer gaunt. He now rode a black stallion and, after three days astride the beautiful animal, convinced himself that it would do. A knowledge of Cain's tactics had guided him in picking up a trail that was many days old. He knew that the outlaw never stayed in one place and was continually on the move.

He had given up riding by night, and now entered the towns boldly in the full light of day. Time after time he peered in through the windows of a saloon before entering, searching inside for a face he knew, then going in and hanging about in hopes that a misplaced word or a gossiping drunk would give him the clue to Cain's whereabouts.

Here in Devil's Run, a wide-open mining town sprawled across the mouth of a cañon, he found Slash Barton. It was night, and Steve had walked to the dirty window of the town's one saloon to look inside. Slash Barton's burly figure was the first one his glance encountered. He watched the man, waited until he had gone over to sit in on a poker game, before he left the window and sauntered inside.

He was halfway across the room before Slash saw him coming and suddenly straightened in his chair. The color drained from Slash's face, and for a moment Steve thought the other would go for his revolver, but Slash had a shrewd respect for Steve Bassett and wisely kept his hands on the table until Steve stood at his elbow.

"Want to see you, Slash," Steve drawled. "Outside. I'll follow you."

Slash got up out of his chair slowly, keeping his hands away from his guns, and walked the length of the room to the batwing doors. As he went through them, Steve was at his right side.

"Where's the outfit, Slash?"

Barton gulped once, answered hollowly: "How should I know, Steve? I thought you and Slim. . . ."

"Slim's dead! You know who beefed him. I want to know who was with Cain that day they dry-gulched us."

"Steve, honest to. . . ."

"Cut it!" Steve barked. "You know, and you'll tell."

Slash wiped beads of perspiration from his forehead, reached with shaking fingers for the tobacco in his pocket. Steve waited, until finally the other blurted out: "Lord, Steve, it wasn't me. I wasn't along. Druro left me and Willis Howard up at the shack. He and the others was gone for two days. When they come back, I heard what had happened. You know I wouldn't run a sandy. You and me always got along. . . ."

"I know . . . I know," Steve put in. "But who was with Cain when they cut down on us, Slash?

"It was Eric Young and Bart Ryan, Steve."

"Just the two of 'em?"

Slash nodded.

"Where were the others?"

"Playin' poker out at Manuelo's place."

Steve thought for a long moment, finally asked: "Where's Druro now?"

Slash shrugged his shoulders in defeat and said: "He's on his way to Three Rocks."

"What for?"

A dry chuckle issued from deep down in Slash's chest. "He's down there to cut hell out of Jim Williams and his deputy. There's a gun-slingin' kid named Rivers who's been cleanin' up the town, cuttin' down on those loose-footed strangers. He's. . . ."

"Go on," Steve growled. "What about Rivers?" A dull warning made itself felt at the back of his mind, and he waited for Slash's next words.

"Hell, I'm tellin' you, Steve! Jim Williams was elected sheriff about a month ago and swore in this Rivers as deputy. Three Rocks has been runnin' wide open and needed cleanin' up. This ranny, Rivers, is doin' it. They say a girl threw him over, and he don't give a damn what happens to him. He run Mike O'Bannon out of town for playin' marked cards. The other night he cut Cliff Farrell off pocket-high in a fair gun fight. Cliff was lookin' for trouble and forced the thing. They buried him the next day."

"What's this got to do with Druro?"

Slash shrugged. "You got me, Steve. Druro's that way . . .

always gettin' loco ideas. He took Eric and Bart and went down there, sayin' he thought he'd look this Rivers *hombre* over."

Steve took Slash by the arm, and his hold was so vicious that the outlaw cried out. Slash had never before seen the look that came into Steve's eyes then.

Steve asked hoarsely: "When did Druro start?"

"This mornin'."

For five long seconds Steve stood there, thoughts seething as he calculated his chances. Druro Cain's streak of cruelty would sometimes creep out in this way; he killed for the sheer love of going against the order of things. Steve had seen him that way and knew that the killer was merciless.

Would Cain keep on and ride the sixty miles into Three Rocks without stopping? If so, there was no way he could help Rand Rivers. But he knew his man, and abruptly he realized that Druro Cain would never ride that distance unless a posse was at his heels. He was inherently a lazy man.

Steve pushed Slash roughly aside, headed for the livery stable at a dead run. The thought that drove him was that he was responsible for Rand Rivers's throwing his life away because of a girl.

V

Jim Williams went down to meet the two o'clock stage and waited the twenty minutes until the mail was sorted. He was a big man, well over fifty, deep-chested, gray-haired, and with a firm set to his jaw that was tempered by the clear brightness of light-brown eyes. The look of the man inspired confidence. It appeared as if Three Rocks had picked the right man for its sheriff.

There was a letter for Jim. He opened it as he sauntered down the street in the direction of his office. As his eyes met what was written on the page, he stopped dead in his tracks and stood that way for a full minute. When he went on again, his steps were quicker.

In the door of the office he paused, looking across the sparsely furnished room to where Rand sat at the desk, his back toward the door. He was sorting through some reward notices and, having recognized the sheriff's heavy tread, did not turn. Once Williams opened his mouth to speak, hesitated, then turned to go out again.

"Jim," Rand called, "take a look. I think I've found an *hombre* here. . . ." He broke off abruptly as he swung around in his chair and caught the expression on Jim's face. "What's eatin' you?"

William hesitated a moment in indecision, glanced briefly at the letter he still clutched in his hand, then came over and threw it on the desk in front of Rand, saying: "I don't know why the hell I'm showin' you this, but I reckon it's your business as well as mine."

Rand took the sheet from the envelope, read the scrawl written on it:

Jim Williams, Sheriff

I here you got law in your town now. I'm comin' over to see.

Druro Cain

Rand looked up, met Jim's level glance. "Trouble?"

"Trouble." Williams nodded.

For a moment neither of them spoke. At length Rand said: "So it's our turn."

Williams let out a smothered oath, jerked off his Stetson, and hurled it into a corner of the room. "Just when we're gettin' this town whipped into shape!" he bellowed, and stood there cursing fluently. "Cain's a killer. He's busted ten towns wide open. Shoots at the drop of a hat. He'll raise hell here."

"Isn't there a reward out for him?" Rand queried.

"Reward? Sure there's a reward. Only nobody's damn' fool enough to try to collect it."

"Let's try," Rand said bluntly.

Jim Williams's eyes widened in disbelief, and, when he spoke, his voice was brittle: "Get this, Rand! We're keepin' out of his way. No reward collectin', do you hear? Let him raise his hell and get gone. He's poison."

Rand thought a moment before he spoke. "Seems like Cain wanted to scare us or he wouldn't have written this letter. If he busts the law wide open here, there'll be others who'll try it. We'd never live it down."

"Damned if I care about that," Williams said. "You've got your orders. Keep out of Druro Cain's way."

Rand said slowly: "I can't do that, Jim."

"Why not?"

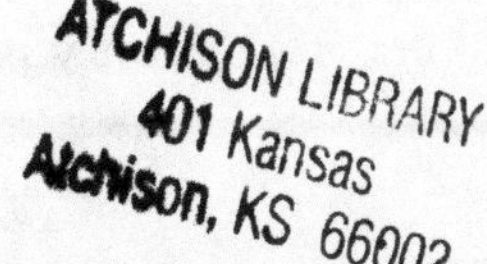

"I'm not lettin' down now."

Jim was breathing heavily, trying to control his temper, for what he had to say was something that had been bothering him ever since he had deputized Rand Rivers. He spoke calmly, pointedly: "Rand, you've got to listen. I've been wantin' to tell you something, and now's the best time. Ever since you started workin' for me, you've been on the prod. You're changed. Somethin's happened so's you don't give a damn any more. Some say you've quarreled with Joan . . . that she's responsible. I don't know about that, and it's none of my business. But don't let anything she's done ruin your life. Those things blow over. You've got a chip on your shoulder, and, if you keep it there, some salty ranny with a quick hand is goin' to let daylight through you. If that happened, I'd be responsible for seein' you murdered. Don't let this go on. I don't want you to run afoul of Druro Cain, and you've got sense enough to see the reason why. Do as I say and stay clear of him."

Jim turned, walked over to the corner to pick up his Stetson, and stomped out of the office. That was the last time Rand saw Jim Williams alive.

After the sheriff had gone, Rand sat at the desk, turning over in his mind what Jim Williams had said. Bitterly he thought back over the past five weeks, of how it had changed him, of the dull, empty ache that was forever with him when he thought of Joan. She had seen him twice since Steve Bassett's departure. The first time she had rebuked him for going against her wishes in sheltering the outlaw, although Rand had tried unsuccessfully to reason with her. The second time he had seen her he had thought he caught a hurt look in her eyes. She had spoken with him, talked for several minutes, but it was not the same Joan. He knew he had hurt her, yet it was not within his power to make amends for what he had done. As if by mutual agreement nothing had been said of their marriage or the changes Rand had planned for the cabin.

That had decided him, convinced him that it would never be the same between them again. He took his work seriously, plunged headlong into the job of cleaning up a town that had gained a reputation for lawlessness. Now, as he thought of Jim's words, he knew how true they were. Some day he would meet a man a little faster. Somehow, it didn't matter.

Rand was eating his supper at the Coffee Pot when he heard the two shots thud hollowly from Thompson's Place farther up the street. He laid down his fork, sat listening for several moments. Then from outside came the pounding of feet on the boardwalk, and a small boy rushed into the restaurant.

"They've killed Jim Williams, Mister Rivers," the youngster gasped, breathless.

Rand sat stunned for the space of two seconds, feeling the blood race through his head, letting the awful truth take root in his mind. Jim Williams was dead. All at once a consuming rage took possession of him, and he rushed out of the place, headed up the street toward Thompson's Place.

He had taken five steps when he felt a hand grip his own. He whirled to confront the man who held him.

It was Steve Bassett.

"Stay away from there, Rand," Steve spoke rapidly, his words clipped and hard.

"It's Jim Williams," Rand said, pulling his arm away. "They've killed Jim Williams."

Steve flicked his cigarette out into the street, watched its glowing arc cut a line across the thick gloom. "Stay away.

Druro Cain's in there."

"I'm going," Rand said flatly. "I'm in a hurry."

"Cain's there with two of his men."

Up the street a crowd began to form in front of the saloon. Abruptly another shot smote out to blend in with the street sounds, jerking their attention to the spot.

"He always does that when he's on the prod," Steve said. "He'll stay till he's ready to leave, darin' anybody to come in after him."

"I'm going after him," Rand insisted. "Jim Williams was my friend."

"Wait!" Steve snapped out the one word as Rand turned away. "Cain's my man. You know why."

Rand shook his head. "It's my fight as much as yours."

"Rand!" Steve's voice took on a chilling edge. "Give this up. You thought I was fast, but Cain's faster."

"This is my duty," Rand said, his drawl holding a finality. "Don't try to stop me." He turned then and walked away. Steve knew there was no stopping him.

Suddenly Steve sprang after him, stabbing his hand downward to his revolver. Rand heard and had half turned to meet him, when Steve's .45 struck down savagely, catching Rand a glancing blow along the side of the head. He sagged to his knees, sprawled slowly out along the walk, and lay without moving. Steve stepped over him, headed up the street toward Thompson's Place.

The crowd standing outside gave way; men stepped aside as they caught the look in his eyes. Looking briefly beneath the doors, Steve saw that the room was empty. He thumbed out the butts of his revolvers, slapped the batwings aside, one with each hand, and took the two steps that carried him into the room.

Three men were at the bar—Druro Cain, standing nearest

the door, Eric Young and Bart Ryan behind him. A cigarette drooped from one corner of Cain's mouth; his scar caught the light and shone in one thin line down the length of his face. He leaned carelessly against the bar, both his .45s in their holsters. Ahead of him Jim Williams's body lay sprawled, inert, face down.

No word was spoken. Cain's gray eyes widened with quick surprise, then smeared over to a shadowy coldness as he moved. Eric and Bart lunged away as Druro's hand was falling toward his six-gun. Steve bent forward slightly, whipped his hand down, and felt the feather touch of the gun butt against his palm as he arced it up out of the holster. His eyes could not follow Cain's draw, yet he had the satisfaction of feeling the pound of his gun against his palm at the precise instant Druro's revolver lanced fire. The crushing thud of the bullet that caught him in the left side of his chest spun him around, but not before he saw the blue hole that suddenly appeared on Druro Cain's forehead.

Steve went to his knees from the shock, turned half around. The pain was like the stabbing of hot iron in his chest, yet he turned back instantly, in time to see Cain go suddenly loose and fold to the floor. Eric and Bart centered in his vision. He thumbed the hammer of his revolver as both cut loose at him. Eric fell suddenly backward over a table and piled up on the floor.

Abruptly Steve heard the hollow crash of a .45 at his side, turned in time to see Rand Rivers, beside him, throw another shot at the still standing Bart Ryan. Ryan fired once before he fell dead across Cain's body, and the slug from his gun took Steve through the stomach.

It was over then, the three dead outlaws lying halfway the length of the room behind Williams's body. Steve huddled over, clutching his stomach as the first terrific pain caught him. Rand Rivers was standing alongside, with a smoking revolver in his hand.

Rand bent down, gently pulling Steve back until he was lying on the floor. He pulled the shirt away, looked once, and then slowly covered the wound again. Nothing could help Steve now.

Others stepped through the doors only to stop and stare, aware that a man was dying, keeping their distance.

Suddenly, from outside, came the startled cry of a woman's voice: "Rand! Rand!"

The crowd opened. Joan Fields rushed into the room, her eyes wide with terror. She threw herself down beside Rand. His arms went about her. For a moment she clung to him, sobbing quietly, until he took her by the shoulders and pushed her away, nodding down at Steve.

She looked down at Steve's face and recognition came. Her glance ran down to where the blood made a crimson patch near his heart.

When she looked up at Rand, he answered her query: "He wouldn't let me meet Cain."

Steve opened his eyes then, looked at Rand, and smiled. "He was mine, lawman." Blood flecked his lips, and his face contorted horribly. In a moment the pain eased. He smiled again, looking at Joan.

She said—"I'm sorry, Steve . . . really sorry."—and tears filled her eyes.

"Don't be," Steve whispered. "This has been a long time comin', but it's the way I wanted to go." He closed his eyes, breathed frantically, as though a terrific weight were crushing the air from his lungs. The spasm passed. He looked up at Rand and Joan again, saying: "Rand was mighty fine to take me in. Promise me you two will be happy."

"We will . . . we will," Joan sobbed. "I didn't understand, Steve. Forgive me?"

Steve nodded slowly. "I don't blame you." His eyes widened then, and Rand turned Joan's head away as the end came quickly.

Bullet Cure

Jon Glidden finished this story in ten days, sending it to his agent on December 14, 1937. Marguerite E. Harper sent it on to Mike Tilden at Popular Publications who quickly bought it for *Star Western*, where it appeared in the May, 1938 issue. The author was not quite sure of the title he wanted for it, deciding finally on "A Medico Prescribes a Bullet-Cure." Prior to its appearance, Mike Tilden changed this title to the more garish (and certainly less apt) "Doc Gassoway Prescribes Hot Lead." The author was paid $124.20 for the story at the rate of a cent a word.

Bullet Cuts

I

Dr. Gassoway was sensitive about his name—always had been. As an under-size kid, resenting the nicknames they gave him, he had been in so many scraps and come home with so many black eyes that his mother had been prematurely gray-haired at thirty-five. Perhaps it had been that early training in the petty meanness of his companions had made the youngster overly fond of his own company. And he was still that way, a solitary, self-sufficient man.

In this small cowtown, where every woman—and man, for that matter—had an over-developed, neighborly curiosity, Dr. Gassoway was close-mouthed and stuck strictly to business. Had he wished to talk, he would have made the town's best gossip; for, understanding how he could be trusted, people either sought his advice or poured out their troubles merely for the sake of relieving their minds.

Tonight, with the tag-end of an all-day wet snow making it uncomfortable outside, the medical man's office hour dragged by without a customer. Toward eight-thirty he was about to lock up for the night when he heard steps on the outside stairway. The door to the waiting room opened and closed, and whoever was out there spent a few seconds stomping the snow off his boots—long enough to allow Dr. Gassoway to open a medical journal and let his face assume a mildly serious expression.

"Come on in," he called, when he was ready.

Phil Orr walked into the room. At his first glimpse of the man's calmly appraising gray eyes, Gassoway knew that any pretense was out of the question. Orr, only three months in this country, should have been a stranger, but he wasn't. So Dr. Gassoway swiveled around in his chair and took out a bottle from his medicine cabinet. "Have a drink?" he said.

Phil Orr shook his head, and it was then that the medical man caught the troubled expression in the man's eyes and knew what was coming.

Orr said: "There's something you've got to do for me, Doc."

The physician was a bit surprised at the meekness of those words, lacking as they did the forcefulness he always associated with Phil Orr, with his good width of shoulder, tough, flat-muscled body, and lean face which gave the impression of being capable of taking care of himself. Because the medical man hated a show of weakness in any strong man, he now cursed inwardly.

"It's because I can't write, Doc," Orr drawled. "There's something I've got to get down on paper. And I'll have to trust the man who writes it for me."

"What makes you think you can trust me?" Gassoway was playing for time in asking that question, for he clearly remembered seeing Phil Orr writing out a shipping order not two weeks ago at the freight office. Orr was lying, and the medical man was asking himself why.

"I know men, Doc, well enough to decide who to trust and who not. Will you do it?"

"A letter?"

"No. You might call it a confession." Orr glanced back over his shoulder toward the stairway door. "I haven't much time, Doc."

Gassoway opened a drawer and took out a sheet of paper, reached for the pen, and, dipping it in the ink, said: "Shoot."

"Start it something like this," Orr said slowly, coming

across to lean over the desk. "To whom it may concern . . . the undersigned, for reasons stated, prefers not to be present when this statement is made public."

Orr hesitated, and after a moment Gassoway growled: "Well?"

"Maybe you can put it in your own words, Doc. Here's what I want said. Two months ago, working the North Creek range, I rode across something I wasn't supposed to see. There was smoke comin' from a clump of scrub oak down in that draw at the foot of the bench, and I went down there to see what it was. It was a brandin' fire. Tracy Powers and two of our crew were down there ventin' our own brands from the hides of half a dozen heifers. It was a gray day, and I naturally wasn't too careful. They saw me, and a fourth man they'd put out as guard got the drop on me. He took me down there, and I had it out with Powers. He offered me. . . ."

"You mean that Tracy Powers, a foreman, was stealin' his own beef . . . Dick Anthony's beef?" Gassoway queried, amazed.

"That's what I mean. Now don't interrupt, Doc. I want to get this done with. Tracy Powers, in some way, had learned that my name isn't Phil Orr. I'll tell you that part of it later. He first admitted that all the critters the old man has been losin' had been re-branded right on Anthony's R A range, by him and these three others. With Anthony crippled up the way he is, he doesn't get around his fence more than once every two or three months . . . never in this kind of weather. Well, Tracy and these others are stealin' him blind. They made me a deal to come in with them, and I had to take it."

As Phil Orr paused, Gassoway tilted back in his chair. He said tonelessly: "Orr, this is dynamite. It answers a lot of questions the law's been asking."

"I know, and that's why I want to get it off my chest. I can't sit by and watch old man Anthony and that girl of his lose everything. There's something bigger than a few head of stolen beef behind this, too.

"That was two months ago," Orr continued. "In that time Powers and the rest of us have changed the brands on at least two hundred head. As you know, a week ago a herd was driven off during that storm and never seen again. The sheriff and his posse spent three days combin' the hills, and found nothing. The reason they didn't is because that herd is right now within ten miles of its home range. The brands were changed to Bar A."

Orr paused long enough to fill a silver-banded pipe and light it. Dr. Gassoway didn't speak. Sam Ackers owned the Bar A, and nothing he ever heard about Ackers surprised the physician. He didn't like the man, never had, and he was a little pleased at having his judgment borne out by this news that named Ackers as a rustler.

Orr let out a cloud of blue pipe smoke. "I'm in town with Tracy and the bunch tonight. They're up to something they haven't let me in on yet. The reason I'm here is to have you bandage a sprained wrist that isn't sprained. So you'd better get to work while I finish talkin'."

Gassoway opened the bottom drawer of his desk and took out two wooden splints, and, as Orr went on, he held out his left arm and let the medical man bandage it.

"Tracy Powers isn't doin' this on his own. He speaks of a boss, but won't say who he is. They're up to something tonight . . . something Tracy says is bigger than swingin' a sticky loop on a few head of beef. I have a hunch that Tracy will use me for a while longer, and then put a bullet in my back. That's why I'm here. If anything happens to me, Doc, you're to take this statement to the sheriff. Until then, let things go along as they are. Maybe I can blow it up without any help."

Phil Orr was through, or so it seemed. He stood there without so much as a word during the next three minutes in which Gassoway efficiently bandaged the unsprained wrist.

When it was finished, Orr picked up the pen and signed the name **William Quinn** at the bottom of the blank sheet of paper, saying: "You fill this in your own way, Doc."

He was turning to leave, when Gassoway stopped him. "You forgot something, Quinn."

William Quinn, alias Phil Orr, stopped just short of the door, his face set in a tight grin. "I hoped you wouldn't ask that. But it's a fair trade for what you're doin' for me. That's my right handle . . . Bill Quinn. Colorado's my home state, and Mercer County's got three thousand dollars on my head for a murder. I won't even try to say that the killin' was framed on me, because that's the story of a man whose luck rides against him."

During the silence that followed, Dr. Gassoway was thinking of Bill Quinn. Finally he asked: "You *were* framed with that killing?"

"Yes. And there's no way to prove it."

"And that's what Powers holds against you?"

Bill Quinn nodded. Then, with—"Thanks, Doc."—he abruptly turned and was gone.

Gassoway spent most of the next half hour writing out that statement over William Quinn's signature. Finished, he read what he had written. Three times he read it, at times pausing to remember how Quinn had looked as he talked. What he now knew of the man increased the admiration he had felt for him since the first time he had met him as Phil Orr. He was remembering one other thing, too. At the dance a month ago he had seen Dick Anthony's daughter, Anne, looking at this

Bill Quinn in a way that wasn't intended to be seen.

The physician, a bachelor who had once been in love and never admitted it, recognized the signs. Crippled Dick Anthony was an old friend of his, and his girl Anne was more than a friend. He wouldn't see her hurt. Thinking this, he picked up the sheet of paper and held it over the chimney of his lamp. One corner charred, burst into flame, and Dr. Gassoway held it until all that remained of Bill Quinn's confession was a curling wisp of gray ash.

He felt better. He walked over to the clothestree behind the door, took down his hat, and came back to blow out the lamp.

Halfway down the street to the Cattle King Bar, his coat collar turned up about his ears, Dr. Gassoway paused at the edge of the awninged walk to scrape a wad of snow off the heel of one boot. It was a good thing he did, for, if he had gone on, he would have been directly in front of the bank when the explosion cut loose.

As it was, the concussion of the blast that blew out the front windows of the bank, made him lose his balance, and stumble out into the mud of the street. Against the chill of the water that seeped in over his boot tops, the physician felt another chill course along his spine. He was just remembering Bill Quinn's words: "They're up to something they haven't let me in on yet."

It took the town a full half minute to rouse itself after the explosion. Then, above the first shouts that shuttled down the street, Dr. Gassoway heard the pounding of several ponies in the alley out back as they got under way, and the Cattle King's doors were emptying a curious, frightened crowd out onto the walk.

Half a dozen men ran down the walk to fire questions at Gassoway, and a few more, having heard the sound of the running horses cutting out of the alley behind the bank, piled into the saddles of their rail-haltered bronchos and headed down the deep mud of the street in pursuit.

Dr. Gassoway didn't answer any questions. All he could say was: "A couple of you keep this crowd out until the sheriff gets here. I'm goin' in there and have a look."

He stepped in through the broken plate-glass doors without opening them, and no one followed. The medical man groped around for a full half minute before he found the lamp on the counter at the rear. It wasn't broken, and he lit it.

The first thing he saw was the litter of papers and books strewn across the floor before the vault's sagging-open door. He went behind the counter, careful to touch nothing, and had a closer look.

Someone outside said—"Here comes the sheriff."—and at the same instant Gassoway saw the silver-banded pipe lying at the center of the vault's open doorway. He knew that pipe, and he thought he knew why it had been left there. And while the voices outside burst out in explanation to Sheriff Pringle, Dr. Gassoway picked up the pipe and put it in his pocket.

When Pringle came in, he stared hard at the figure behind the counter. Then, as recognition came, he said in relief: "Oh, it's you, Doc! Goddle-mighty, ain't this a mess?"

"Better send for Mel Anthony," Gassoway said.

"I did already."

Mel Anthony was president of the bank, the younger brother of old Dick Anthony, owner of the R A.

Dr. Gassoway liked Dick as much as he loathed Mel. He wasn't alone in his feeling toward the banker, who had made it hard for ranchers these last four years of poor grass and falling beef prices. But Dr. Gassoway, like everyone else, grudgingly respected Mel's business ability.

In the next five minutes Harry Pringle made a hasty, ineffectual survey of the blown vault. Once he called out to Gassoway—"Looks like they got all there was."—and another time he mumblingly cursed Mel Anthony for being a fool in not spending a few dollars to have a bigger and stronger vault installed.

"He won't spend a dollar that ain't bringin' in two," Pringle grumbled.

"Business, Harry," Gassoway reminded him. "Did you ever know a banker who wasn't tryin' to corral every dollar in the state?"

"You're wrong, gentlemen . . . every dollar in the United States," came Mel Anthony's voice from the front.

Gassoway and Pringle both turned red in the face. Pringle stammered an apology, but the medical man held his silence and felt a cold flood of anger rise in him as he thought what a money-grabbing fool Mel Anthony had been these past few years. Knowing the shape the bank was in, Dr. Gassoway felt an acute dread over what might be coming.

He was surprised to see Anne Anthony follow her uncle in through the doors, since Dick and Mel were near enemies. But as Anne came alongside him, Gassoway forgot all this.

The girl was pretty, as always, Dr. Gassoway was thinking. She wore no hat over her taffy-colored hair, and her strong face was flushed from the excitement and her blue eyes were bright. Had Gassoway been a younger man he might have instinctively resented the look he had seen this girl give Bill Quinn the other night. As it was, he was thankful that they had both made a strong choice.

He thought of Quinn's pipe in his pocket. When no one was looking, he took it out and turned to Anne. "Phil Orr stopped in at my office tonight," Dr. Gassoway said in a low voice. "He left this. Would you mind takin' it back out to him tomorrow?"

She took it, and Gassoway thought her color heightened. When she didn't answer, he said bluntly: "Put your brand on that cow-nurse, Anne. You'll never find another better."

Surprise widened her eyes. Then, in a sudden burst of confidence, she smiled and looked proud and happy. "I've decided that already, Doc," she answered. "Only I didn't know you felt that way, too." She paused then, seeing that her presence needed explanation, and added: "I came in to try to patch Dad's quarrel with Uncle Mel."

It was Mel Anthony who interrupted their conversation. He came up and stood spraddle-legged before the sheriff, and said sarcastically: "I suppose you'll have caught whoever did this by sunup tomorrow, Pringle."

The sheriff's face turned beet-red. "I'll do what I can, Mel."

Anthony snorted. "The same as you did for Dick last week when that herd took wings and flew away."

Pringle was riled, and looked it. But he had taken tongue-lashings like this before. Now, facing the man who controlled half the votes in this county, was no time to forget himself. "When there's light enough, I'll round up a posse and follow the sign, Mel. That's all any man can do."

Dr. Gassoway left a minute later. He didn't go directly home, but by a roundabout way that took him to the train station. He found a light in the ticket-agent's office and went in and sent a telegram to the sheriff of Mercer County, Colorado.

II

The next day, Dr. Gassoway wasn't hopeful of the results the sheriff would get. It had snowed a good two inches since midnight, and, unless the sheriff's nose was keener than his eyes, he'd be out there all day in the cold for nothing.

As Dr. Gassoway was going to his office, he saw Anne Anthony drive her buckboard down the street and head home, out the north trail. The physician wondered what old Dick Anthony would say when he heard the news. He wondered, too, who Tracy Powers and his men were working for. And why did Powers's unknown boss want Dick Anthony's outfit?

Already, at this early hour, two people had stopped him and asked if the bank was going to open its doors today. Dr. Gassoway didn't know, but he lied like an expert. Sure, the bank would be open, and what kind of a loco notion was it made people think the world had come to an end simply because a bunch of drunks had broken open a vault? Harry Pringle was on the job, wasn't he?

This helpless curiosity on the part of people who could neither think for themselves nor take their medicine without a howl irritated the medical man. His office would be a meeting place for the grouchers, the frightened, the belligerent, and he wasn't feeling equal to the task of playing his part of public comforter today, especially since no serious patients were due in.

At the livery barn he saddled his bay mare and was out of town before it was fully awake. His black kit was tied to the cantle. He always carried a gun in his medicine bag, and for the first time in years he wondered if he hadn't ought to take it out and clean it, get it in working order. He was riding for the R A, and on the way he could stop by to see his only seriously sick patient, the Widow Mulford.

He arrived at the Anthony ranch house at eleven, his doctoring for the day finished. As he pulled into the yard, he saw old Dick and Anne and four or five others standing down by the corral. So he rode down there.

Anne ran to meet him, her father hobbling along behind more slowly. She was breathless as she stood alongside Gassoway's stirrup and looked up at him, agony in her glance.

"He's gone, Doc," she said brokenly. "It's Phil! His pony is down there at the corral, blood all over the saddle, broken reins, lame. . . ."

Gassoway swung around and took her by the arm. "Let's have a look."

They met Dick Anthony halfway to the corral. The grizzled rancher shook Dr. Gassoway's hand, a lurking worry behind his glance. "One thing after another, Doc," he observed. "This time it looks like we've got a bushwhackin' on our hands."

It looked that way to Gassoway, too, a minute or so later. It was Bill Quinn's palomino gelding, and the hull was smeared with enough blood to make the physician assume a stony-faced expression.

He tried to be casual about it, but somehow his effort fell flat as he said: "He's hurt, sure. But a man can lose a lot of blood and still grow it back again. Get your men on his sign, Dick. He can't be far."

"Five have already gone," Anthony told him. "The gelding came in a half hour ago."

They had done all they could do. All but Anne, and she

saddled her bay and ten minutes later rode out along the trail to town, knowing that Bill Quinn—Phil Orr to her—had been in town last night.

Dr. Gassoway and Anthony went up to the house and took chairs before the big stone fireplace in the main room. Anthony offered his friend a cigar, and, after both men had got their smokes going, the rancher asked: "Well, how does it look, Doc?"

This was no time for evading the issues, so Gassoway replied: "Not so good. Mel claims he thought he was savin' the bank money by not takin' out insurance. Unless Pringle has a run of luck and brings back what was in that vault, it's likely to be hard on some of us."

Old Anthony was silent for a moment. At length, he sighed: "This was a good country when I first came in. There were rustlers and thieves, but we hunted 'em down and strung 'em up to the first handy cottonwood. If I were a younger man, maybe I could do something about all this."

"Mel wouldn't foreclose on his own brother," Dr. Gassoway ventured, coming directly to a point they had been circling these past few minutes.

Dick Anthony chuckled grimly: "Doc, Mel's harder with me than he is with a stranger. Maybe you didn't know it, but Mel wanted to buy a half interest in this spread three, four years ago. He wanted a finger in everything, and I was stubborn enough not to want him interferin' with my business. So, instead, he loaned money to all the outfits around me. He claims that land is a man's best investment. He wants something besides money to leave his family when he passes on. Sometimes I think he'd rather run his own outfit than sit at that desk in the bank. I was damn' fool enough to make it possible for him to get mine by borrowin' money from him. Now it looks like I'll be payin' him rent instead of interest. . . ."

Gassoway took his leave shortly after the noonday meal, promising to send out word of any new development. He was two miles out along the trail when he saw a group of riders top a rise ahead. It was Anne and four of the crew. Closer, Gassoway recognized Tracy Powers's rangy buckskin. He pulled aside and waited for them, and Anne, who came on ahead of the others, reined in alongside.

"The snow came after midnight. We lost the sign."

The agony mirrored in the girl's eyes set up a knifing hurt in Dr. Gassoway. Anne loved Bill Quinn. But as he sat there, watching Tracy Powers and the other riders come up, the medical man's first emotion was wiped away in a flare of quick anger.

He looked across at Tracy Powers and queried: "Who would have wanted to shoot Phil Orr?"

Powers, tall, lanky, and with dead-looking, pale-blue eyes smiled and drawled: "After all, he was a stranger, Doc. He never told me who he ran with before he drifted in here for a job. From the way he wore his cutter, and the habit he had of watchin' his back trail . . . I'd say he'd been expectin' what's happened."

"When was the last time you saw him?"

"Last night, right after he came from your office with his hand all wrapped up. We started for home, but he claimed he wanted to sit in at a game of stud at the Cattle King."

Powers was honest in his answer, so far as Gassoway could make out. But the physician had a few ideas of his own and was impatient to be on his way, so now he turned to Anne and said: "Phil's all right. Take my word for it. You get on back and stop worryin'. I'll ride out tomorrow."

She nodded and wheeled her horse from him as tears filled her eyes. The rest filed on past, following her. Tracy Powers, as he rode by, smiled wryly and said: "A man can't outride his past, Doc. I reckon Orr's caught up with him."

Dr. Gassoway had risen to a profession that called for an analytical mind. And now, his horse plodding back along the trail, he told himself that one of two things could have happened. Bill Quinn was either dead from a bullet from Tracy Powers's six-gun, or Quinn wanted him, Gassoway, to think he was dead, so that the information he had given last night would be made public. Gassoway discarded the first answer as an impossibility. The dynamiting of the vault had taken place no longer than half an hour after Bill Quinn had left the office—too short a time for Tracy Powers to have taken Bill out of hearing of the town and bushwhacked him. Sure of this, Gassoway accepted his second theory as fact, and acted upon it.

The trail out from town ran string-straight across country as flat as the back of a man's hand, in all but two places. At one point, the trail dipped down across a broad dry wash and ran for a hundred yards across a rolling stretch of piñon-studded, sandy waste. Looking down at it from the far bank, Gassoway decided that it wouldn't have suited Bill Quinn's purpose.

Then it's Table Rock, Gassoway thought. And at that thought he put his mare into a swinging run that took him on toward town. He rode hard for two miles and walked the mare another two. There, its precipitous sides rising for sixty feet above the trail, stood a gaunt, high shoulder of rock. Its base ran back from the trail, stood for nearly a hundred yards, sloping gradually up to the top at the back, but its other three sides were sheer and steep. Close in back grew a tangled mass of brush and stunted trees that followed the banks of a deep wash back for over a mile north.

Dr. Gassoway circled to the back and set his mare to the climb. Toward the top, he got out of the saddle and examined the spot. Up here was a jumble of eroded, sandy rock, a few large boulders, and several thickets of leafless scrub oak and a few low-growing, stunted cedars. Selecting what seemed to be the best spot for a man to hide himself, Gassoway walked over to a scrub oak thicket and pushed his way into it.

He was in luck. Behind the screen of bush was a four-foot-high bench of rock. Below it, on a bare patch of sandy soil, lay the snow-ringed black ashes of a fire. Dr. Gassoway held a hand over the coals and felt a hint of warmth. A smile took possession of his face as he stepped over and found a pile of chicken feathers and the remains of a cooked carcass under the ledge.

"A man doesn't usually bleed a chicken over a saddle, but I reckon that's what Bill Quinn did last night," he mused shrewdly. "I wonder who this hen laid an egg for yesterday?"

He climbed a little higher and had a look around. His glance followed the twisting line of the brush-bordered wash to where it cut through a clump of poplars, crowning the crest of a low hill. His smile broadened as he looked over there, and once he raised a hand and waved, although, as he did it, he felt a bit foolish.

In town a half hour later, Dr. Gassoway stoically faced what he knew was coming. Riding past the bank, he saw that the doors were closed, that a sheet of printed paper was tacked on them. He didn't stop to read that notice; he didn't need to.

Now that he was sure Bill Quinn was alive, he debated for many minutes on doing what Bill Quinn evidently wanted done—turning over to the sheriff the information he possessed. But Harry Pringle would want proof, and that proof couldn't be given without exposing Bill Quinn for what he was—a wanted man. No, Gassoway decided, this would have to work itself out some other way.

The waiting room of his office was crowded. He took one look and announced sharply: "Anyone who's sick step on into the office. The rest of you will have to leave. This is pneumonia weather, and I'm busy. If you're wantin' to know about the bank, I can't tell you a thing."

Later, finished with his last patient, Gassoway locked the stairway door and went into his back office. He settled down in his leather chair with his eyes closed, hoping he could catch a nap. But he wasn't sleepy, and he couldn't think straight. Even though he knew Bill Quinn wasn't dead, he was irritable, and he couldn't see how this was all coming out. "Maybe I'm gettin' old," he muttered.

Finally he went to a front window of his waiting room and called to a youngster on the walk below.

When the boy appeared at the door, Dr. Gassoway handed him two dollars and said: "Go to the Cattle King and tell George to send me up a bottle. You keep the change."

Ten minutes later he was once more slumped in his leather rocker, a full bottle in his hand. Ten more minutes, the liquor was warming his insides, and he was thinking a little clearer.

Tracy Powers, late that afternoon, rode into town alone. He whistled tunelessly as the miles dropped away under his pony's hoofs, thinking not at all of the reason for this ride—to inform the sheriff that Phil Orr was missing.

At the jail, Harry Pringle listened to Powers's story with a scowl growing deeper along his weathered cheeks.

"A hell of a note," he growled, when Powers had finished. "All day out in the cold tryin' to find sign that wasn't there, and now this. And why in tarnation would anyone want to beef Orr, a stranger?"

Powers smiled knowingly. "No one knows where he came from."

"Then it's none of my business what trouble he brings with him. If his saddle was as bloody as you say, he's dead now. And lookin' for him won't help me any. I'll let the buzzards find him."

Tracy Powers was in agreement. He didn't know what had happened to Phil Orr—Bill Quinn, rather—and he didn't care. A good break of luck had relieved Tracy of a job he knew wouldn't be easy. If Bill Quinn was dead, then it saved him the bother and several days in the company of a troubled conscience.

Powers ate a leisurely supper at the back counter in the Cattle King and, afterward, sat in for an hour and a half in a stud game. Then, forgetting his losses with a good humor that surprised the others at the table, he sauntered out front and climbed aboard his buckskin.

He took the trail north out of town and held it for nearly a mile. There he left the trail and cut directly east, his pony finding it heavy going through the drifts. That was the beginning of a three-mile swing that took him far to the other side of town.

Over here the country was broken by a long line of barren hills that swept on toward the mountains. Powers picked his landmarks in the snowy half light and made for a tall, dead cottonwood gauntly outlined against the slope of a high knoll.

At the foot of the cottonwood stood a cabin with its roof line sagging and its two front windows jagged with broken glass. To all appearances, this cabin had not been lived in for years. There was nothing up here to attract a man, and the fact that someone had built this place proved only that fools leave their mark behind them.

Powers knew what he was doing. He made a circle that brought him to the cabin's rear door. Thirty feet out, he reined in on the buckskin and sloped out of the saddle. As he walked toward the door, a shadowy figure was outlined in it.

Mel Anthony said: "You're late, Tracy. It's damned cold standin' here."

Powers answered flatly, "If it wasn't worth it, maybe I could take that stuff and put it back in your vault." His tone lacked the respect one ordinarily expected a man to use in addressing Mel Anthony.

"I've got your money." Anthony disregarded the tone and the sarcasm. He held out a small package which Tracy Powers took. "There's four thousand."

"You said it would be five."

"I was wrong about the insurance," Anthony explained. "It covers only seventy percent of the loss."

Powers was sneering openly now. "Only seventy percent of your loss, eh? You get what we took . . . you get the insurance . . . you foreclose on half a dozen outfits, and then you try to beat us out of a thousand. Mel, you're crooked enough to. . . ."

"There's that note of Sam Ackers's I've got to cancel," Anthony broke in. "That was the agreement. I was to tear up that mortgage, if Sam came in with us. That cost me five thousand."

"You're still ahead of the game. Lay that extra thousand on the line, Mel, or I'll . . . well, you can guess." Powers's tone wasn't pleasant.

Grudgingly Mel Anthony reached into a pocket of his coat and lifted out a sheaf of banknotes. He counted them carefully and finally handed them to Powers. The R A ramrod grinned as he took the money, not letting his glance leave Mel Anthony's hands.

"Any other little jobs you'd like done, Mel?"

"Tell Ackers to hurry and drive that herd north to the spur. You're to get your split from him this time. We shouldn't be seen together."

They didn't ride away together. Mel Anthony didn't trust Powers, and he was nervous as a cat tonight. So he let Powers go on ahead, and went back to the shed at the rear for his own broncho only after Powers was out of sight.

He had led the animal out of the shelter and had raised a foot to his stirrup, when a voice behind him suddenly whispered harshly: "Wait a minute, friend."

Mel Anthony, in a paralysis of fright, turned his head. There, standing at a corner of the shed so that his tall outline was etched against the snow, stood a man with a leveled gun in one fist.

Before the banker could release his foot, the figure behind had stepped beside him. In a short, choppy blow, the barrel of his .45 caught Mel two inches above his right ear. Mel fell slowly, caught from behind.

The man who had struck the blow laid the banker carefully on his back and spent three minutes going through his pockets. Then, by the light of a half dozen flaring matches, he examined a sheaf of papers he had taken from Anthony's wallet. Finally he found what he wanted, for he returned the wallet, saving out only one slip of paper.

Two minutes later he had walked the crest of the steep slope behind and was climbing into a saddle that fitted Dr. Gassoway's broad dimensions better than it did this stranger's. It was Gassoway's mare, too, and, as the rider disappeared into the darkness, he didn't bother using the stirrups that were too short for him and that he hadn't taken the trouble to lengthen.

Dr. Gassoway had a rush call that night. The Widow Mulford was worse, and one of her boys had ridden a blown horse down the street ten minutes ago to pound at the physician's door and wake him from a liquor-deadened sleep.

Dr. Gassoway had sent the Mulford boy on home, saying that he'd overtake him on the trail. He found the livery barn locked and had to waste two minutes rousing Joe Jacobs. Joe let Dr. Gassoway inside and went back to his cot, knowing that the physician would lock up as he left.

But Joe was barely asleep when he was once more jerked rudely awake.

"Where's the mare, Joe?" Gassoway asked.

Even half asleep, Joe Jacobs could remember the details of what went on at his place. So now he promptly answered: "She was out when I got back from supper, Doc. You must have left her out on the street. I thought maybe you had a call."

"So I did," the physician agreed after a moment's deliberation. He didn't seem particularly alarmed over the mare and added an explanation that came out so smoothly it surprised him. "She went lame, and I had to leave her out at the widow's place. Lend me your team and buggy, Joe."

"Go ahead . . . take 'em." Joe was already sliding down under his blankets.

So Gassoway hitched Joe's team of blacks to the buggy and locked the barn as he left. He drove out to the Widow Mulford's and stayed with her until she died early that morning.

When he got back to town, just at daybreak, he found the street alive with people and a crowd at the front of the bank. As he drew abreast the open doors of the bank, an ominous foreboding flooded through him. Harry Pringle came out.

Gassoway called: "What's the matter, Harry?"

The lawman came to stand at the front wheel hub, and the look on Pringle's face was a mixture of weariness and bafflement. "Doc, maybe I'm dreamin', but you look over there and tell me what you see."

"The bank doors are open, and there's a crowd standin' there, watchin' us." The physician didn't know what to make of all this.

Harry Pringle sighed. "I was afraid it was real. At four o'clock this mornin' Bathhouse Rayburn happened to wake up out of a drunk in the pool hall across there and to look out the front window. He saw a light in the bank. He kept on lookin' and saw someone movin' about inside.

"It scared him sober, and he ran down the alley to my house and got me up. I came up here, and the light was gone. I wanted to go home, but Bathhouse made me bust in them board doors and have a look. And, sure as hell, after Mel Anthony spendin' all yesterday with a crew of men fixin' that vault door, it was open again."

"You mean the bank has been robbed a second time?"

The sheriff nodded.

"What was taken?"

"Papers this time. We don't know exactly what yet. Mel ain't home . . . his wife don't know exactly where he is . . . and all I can get out of the clerks is that the file cabinet where they kept the bank's mortgages has been opened. They won't touch 'em without Mel's authority."

The medical man tried to smile, hoping it would cheer the man who was shouldering all the trouble.

The smile wasn't genuine, and Harry Pringle was not only bewildered but boiling mad. "I turn in my badge today, Doc! This has got me wound up till I don't know the difference between a hand and a foot."

"That won't help, Harry. Stay on the job and maybe it'll straighten out all of a sudden." And Dr. Gassoway went up to his office after returning Joe's team to the barn.

He wasn't on the street when Mel Anthony rode into town, so he got the story of Mel's arrival second-hand. But by sifting several versions, he knew that Mel hadn't seemed surprised when he heard the news of the second robbery. And Dr. Gassoway didn't believe the banker's story that he had ridden out to see a client the night before, that he'd been pitched off his horse and lit on his head and was knocked unconscious. Dr. Gassoway wondered if Mel could explain where he'd been pitched off his horse. He decided finally to keep a tight rein on his curiosity and find out for himself later on.

He worked hard that day, doctoring the new cold crop. After supper he went to the livery barn and borrowed one of Joe's blacks and a saddle. Then, with his coat bundled tightly about his neck, his medicine kit tied to the saddle cantle, he headed north from town to see what he could see.

It was cold. No snow had fallen today, and with only the light of the stars he could see plainly a hundred yards ahead. No man could travel far through snow like this without leaving sign; a man who had sat behind the desk of a bank for the last twenty years wouldn't be at all clever about hiding his sign, anyway. Mel had certainly ridden north last night, for all his clients lived that way from town.

Sure enough less than a mile out of town a horse had cut off to the right of the churned up trail. Dr. Gassoway wasn't expert enough to guess how long ago those tracks had been punched through the snow's tough crust, but he was thorough enough to decide that he'd follow any and all sign that didn't stick to the trails.

It might take him a week, maybe longer, but he was after the answer to a lot of questions that it troubled him to leave unanswered. And right now he wanted to know where Mel Anthony had been punched off his horse.

IV

The news of the second robbery reached Dick Anthony and his crew late that afternoon. The man who brought it—a wrangler headed north into Utah—didn't have all the facts and wasn't particularly interested.

"All I know is that some mortgages was stole. That sheriff of yours is about ready to lock himself in his own jail and give himself up. It's a powerful big job he's got, from what I hear."

Tracy Powers was present as the wrangler told his story. As soon as he could slip away unnoticed, the R A ramrod went to the corral and saddled his buckskin and took the trail to town.

Powers didn't whistle as he made the ride today. He was worried. The most ominous thing about the wrangler's story had been the news that whoever had opened the safe last night hadn't used dynamite. To all appearances the robber had opened the door by using the combination to the lock. Common sense told Powers that a tight-fisted man like Mel Anthony would be the only man who knew the combination to his own vault. And what was this about Mel's drifting into town this morning with blood smeared all along one side of his scalp and a trumped-up story of how his horse had pitched him and knocked him unconscious?

"He did the job himself," Tracy Powers breathed, half aloud. "He's figurin' some way to frame me."

It was a thought he couldn't put down. He had worked for many months with Mel Anthony, helping the banker frame a brother he had never liked and whose outfit he wanted so badly he could taste it. And now that the job was nearly finished, Mel Anthony couldn't run the risk of keeping a man who knew as much as Powers did.

Powers had already decided to stay in the country and depend on Mel if he ever ran short of cash. For what was the use of doing work like this unless a man could cash in on some easy blackmail? That was it! Mel knew he'd be blackmailed, and this was the beginning of a frame-up that would get the men who had worked with him out of the way.

Dusk was coming on, and Powers hurried, all at once impatient to get this over with. He'd go directly to Mel's house this time and either find out what was what, or. . . . Suddenly he felt a faint current whip the air before his face. An instant later the *crack* of a rifle sounded from far to his left.

He rammed his spurs into the buckskin's flanks and bent low on the off-side of his saddle, looking to see where that shot had come from. A grove of tall poplars crested a low hill, and he saw a bluish puff of smoke blossom out from the shadowed tree margins. A full second later a puff of snow in line with him told him where the second bullet had struck.

Tracy Powers rode for his life for the better part of a minute. And in that interval that seemed to him an eternity, the rifle behind spoke two more times. A mile farther on he pulled in and let the buckskin blow, thankful that the settling dusk made him a poor target. He pressed on, holding the buckskin to a stiff trot for a full ten minutes before he spurred him to a run again. Mel Anthony was forcing his hand. Powers had no doubts as to who it was that had fired those shots.

In town, Powers took the back alley to the rear of Mel Anthony's big frame house. He climbed out of his saddle, crossed the open yard warily, and softly mounted the steps to the back porch. He knocked loudly at the door and stepped to one side, his hand under his coat closed on the butt of the short-barreled Colt.

Mel's gray-haired housekeeper opened the door. When Powers stepped into the light, she started in surprise and caught her breath and said: "Oh, you frightened me, Tracy! Won't you come in?"

"I want to see Mel."

She looked faintly puzzled. "You should have met him on the way in. He started at least two hours ago. Said he was going out to see Dick and be there all night. I think he had some bad news."

Powers thanked her and left. Here was the proof he wanted—proof that Mel had been the bushwhacker. He wasn't in a hurry now. After a stop at the Cattle King, he mounted up and headed out the north trail for home. Sooner or later he would settle things with Mel Anthony.

A mile beyond town he saw the sign that cut off at right angles from the trail. Two riders had cut east across the country, and from the looks of them one sign was old, the other fresh. Then he remembered that this was the way he had come last night on his ride to the cabin.

Curious, worried, he guided his horse off the trail to follow the sign.

Far back, well out of hearing and barely within sight, Mel Anthony saw Tracy Powers make the swing that took him toward the deserted cabin. Mel, never an overly brave man, was riding with a gun clutched in his fist. He hadn't ridden out to Dick's tonight, as he had told his housekeeper he was going to do. Instead, he'd hidden in the bank until he saw Powers ride into town and out again. He had been expecting Tracy Powers. It wasn't hard to figure what had happened last night. Powers had circled the deserted cabin and had been the man who had gun-whipped him and taken the combination to the vault. Tracy had stolen those mortgages, was probably going to use them as a means for blackmail. He had ridden in tonight, as Mel had known he would, to make his bargain for the return of the mortgages.

Mel had thought this matter through today. He had never killed a man. But this was too far along to have everything ruined by a gent like Powers. Powers needed a fast killing.

When Powers swung down the hill that fronted the cabin, Mel circled so as to come up on it from the other side.

V

Dr. Gassoway, coming within sight of the deserted cabin alongside the cottonwood, remembered how Charlie Van Neussen had come here fourteen years ago and taken up these four sections of poor grass and built this place. Charlie had stayed out here, bull-headedly running a small herd for nearly five years —until a drought dropped every head of his already gaunted herd. Charlie had moved out and left his place, and, as far as Gassoway knew, no one had lived in it since.

The medical man had his share of brains, and now, faced with the necessity of finding out why Mel Anthony had visited this out-of-the-way place last night, he rode on directly to the cabin. The tracks he was following made a wide circle, so he circled. Once in the back yard, still sitting the saddle, he looked around. A man's boot sole prints led to the door, came out again. Another, a smaller pair of prints, joined the first, leading out back to the shed. So Gassoway wheeled the black around and rode to the side of the shed.

There he saw a dark smear in the snow. He came out of the saddle and knelt beside it. Against the snow, the frozen blood still showed a bright red under the flaming light of the match Gassoway held over it. Here was what he had been looking for—the place where Mel Anthony had been pitched from his horse.

But as Dr. Gassoway looked about him, he mumbled his surprise: "Pitched, hell! He walked out here."

There was a mystery in this too deep for his reasoning. Finally, he gave it up and walked over toward the ground-haltered black. He was halfway to it when a voice froze him in his tracks.

"Hold it, Doc!"

Gassoway turned, rigid in fright. And when he saw Tracy Powers standing there, his fright didn't leave him.

Powers stepped out from the rear corner of the cabin. He held a blunt-nosed .45 in one gloved fist, and, as he came nearer, the physician felt his spine crawling as he drew an imaginary line between that gun and the second button of his coat.

"Snipe huntin', Doc?" Powers drawled, not unpleasantly. The R A ramrod tried to overcome the surprise at discovering whom he had followed, tried to see why Dr. Gassoway should be interested in a day-old sign.

The medical man's voice was thick-toned as he answered: "Not snipes, Tracy. In fact, I wasn't huntin' a thing. A man's got to have his exercise. This is the way I take mine."

"By followin' sign?"

But Gassoway didn't have time to answer, for simultaneously both men heard the crunching of snow out in front of the cabin.

Tracy Powers whirled, and, as his eyes made out a shadowy figure in the yard before the cabin, his hand streaked up his .45. Before he had time to swing it into line, a tongue of gunflame spat at him from the hand of the man out front.

Powers fired an instant later, and the booming of those two shots went slapping out across the hills. Powers grunted faintly and staggered backwards. The figure out front fell face down and lay still.

Powers said—"Stay where you are, Doc."—and walked across and knelt beside the prostrate figure.

Gassoway saw him take the gun out of the man's hand and then heard him call: "Come over here, sawbones."

When Gassoway stood above Powers and looked down

into Mel Anthony's upturned face, the puzzle that had been baffling him for the past three days began to take on shape, although not definite shape as yet, for Tracy Powers's shooting of Mel Anthony didn't fit in with the rest.

Mel's face was gray against the whiteness of the snow. He opened his eyes and looked up at Powers, then at Dr. Gassoway, and there was fear in his eyes. He mumbled thickly: "Don't shoot, Tracy. You can have anything you want."

Bill Quinn, standing in the window of the cabin, heard Mel Anthony say this. Quinn had played a lone hand these last two days, and had picked this deserted cabin as his safest hiding place, after watching Mel Anthony ride away this morning. If Dr. Gassoway had taken the trouble to make a wide circle of the hill behind the cabin, he would have found his mare staked out in a grove of poplars a quarter of a mile away. So would Tracy Powers, or Mel Anthony, for that matter.

Quinn couldn't figure what had brought these three here tonight. Perhaps those four shots he had thrown so close to Tracy Powers late this afternoon had something to do with it. And perhaps that second robbery of the bank had played its part. He had been counting on Powers and Anthony having it out between them; but he hadn't been counting on Dr. Gassoway's being involved.

And now, as he stared out at those three, wondering what would come next, he heard Tracy Powers snort his disgust at the banker's words and say: "You're damn' right I can have everything I want!" Tracy looked up at Gassoway and added: "Take a look at this polecat and see how bad he's hurt, Doc."

Gassoway unbuttoned Mel Anthony's coat and ripped away the right sleeve of a shirt. He was busy for a half minute or so, and then folded the coat back and told Powers. "A busted shoulder. He needs attention."

"He needs another bullet through him . . . this time

where it'll do more good."

Powers seemed to be honestly considering this, but abruptly some thought changed his mind. "Let's carry him inside, Doc. You'll have to patch him up the best way you can. He's got to live a bit longer. There's a lamp in there with some coal oil in it and that big fireplace still works. You'll do your doctorin' right here."

Between them, they lifted Mel Anthony and carried him around to the front and in that door. Bill Quinn moved out of the window, palmed the Colt out of his holster, and waited there in the darkness. This was going to take some planning—with the physician in the way.

He heard them moving about, and suddenly a match flared. Powers, his back to Quinn, walked over to a low shelf and lifted the chimney off a blackened lamp and touched flame to its wick.

Quinn waited until the chimney was back on the lamp again before he said quietly: "Powers."

Tracy Powers wheeled around, his right hand clawing in under his coat. But when he saw Bill Quinn standing there, a gun lined at him, he went rigid, and said hoarsely: "So you ain't dead!"

Gassoway wasn't as surprised as Bill Quinn had expected him to be. He wasn't so surprised that he couldn't move, for now he stepped over and said quietly: "I'll have your gun, Powers." He reached and got the weapon.

Mel Anthony raised his head where he lay near the door. He took one look at Bill Quinn, and a little of the fear went out of his eyes while anger took its place.

"It's him, Tracy!" he cried, and his voice had a note of triumph. "He's the one who's framed us . . . the one who gun-whipped me last night. He got that vault combination and broke into the bank."

VI

No one spoke for long seconds. Each man there was thinking out his own answers, particularly Dr. Gassoway. He was the first one to speak, and what he said was: "The only thing I don't get is why you wanted Dick's layout, Mel."

Anthony's self-confidence—and his cunning—were returning. The man he feared here was Tracy Powers, and now Powers was helpless. So Mel bluffed. "Who said I wanted Dick's outfit?"

Powers breathed a string of profanity that Bill Quinn cut short. "Doc, get to work on Anthony. Powers, you be quiet, or I'll cut down on you. We'll get this straight before we leave here, but right now we're workin' on that shoulder."

Bill Quinn was sure of himself. They were alone here, and, before the night was out, he meant to have every fact to explain Mel Anthony's motives, enough to hang the banker. But the law can't hang a dead man, and from Gassoway's tone of a minute ago Bill Quinn knew that Mel's wound was serious.

"Get a fire goin' . . . some water to boil," Dr. Gassoway told Powers. "You can heat it in that old basin over there. Only clean it out before you use it."

Powers spent a minute starting a fire from some rotten boards lying on the floor. Then he picked a battered basin and hesitated. Bill Quinn saw what it was and held out his hand and said: "I'll go out and scrape up some snow."

All the life had gone out of Tracy Powers these last few minutes—or so it seemed. That perhaps accounted for Bill

Quinn's carelessness. When he stepped too close to Powers in reaching for the basin, his gun wasn't lined.

Powers lunged as quickly as a striking rattler. He got a hold on Bill Quinn's wrist and twisted into him, wrenching the gun loose. Quinn caught a hold on Powers's shoulders and pulled him over backwards. But Powers twisted as they fell together and managed to roll clear. When Powers lit hard on one shoulder, he had the weapon lined at Quinn.

Powers said softly: "It wouldn't take much to make me blow a hole through you, friend."

Bill Quinn didn't answer and didn't move until Powers himself stood up. Then slowly he sat up. Powers stepped back and looked across at Gassoway, who knelt beside Mel Anthony with his open kit on the floor beside him. "Let that go, Doc," he said.

"He's hurt bad," the medical man protested.

"I say to let it go." Powers took two steps that put him where he could look down into Mel Anthony's face. He stared hard at the banker, swung his gun around, and drawled: "Now you'll tell me why you wanted your brother's layout."

Anthony raised his head off the floor, glanced helplessly at Gassoway and Quinn, and then said in a small voice: "I've never liked Dick. Everyone else does. I wanted to see him squirm."

Powers shook his head. "You wouldn't go to all this trouble for a thing like that." He thumbed back the hammer of the weapon. "Talk, Mel, or I'll let you have it."

The banker weakly raised a protesting hand, his glance full of terror. "I'll talk," he croaked. "I'll tell everything. Last year I had a man from a mining company in to look over some of the bank's property. I had him take a look at that north end of Dick's place, on the off chance he'd find something. It might have been worthless, but I'd seen some things up there that made me curious."

In the pause that followed, Powers queried bleakly: "And what did he find?"

"Gold," came Mel's hoarse answer. "Enough of it to make us all rich. I'll make a deal with you, Powers. We'll all of us get a split on it after I've foreclosed, and. . . ."

Tracy Powers's thumb accidentally slipped off the hammer of his gun. It couldn't have been anything but an accident, for Powers was as greedy as the banker, and what he was hearing had already set his brain to scheming. That gun was lined at Anthony. Its blasting roar cut short Anthony's words. His body jerked in a spasm, and he suddenly went limp. His head rolled to one side.

Powers, appalled at what he had done, breathed a curse and said frantically: "Take a look at him. Quick, Doc!"

Gassoway, seeing the red smear spreading across Mel's shirt, ripped it away and took one look. Then he turned and reached into his medicine bag. His hand came up, closed over a short-barreled .38. Before the gun swung up in the medical man's hand, two things happened. Powers jerked himself out of his paralysis and swung his own weapon around to cover the medical man. Bill Quinn, acting on a slim chance, lunged and knocked the lamp to the floor.

Behind Quinn two guns blasted out in one double explosion of sound. Quinn dove toward the spot where Powers had stood a moment ago. His shoulder collided with Powers's leg a split second before Powers shot again.

Quinn felt Powers's frame give way, and a moment later the man's weight smashed down onto him. Groping wildly with one hand above his head to ward off the expected blow, Bill Quinn winced from the pain of the gun barrel as Powers swung it down at him. He caught the barrel, the blow numbing his hand.

There was one awful second when Quinn thought he would lose his grip on that weapon. But he forced the gun tightly in toward Powers's waist and held it there against the man's tearing grasp. He rocked back the hammer.

When the muffled blast of the gun cut loose, Powers's frame went rigid, then limp.

Bill Quinn pushed the sprawled figure away, and stood up, saying: "It's all over, Doc."

There was no answer. Quinn lit a match, almost afraid of what he was going to see.

Dr. Gassoway wasn't dead. Powers's shot had dug a wicked gash along his scalp and knocked him unconscious. Bill Quinn worked over the medical man, went out once to get a handful of snow which he rubbed on his friend's face. The shock brought Gassoway to his senses.

Mel Anthony was dead from a bullet through his heart. Powers, with a slug from his own gun in his spine, lived only a few minutes.

Later, in town, after they had delivered the two bodies to the sheriff and tried their best to explain things to the amazed lawman, they climbed the stairs to Dr. Gassoway's office.

As he opened the door, Gassoway leaned down to pick something off the floor. It was a telegram that had been pushed under the door.

It was signed by the sheriff of Mercer County, Colorado, who was evidently a stingy man, for he had used only nine words in his message:

Quinn not wanted. Confession of frame-up clears him.

Gassoway handed the slip of paper to his friend. As Bill

finished reading it, the medical man said: "So you can keep your name and stay here with Anne."

Bill Quinn nodded, a hard man, but too full of emotion to speak.

"Damn," Gassoway breathed. "If I could only change my handle that easy."

The Echo Herd

During the Second World War, Jon Glidden served with the U. S. Strategic and Tactical Air Force in the United Kingdom. When he returned to civilian life, he resumed his life in the *hacienda* he and his wife, Dorothy, owned in the Pojoaque Valley near Santa Fé. His Western novels were by this time being serialized in *The Saturday Evening Post.* "The Echo Herd" was completed in June, 1947 and sold to Mike Tilden, editor of Popular Publications' *New Western,* on July 1, 1947. The author was paid $375.00 for it. When this story was published in the November, 1947 issue, the title was changed to "The Devil's Night-Hawk," but for its appearance here the author's original title has been restored.

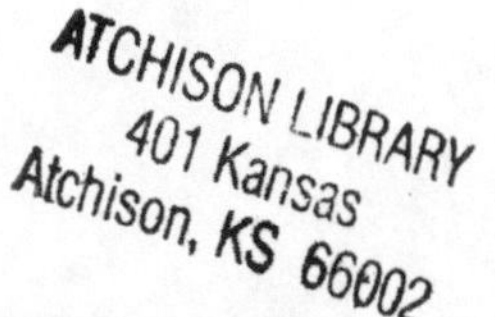

1

It wasn't so bad at first. They were grouchy about being wakened in the dead of night, but that was natural. The cook and Ed Buford were the first ones out, and they went up to the house, Ed to waken the boss. And while he waited for Cass Waite to pull on some clothes, Jim Rush stood by the bunkhouse stove, soaking in some of its feeble warmth.

He was cold, chilled to the bone. His shoulders were wet from a hole ripped in his poncho on that wild scramble through the scrub oak and alder thickets. A wavy streak of blood glistened along his flat cheek, running down a deep gash showing through the blond hair above his temple. But there was nothing wrong with him that a good night's sleep wouldn't fix. He looked lean and tough as rawhide, even though tiredness showed in his eyes and in the drawn look of his angular face.

Finally Cass was ready, and they stepped out into the rain and trudged up to the house. A lamp came on in the office. They found Ed Buford and Mark Ames in there, Ames standing by his rolltop desk. The rancher had no more than put the chimney back on the lamp than the cook brought in a pot of coffee and some tin cups, setting them on a table by the window. Ames hadn't bothered putting on a shirt, and he looked skinnier than ever in his long-sleeved underwear as he reached down to fill a cup and offer it, saying: "Drink this before you try and talk. Lord, you look played out."

Jim Rush was even more played-out than he looked. Three

miles afoot over rocky going in a driving downpour can take a lot out of a man. Ten more miles of riding a skittish, caught-up mare bareback—with a halter fashioned from his belt—had left him sore. His leg muscles felt sprung. He wanted nothing so much as to sit down or lie down in a chair or a bed or even on the ground, anywhere. But before he did that he'd have to give Mark Ames his story, and he could stay on his feet while he did it.

Now, as the first swallow of coffee eased the chill of his insides, he asked: "How much did Ed tell you?"

Ames glanced at his foreman, his steady gray eyes squinting against the lamp glare. "What was it you said, Ed? The herd driven off up Echo?"

All at once, seeing the way Ed was staring at him, Jim had his first hint of something wrong. Bell's foreman was big and trigger-tempered, and, if he didn't like you, his eyes would get the way they were now—narrow-lidded and smoldering. Why he should have a chip on his shoulder tonight, Jim didn't know. No rule in the book said you had to like the ramrod you worked for, and from the first he'd disliked Buford. But something was really wrong now.

"Let Idaho tell it," Ed drawled tonelessly, calling Jim by the handle he'd given him the first day he signed on.

"Go ahead, Idaho. Let's have all of it," Ames said. Over in the corner Cass Waite eased lower into the rawhide-backed chair, his spurs setting up a whisper of sound over the drone of the rain on the shingles. He, too, was staring at Jim oddly, coldly. None of them was interested in the coffee.

"It was along about ten when I heard something soundin' over the storm and raised up to see what it was," Jim began, a vague uneasiness and anger stirring in him. "I'd rigged the tarp so it would shed most of the water and shoved the Forty-Five under my hull to keep it dry. While I was reaching for it, tryin' to see out, something belted me alongside the head. That's the last I knew for a while."

"So you just let 'em walk right in on you," Buford drawled in a voice as cold as winter granite.

Jim's angry glance swung around. "No one told me to night-owl that bunch of steers." He nodded across to Cass Waite. "When Cass left after supper, all he said was to watch for lightning spookin' 'em through that brush we'd thrown across the narrows. I waited until the storm steadied down and then turned in."

"Then what?"

Mark Ames's two words brought with them far more surprise than either Ed's or Cass's strange manner. The rancher spoke in a clipped, hard way. Ordinarily he was mild and easy-going. But a subtle change had come over him. As Jim answered, he was trying to grasp what lay beneath this sudden hostility.

"By the time I was on my feet again, they were moving the herd out up the cañon. I counted three of 'em before I made a run for it. Someone took a shot at me. Guess they thought I wouldn't come to so soon."

Ed Buford looked pointedly at the clock on the wall above the desk. "That happened about ten? Where you been between then and now?" The clock's hands said one-forty.

"Hoofin' it out. They drove off the gelding. There was a bunch of nags standin' out of the wind below the dam. It took some doin' to catch up one. What the hell would you have done?"

Ed Buford's square face reddened at the studied insolence of Jim's question. No one on the crew talked to Ed this way, not even Cass. But the next moment Jim saw Ed wasn't to be prodded into showing his hand yet. Then Cass was saying bluntly: "Any damn' fool would know enough to keep an eye on that much beef with those nesters on the prowl like they've been."

"Cass, one day you'll run off at the mouth to the wrong man," Jim drawled softly. He was mad now, mad clear through.

"See if I got this straight, Idaho," Mark Ames said with a mildness that didn't deceive. "You claim you didn't hear anything until it was too late. They knocked you out and went about their business. Didn't even leave a man to watch you. So you just up and walked out of there."

Jim was holding a tight rein on his temper, all at once seeing what a spot he was in. "Maybe they thought I was done for. It was black as the inside of a jug, and stormy. If you had bent your barrel over a man's skull, you might think he was taken care of."

Ames glanced at his foreman, and the look that passed between them meant they'd settled something in their minds. Ed Buford spoke. "You hired on here two months ago, my friend. With a tall story about hatin' sodbusters. So we trusted you."

"You can still trust me." Jim knew before the words were out that they meant nothing to these three.

Cass Waite came up out of the chair and stepped over to the door, behind Jim, leaning lazily against the frame. His move had an unmistakable meaning. Ed went on tonelessly: "This was the first time we'd left you alone where you could do us any harm. You saw your chance and rode over to Flint Creek and spread the word. You probably went straight to Morgan Long, knowin' he's their big augur. The rain made it easy. Come daylight and we'll play hell findin' any sign. When your sidekicks showed up, you probably helped 'em pull that brush clear. By mornin' those steers'll be far enough out of. . . ."

His words broke off as Jim suddenly lunged at him. Jim, knowing things would only get worse instead of better, swung fast and hard. His knuckles slashed across Buford's thick lips, and the next instant he brought in his left, brought it in low to catch the Bell man in the groin.

He was watching Ed fall, a wild surge of sheer gladness in him, when Mark Ames broke the chair over his head.

The water runneling down over his cheeks and off his chin brought him back to consciousness, and for a time his senses gave him only a half awareness of what was happening. He was tied onto a saddle, boots roped to the cinch, wrists to the horn. He was colder than he'd ever been. For a time he imagined this to be a night long ago when a blizzard had caught him and his father, riding out from town. They'd traveled the line of a rail fence to find their cabin. Something was wrong, and it took him a long interval to figure out that it wasn't snowing tonight, but raining instead.

He found the strength to lift his head, and a moment later a shadow came in at him from his right side. He heard Ed Buford's voice sounding from a great distance. "The pale-haired devil's come to." The next instant a shower of fiery sparks exploded across his consciousness, and he had a split second's realization of stabbing pain at the hinge of his jaw.

Sometime later the ache of the horn digging into his chest brought him back again, and this time he didn't have the strength to straighten. He only sat there with the jolt of the horse rubbing his ribs raw against the horn. His tall frame still trembled with the cold, although it wasn't raining now. He couldn't seem to close his mouth. The whole right side of his face throbbed dully. He had no connected thoughts. For what seemed an endless time the pain held him on the verge of terror. Finally the horse stumbled along a steep stretch of trail where it crossed a wash; the horn dug suddenly and hard into his chest, and he fainted.

When he was next aware of anything., he could feel that he was lying on something soft. His head throbbed dully, and there was a light shining on his face, a light too bright to open his eyes to. He could hear voices, indistinctly at first, but then with growing plainness. The first words that made any sense to him were drawled deliberately and close at hand. It was Mark Ames saying: ". . . law won't do something, we damned well will. There'll be a hangin' jury, if I have to buy one!"

"Now, Mark, for the love of God, give the man a chance! You'll blow the lid off this thing now, and we'll need a bigger buryin' ground."

"I'll blow it off! Tonight! Beginnin' at Morg Long's layout."

Jim could hear boots thudding across a plank floor. Even though the light glowed rosily through his closed lids, he opened his eyes. He was staring straight up at a lantern hanging from a beamed roof. He turned his head in time to see Mark Ames and Ed Buford going out through a door. A strong wind and a spray of rain slanted in through the door until it closed behind them, leaving a stillness settling over the room.

Then a voice at Jim's other side intoned: "Your patient's comin' to, Len. Better have a look at him."

Jim rolled his head the other way to see George Crosley's full-mustached face staring soberly down at him. The nickeled star on Crosley's open vest glittered blindingly. Beyond the sheriff now a black-garbed figure rose from a caboose chair in front of a flat, scarred desk. Although Jim had never seen him, he had heard of Dr. Leonard Olds.

The medical man came across and looked down at him, asking: "How do you feel?"

"I've felt better." Jim heard his words come out shaky and weak.

"Your skull must be the next thing to rimrock, son. Why it didn't fracture, the Lord only knows. It took thirty-four stitches to close that one big rip and ten for the other." The doctor looked around at George Crosley. "By the way, they didn't say how he was hurt, did they?"

The old lawman shook his head, and, looking beyond him, Jim could see that the far wall of the room was a row of thick iron bars centered by an open door of steel grillwork. This was Crosley's office, with the jail backing it. Jim quickly gathered that they had stretched him out here on this cot only for the doctor to treat him. The jail door was open, ready for him—if Mark Ames's words were to be taken at their face value.

So now he summoned the strength to speak again. "What're they chargin' me with, Sheriff?"

"Aidin' and abettin' the rustling of a Bell herd. Idaho, you're in bad trouble."

The gravity written on the lawman's face was more convincing than his words. Thinking back on what he knew of George Crosley—or rather on what he had heard, being a comparative newcomer—Jim could see nothing that improved his chances. Crosley was honest. But he was too old for his job and, most important of all, had been sustained in office chiefly by Mark Ames's friendship for him. Notwithstanding his honesty, cattlemen like Ames looked to George Crosley to support their interests against homesteaders who had recently filed on quarter-sections along Flint Creek to take up grass that had always been Bell's. Now it looked as though time was near for a showdown between the homesteaders and Bell.

Jim thought it through logically and deliberately, seeing how Ames was using him as the trigger to set off a range war. The unfairness of it, along with Mark Ames's cold-blooded refusal to believe his story, made Jim push up onto one elbow.

"Look, Sheriff. I had nothing to do with this. They'd left me to hold the herd till mornin' while the rest worked the big bunch over at Arrow Springs. I was gun-whipped, left for crow bait. I got away and rode across to the layout. They thought I was lyin' when I told it. The three of 'em . . . Ames and Ed and Cass Waite . . . beat the daylights out of me, hog-tied me, and brought me in here. Now I'm framed."

Crosley considered this a long moment and finally lifted his spare shoulders in a shrug. "Mark's sworn out a warrant on you. There's nothin' I can do about it."

"You're the law. It's up to you to see that it's honest law, not crooked." Jim swung his legs to the floor, leaning over and holding his head in his hands as a sudden dizziness hit him.

"Careful there," the doctor said, a look of alarm crossing his face. "You're in no shape to be off your back, man."

Jim ignored the warning, looking at Crosley. "I've heard you're straight as a string, Sheriff. But there's nothin' straight about this."

"You'll be given a trial, Idaho."

Jim smiled crookedly. "You heard what Ames said about a jury."

"Sometimes Mark talks too big." Crosley's hawkish face showed a tinge of stubborn anger.

"Does he?" There was mockery in Jim's tone.

Abruptly Crosley reached down, taking Jim by the arm, saying irritably: "You need rest. So do we. It's close to four o'clock, and this is goin' to be a bad day, unless I'm wrong.

Here, Len, give a hand."

The medical man moved in on the other side. As they helped him to his feet, a feeling close to panic hit Jim. He had no illusions on what the closing of that cell door meant. Once they had him locked in there, he was at their mercy. Right or wrong, Mark Ames intended to make an example of him, instead of untangling the mystery lying behind the stealing of the herd.

His jumbled thinking searched frantically for a way of escape. But the unsteadiness of his legs, the dizziness, warned him against any violence. He would have fallen, if they hadn't held him erect.

Just then his glance went to the sheriff's littered desk, to the rack above it where two carbines slanted against the wall. Lying on the rack was a .45 Colt, its walnut handle cracked and dusty.

Sight of that made him drop his head and lift a hand to his forehead, saying weakly: "Give me a minute to steady down."

"Sure, no hurry," George Crosley answered, concern in his tone.

Gradually Jim's vision cleared, and the floor stopped swaying beneath him. He felt a tired strength slowly returning to his legs. When he drawled finally—"O K, give it a try."—and let them lead him toward the cell door beyond the desk, he stumbled more than necessary and let his knees buckle a little. Coming up on the desk, he lurched into Crosley all at once and seemed about to fall when he reached out and caught himself on the desk's edge. He stood there for several seconds, letting his head sag to his chest, mumbling: "The floor won't stop spinnin'."

"Take a rest," the doctor said, standing on Jim's right, between him and the gun rack on the wall.

For a brief moment Jim considered making a try for the

weapon at the sheriff's thigh. But he knew that even Crosley would be quicker that he was right now. So he straightened, crowding abruptly against Olds. And the doctor moved out of his way.

He said—"I'll hang onto this."—and took a step toward the cell door, supporting himself by a hold on the desk. He didn't look toward the gun rack as he stepped out and reached for the break in the wall at the door's edge. Suddenly he let himself sway in toward the desk again, his hand going up to the rack and snatching up the Colt. He wheeled around, leaning back against the wall, and leveled the .45 at the startled Crosley, drawling: "I'm going out of here."

There was a second in which Jim was sure that the lawman's glance wavered, that Crosley was trying to trick him. But then his thumb drew back the hammer of the weapon. There was no tension in it. He knew he was finished.

"Should have been fixed a long time back," Crosley muttered in an almost apologetic way. And he nodded to the cell door.

Jim laid the Colt on the desk, stepped around the doctor, and in through the cell door. Crosley tossed him the blanket that had been on the cot in the office. He handed in the lantern. "You sleep easy, Idaho. Nothin's going to happen to you that shouldn't."

"No?" Jim drawled dryly.

After they had gone and he had blown out the lantern, he lay on the cot with the blanket pulled up over him, trying to figure out what was to happen. But his thinking wouldn't come straight. Finally he let sleep crowd in on him.

II

The scuffle of boots and the drone of voices brought Jim awake at mid-morning. He was stiff all over, his head and chest ached dully, and he was hungry. But, as he lay there, listening, turning his head a little so that he could peer through the bars into the office, he soon forgot how badly he felt. There were four men out there besides George Crosley, two of whom he had never seen before, one whose face was vaguely familiar, and the last a man whom he knew slightly. Bob Stoneman was a homesteader who had three months ago moved onto the quarter-section highest along Flint Creek. It was Stoneman, spade-bearded and chunky, standing alongside Crosley's desk who was now saying: ". . . doesn't add up to what you say it does, Sheriff. Here we are, all four of us. Accordin' to Ames, we lifted that herd last night and drove it off. Where could we have hidden it so's to be here now? Besides us, there's no one left but my youngster and Fred's daughter to be holdin' those critters for us. Unless you want to count the other womenfolk."

Crosley tilted back in the desk corner in his caboose chair, looking harassed and worried as he muttered: "I'm only tellin' you what Ames told me."

"Which is a damned lot of trumped-up nonsense!" flared the man standing alongside Stoneman. He was a brindle-haired scarecrow individual of middle age, his bib-overalls mud-stained with the legs tucked into oversize flat-heel boots. Now he ran the back of a hand over his tobacco-browned longhorn mustache, saying flatly: "Get your self a horse and ride up to my place, if you don't believe us. What's left of my barn's still smokin'. Bob and Fred and Tom were all there with me from four on this mornin', fightin the fire. On the way down to my place Bob found ten rod of his south fence cut, the wire so tangled he can never use it again. And Ames claims we were out swingin' a sticky loop on his critters."

"Any tracks around? Anything at all for me to go on, Morg?" the sheriff asked tiredly.

And the lanky man—Jim remembered his name now, Morgan Long—nodded to the window where the rain was still steadily pelting the glass. "Tracks? With that much water comin' down?"

Crosley now looked at the other pair of homesteaders. One of these was a young man in his twenties, barrel-chested and blond, his ruddy face pleasant-looking; the other was the oldest of the four, stooped, white hair showing from under a black flat-crowned hat.

"Kirkman," the lawman said, eyeing the oldster, "I've known you the longest. I'm askin' you this just for the record. Is what Bob and Morg claim the truth? Every word of it? If you say so, I'll believe it."

"Every word," Kirkman answered.

George Crosley let out a gusty sigh, rocking his chair to the floor. "Ames claims you boys got away with his herd, Idaho in there helpin'. You claim you were all at home nicely tucked in bed till Morg here woke up hearin' his mare tryin' to kick her way out of her burnin' stable. He sent his youngster after help, and you all gathered at his place along about four. Damned if I make head or tail of it."

"I do."

Jim couldn't keep the words back and immediately regretted them as the glances of all five men swung around toward the cell. He was confused now, wishing he hadn't spoken. Then a stubbornness rose in him, and he decided to go through with it. Something Morg Long had said a minute ago didn't quite tie in with what he remembered of last night. He had a right to know why it didn't.

"What's on your mind, Idaho?" Crosley asked as the others eyed Jim with suspicion or outright hostility.

"Something you just said. Long mentioned it, too. Something about their all being at his place at four this morning."

Crosley looked at Morgan Long. "That's what you said, wasn't it?"

"Four it was," the homesteader said positively. "The mare woke me along about three. It took me near an hour for the boy to get back with the others."

"That makes it even worse," Jim said.

"Makes what worse?" Crosley was leaning forward in his chair now.

"Last night, before you locked me in here, you said it was close to four. Ames and Ed hadn't been gone more than ten minutes. Ames had told you he was headed for Long's to blow the lid off this thing. It's all of twelve miles from here to Long's place. How did Ames and Ed make that ride so quick?"

Surprise, then a puzzled frown, patterned Crosley's lined face. Abruptly his expression softened. "Cass Waite must've been the one. You said he was in on that whippin' they gave you at Bell."

Jim smiled, shaking his head. "It wasn't Cass. He's not the man to fire a barn and pull down a fence all by himself."

"Then how do you figure it, Idaho?"

"Cass had help."

"Where'd he get it?"

"From the rest of the crew, working the herd at Arrow Springs."

The homesteaders were listening intently now. Morg Long's expression of dislike for this Bell crewman had thinned to a look of interest. "That could be," he softly drawled.

"Another thing," Jim went on, watching Crosley's doubt weaken, making a wild spur-of-the-moment guess. "If the rest of the crew at Arrow Springs were handy to help Cass, they could have been just as handy for stealin' that herd earlier. The whole thing could have been planned out beforehand."

Jim saw his words shock the lawman into open-jawed wonder. But Crosley was quick to disbelieve, and he vigorously shook his head. "Mark Ames . . . rustle a herd of his own to bust this thing open? Unh-uh. I won't buy that, Idaho."

Bob Stoneman asked: "Why not?"

"Why the hell won't you?" Morg Long echoed. "See here. Ames has pecked away at us for a year now, tryin' to bring this on. We took all the trouble he threw at us and never lifted a hand against him. Why, last spring I counted eight of my calves burned with his Bell brand after roundup."

"This is the first time I've heard about it," the sheriff bridled. "Why didn't you come to me?"

Morgan Long's thin face took on a twisted smile. "You'd have taken that just like you're takin' this, George. You may not know it, but you've chose sides. Against us."

"That's strong talk, Morg." Crosley's eyes were bright with anger and his face had reddened. "My side's the law, and don't any of you forget it! Anyone that bucks the law gets hurt."

"Then, listen," Morg told him. "See if this holds water. Bob and Fred and Tom have all taken as much from Ames as I have. Never once have we hit back at him. So now Ames finally sees we won't give him an excuse for pushin' us off what was his grass. What does he do? He trumps up this play that'll let him run us out. Rustles his own beef . . . like you just said." The homesteader's glance left Crosley and swung toward the cell. "Stranger, until now I had you figured as bein' with Ames. I've changed my mind. We're all obliged to you for helpin' us see how Ames's dealt his cards in what looks to be a crooked game."

George Crosley banged his fist on the desk. "Hold on! Nothing's proven. You're makin' a bunch of wild guesses. Idaho, I said before I wouldn't buy this. I won't! It's too damn' far-fetched. I've known Mark Ames eighteen years. He's straight."

"Does that hold for Ed Buford?" Stoneman asked quietly.

"Yeah, there's a mighty salty understrapper for a man to have, if he's tryin' to get along with his neighbors," put in the youngest of the quartet, speaking for the first time.

"Dennis, you had that run-in with Buford last summer, and just plain don't like him," Crosley said.

"Tom Dennis's not the only one." This from Fred Kirkman.

Jim, watching the sheriff, could see him definitely close his mind to the possibilities. Crosley now came up out of his chair, once more shaking his head. "The whole thing's too loco. I won't listen to you till you bring me something to go on."

"Like what?" Morg Long asked.

"Proof of some kind against Ames." The lawman looked across at Jim with an angry eye, adding: "Not the first notion thought up by a man bearin' Ames a grudge."

"These men didn't drive that herd off, Sheriff," Jim drawled, intending that his words should annoy Crosley more. "If they didn't, who did?"

Crosley thumbed his wide hat to the back of his head and

ran the thumb into the edge of his thin, sandy hair, glaring at Jim. "Right now I don't know. But I will." He nodded to Long and the others. "Don't worry, I'll have something in a day or two."

"George, we came in here to swear out a warrant for Ames," Fred Kirkman said. "Will you serve the warrant?"

The sheriff's patience had worn too thin. He flared: "No, by God! Not with what you give me to go on."

"So we're fightin' Bell *and* the law," Morg Long said tonelessly.

Crosley swung sharply around on him. "Morg, any more talk like that and you and me are goin' to tangle."

Morgan Long shrugged his bony shoulders and looked at the others. "Let's move, boys. The air's gettin' bad in here."

George Crosley was speechless with anger as they buckled their slickers and filed out of the door. As it slammed shut behind Tom Dennis's broad back, the lawman wheeled to face the cell.

"Now see what you've done!"

Jim grinned. "What have I?"

"You saw 'em stomp out of here. Now they're against me."

"They ought to be. As long as you stand by watchin' 'em get kicked around."

"Damn it, I'm not lettin' anyone kick anybody around!"

"You are, if you don't do something about this."

Crosley caught himself on the point of making a sharp retort. He was obviously trying to control a temper gone too wild. He asked with a surprising mildness: "Just what would you do?"

Jim thought a moment, saying finally: "If I had a prisoner as hungry as yours, I'd feed him. Then I'd get on a horse and ride up Arrow Springs way and count noses. There ought to

be six men workin' the herd up there, not countin' Ed or Cass or the boss."

"Arrow Spring's twenty mile from here."

Jim nodded. "And it's twenty miles back. Which means you'll be all day at it. So you'd better bring in a big meal."

Crosley snorted and reached up to clamp his Stetson low on his head. He crossed the room and took his poncho from a wall hook, not saying anything. As he opened the door and stepped out into the steady drizzle, Jim called after him: "You might bring me some smokin', too."

The way the lawman slammed the door—hard enough to make the window rattle—made Jim feel better than he had all day. If nothing else had been accomplished since he had awakened, he had prodded Crosley's curiosity. Anything, or nothing, might come of that.

Jim was eating his second meal. Carson, from the restaurant across the street, had brought it in a small bucket. It was a beef stew, tasty with potatoes and rich gravy, and as he unlocked the cell—using the key the sheriff had given him in the morning—Carson had held a cocked .38 in his hand and stayed out of Jim's reach, setting the bucket down on the floor. He didn't know when Crosley would be back. No, there wasn't much doing in town. None of Bell's crew had been in today, and Morg Long and his friends hadn't hung around long this morning after leaving the jail.

"It's just too damned wet for anybody to be out in it," was the way Carson put it.

For a while this afternoon, Jim had pulled the cot to the cell's back wall, opened the small, high window, and stood on the cot looking out through the bars along the alley, watching the rain dappling the muddy water overflowing the wheel ruts and the gush of water dropping from the eaves trough of the

hardware warehouse across the way. The cool breeze had eased the dull and throbbing soreness of his head and thinned the staleness of the air in the jail. A rain like this, he had supposed, seldom struck the range during the fall. He had idly wondered who the man could be who had so rightly judged the storm's length and gambled on it in stealing the herd and using the rain to wash out the sign. Leaning there with his elbows on the window's deep rock sill, he had also remembered a couple of things that might interest George Crosley.

One was the oddity of finding Ed Buford fully dressed there at the bunkhouse last night. Jim had taken several seconds to get the lamp going, but, when the light came, he now recalled, Bell's ramrod had been pulling on his second boot. Getting into his clothes after Jim had awakened him would certainly have taken Ed longer than that brief span of time. And Jim knew that it wasn't the man's habit to sleep in his clothes. He should have noticed this last night. But he'd been too much on edge over what he was about to tell Ed.

The other thing he saw as strange was the cook's presence at the layout. At mid-afternoon yesterday, before he and Cass left Arrow Springs to look over the Echo Cañon gather, Soapy Henderson had been at his chuck wagon in the pines, building up his fires for the evening meal. Had Soapy ridden back to headquarters after supper so as to be on hand with a breakfast in the cook house this morning for the crew? Echo Cañon and Flint Creek, scenes of trouble last night, were both much closer to the ranch than Arrow Springs.

Soapy's being there in the bunkhouse, Jim had decided, somehow tied in with Ed's being awake and out of his bunk. Had he only noticed these two things and mentioned them to the sheriff, George Crosley might have ridden out to Bell this morning to see what was going on. Jim's hunch that the crew had eaten there this morning was just as strong as his hunch

that his turning up at Bell last night had been unexpected, and had surprised Ed and Cass. He was halfway convinced it was never intended that he should leave Echo Cañon. Whoever had hit him had meant to kill him.

So now, as the last gray light faded from the street window before night's blackness, Jim was impatiently wanting Crosley to get back so they could talk things over. Nothing was right about his being cooped up in jail. The sheriff was going to have to find a better reason for holding him. Time and again, after he had lit the lantern, he had looked about the cell, trying to see a way of breaking out. But the walls were of adobe and rock, nearly three feet through, and it would take a crowbar to do anything with the bars at the window. He might, using the coal oil in the lantern, set fire to the *vigas* or the roof sheathing above them. But he couldn't burn his way out through the roof without someone in the street discovering the fire.

There was no one he could count on to help him. He had drifted onto this range from across the desert only two months ago. He didn't know anyone here at all well, not even any of the Bell crewmen. Most of them were of a hardcase breed he had never had much to do with. Lately he'd been thinking about drawing his wages and drifting on to some other job that would carry him through the winter. So now he saw himself as friendless, not out of self-pity but simply as he weighed his chances of getting out of here.

It looked like he was here to stay just as long as Mark Ames wanted to keep him. How long that would be he had no way of knowing.

Two or three times during the next hour he got up from the cot and went to the front of the cell at the sound of boots thudding past along the plank walk. But each time whoever it was went straight on, not turning in. When someone finally did stop, it was Dr. Olds who came in, folding a black umbrella and shaking the water from it.

"Miserable night," the medical man said as he came across to the cell. "How's the head?"

"Good enough."

"Lean over so I can see."

Jim tilted his head down, and, after a long look at the biggest gash in his scalp, Olds said: "Coming along fine. We'll take the stitches out in about a week."

"When's Crosley getting back?" Jim asked impatiently.

Olds's brows lifted in puzzlement. "Has he gone somewhere?"

The doctor's question served to drive home Jim's disappointment and disgust, his feeling that everyone, even Crosley, had forgotten him. That feeling held on long after the medical man had left the office, until he had blown out the lantern and stretched out on the cot. He didn't particularly want to sleep, but after several minutes of lying there he could feel himself dozing off.

The tapping on the window startled him out of a half sleep. At first, coming wide awake, he knew only that he had heard a sound. When the tapping came again softly, regularly, he swung erect. Standing warily to one side, he reached up and unlatched the window.

As it swung open, a voice from outside whispered hoarsely over the sound of the rain: "Get ready, Idaho. You're comin' out!"

That first wariness grew stronger in Jim as he tried to recognize the voice and couldn't. His back hugged the wall as he asked, low-voiced: "Who is it?"

"Me. Morg Long. Along with Bob and Tom," came the answer. "Hang on a minute while we give a pull." And there came the sharp ring of metal striking metal, followed by the muttered oath of the man.

As Jim pulled the cot in under the window and stepped up onto it, his wariness draining away, a slow excitement was building up in him. He couldn't recognize the voice as Morgan Long's, but the implication that the homesteaders were breaking him out of this jail was reassuring. He had found some friends.

It was pitch-black outside. He couldn't begin to see anything. But as he once more caught the soft grating of metal, his hand went to the bars, and he finally touched what he recognized as the hook of a block and tackle fastened to the bottom of the middle bar. Several moments later he heard the squeal of a wooden pulley sound from the alley and felt the hook tighten.

The bar popped from its deep anchoring with a loudness that made Jim draw back. Then the man outside was saying: "One more and you can make it, Idaho. You ready?"

"Plenty ready," Jim answered.

Once again he heard the hook being attached to a bar, and a second time there came the complaining squeal of the pulley as the rope put tension on it. This time the bar that was being pulled bent and pulled away, clanking to the ground outside, hitting a rock with a loudness that hurried Jim as he pulled himself up and went belly down across the sill.

The rain was pelting his shoulders as hands took a hold on his arms. The same voice whispered: "Just hang on. We'll get you out."

Panic hit Jim then, a wild surge of it that stiffened his long frame. For the voice, disguised by its whisper, was one he knew. It was Cass Waite's, not Morg Long's.

He threw himself sideways, twisting away from Cass's grip, wriggling clear of the window ledge. He thrust his hands out as he felt himself falling. He suddenly struck the ground, wrist-deep in mud. His left shoulder hit and took up his weight.

Cass cried: "He's loose! Get him!"

A shadow showed vaguely against the blackness close to Jim's left as he lunged back against the jail wall. Cass was to the right of him, he knew, and this other man was closing in on his left. He stood there, unmoving, for possibly two seconds, seeing now how they had tricked him, knowing they would try to kill him. But suddenly it came to him that they were as blind as he in this darkness.

He took a step out from the wall and collided with a horse's flank, wheeling away and swinging at the animal with a hard jab. He struck and heard the horse lunge away with mud sucking at its hoofs, his rider cursing explosively.

Then, from behind him, Cass was calling in a hushed, furious voice: "Damn you, Billy, he's got away!"

Bill Whipple, Bell's youngest crew member, retorted hotly: "Then he went your way, not mine!"

They were thrashing around in the dark as Jim edged around the corner of the jail and took the narrow alleyway between the buildings in the street, walking instead of running, afraid they might hear him. By the time he reached the plank walk, his head and shoulders were wet.

The walk seemed empty, as did the tie rails. But far down the street he dimly made out what he thought was a horse, standing at the rail in front of the Cattleman's Bar. He headed for it.

He was halfway to the saloon when Cass and Whipple came out of an alley below him and rode into the street, turning up toward him, their shapes indistinct in the pale wash of light shining from a store window. He faded off the walk, stepping into the deep obscurity of a store doorway.

Cass and Whipple, riding slowly and looking over the walks on both sides of the street, came on past him and finally turned in at the jail.

He heard Cass call loudly to someone across the street, probably at the restaurant which was still lighted: "Where's Crosley?"

A voice from over there answered: "Out somewhere. Why?"

"Got some things here for Rush. How do I get 'em in to him?"

"Carson's got the key. Hang on and I'll get him."

Jim moved then, knowing it would only be a matter of minutes, perhaps seconds, before Cass had raised the alarm. The cell would be empty, and Cass, the man who had emptied it, would be leading the hunt for the escaped prisoner.

There was an interruption Jim hadn't counted on when a man came out of the saloon and turned up the walk toward him. Once more he took to the darkness, this time in the passageway alongside the bank, and the seconds it took the man to walk on past seemed to Jim to drag interminably.

Then, finally, as he went on, it was to see a lantern bobbing across the street from the restaurant, Carson's blocky shape outlined in its light. Jim walked faster.

The lone bay horse tied at the saloon rail stood hip-shot, rump to the slant of the rain. There was a slicker draped over the saddle.

Jim was pulling on the slicker, when the first shouts came from upstreet. He yanked loose the reins and swung up into the saddle, his legs bent to the too-short stirrups as he put the horse down the muddy street.

He was beyond the stores, riding between the cottonwoods fronting fenced-off yards, when three close-spaced shots sent sharp echoes riding all over the darkened town.

Now they would be hunting him.

III

It had been a hard day for George Crosley. He was half a mile out the west trail from town, cold and tired and disconsolate, wishing he were in bed, when the muffled echoes of the three shots came to him over the whisper of the rain. At any other time the lawman would have paid them hardly any attention. But now, with a strong foreboding, he prodded the tired horse into a trot, and by the time he rode up the street a crowd had already gathered at the jail.

While the others talked, giving him half a dozen versions of how it might have happened, he had his look at the open window, its broken sill, and the empty cell. Someone found the block and tackle outside, but that didn't mean much. It always hung from the beam over the warehouse platform, handy for lifting heavy loads from wagons.

Crosley was listening to Cass Waite's telling how he and Whipple had ridden in with a few things for Jim Rush—his razor, a clean shirt, and socks now lying on the sheriff's desk—and how Carson had come with them into the office, saying that his bay horse had been stolen from in front of the Cattleman's Bar. He claimed he'd make the county pay for the animal.

It was when Cass Waite inserted the suggestion that the Flint Creek homesteaders were the likeliest bet for having broken the prisoner out of jail—and that a posse should ride for Flint Creek at once—that the sheriff finally lost patience. "Cass, you can forget that talk," he bridled. "I had supper with Long and his family. If anyone from up there did this, they'd have passed Long's cabin. No one's come down from there since five this afternoon."

"They could've come down before that," Cass said with a pointed meaning. The crowd took up the idea and embroidered on it.

Soon Crosley could see the situation was getting out of hand. So he shrewdly decided to put the hotheads to work and, his mind made up, went over to his desk and banged on it until the packed room went quiet. "All right, we'll get started at this thing now," he told them. "Al, you take four men and get up to the pass at Summit quick as you can. Another bunch ought to cover those trails down toward the Sink. Six men can handle it. They'll go with you, Whipple. Cass can come with me up Flint way. We'll need a couple more men. All of you are drawin' wages from the county, and you'd better take along grub for at least two days. Rush is to be brought in alive. Get that? *Alive.* You're all deputies. Now raise your right hands and say what I tell you to." And he swore them in.

It was another forty minutes before he left town on a fresh horse, Cass Waite and a pair of townsmen siding him. And once his spare, sore frame had eased to the steady sway of the saddle, he let his mind turn to certain matters he'd postponed thinking about until now. Chief of these, and the most confusing, was that Jim Rush's hunch on what he would find at Arrow Springs had paid off. Early this afternoon he'd waited in the timber above Bell's camp a good hour or more for the two riders slowly circling the herd to show up. But no others had, and by two-thirty Crosley was forced to the conclusion that Ames's two hands were holding the herd by themselves. He had wondered at the absence of the other four men Idaho had claimed should be there. The wondering didn't help his peace of mind much. Where they could be was anyone's guess, and Crosley didn't like guesswork—especially the kind that pointed strongly to an old friend's doing the things Idaho hinted Mark Ames might be doing.

Just now, so as to make sense of the thing, he slowed his horse and let Cass Waite come alongside. He was wishing he could see Cass's face in the darkness as he asked off-handedly: "How's the shippin' herd shaping up, Cass?"

"Fair."

"Most of the boys workin' it?"

"Every man."

That looked like the answer Crosley hadn't wanted. There was one other possibility he had considered. "Didn't Ed send any of the crew up Echo today?"

"Went up himself. Couldn't find a thing."

Now the sheriff was really worried. Here was Cass, claiming that the entire Bell crew was working the main herd, when he himself had seen the herd being held by only a pair of men. Something was wrong. Was Idaho right about Ames's having stolen his own beef up Echo? Or did Cass know what he was talking about?

The ride to Morg Long's cabin took the four of them a good hour and a half, and, long before they reached it, the rain stopped and a stiff chill wind sprang out of the northwest, the sky clearing a little to show patches of bright stars. That starlight was reflected from the still surface of the beaver pond as they forded the creek close below it, and the racket they made brought a pair of dogs down from the cabin, yapping. A light came on in the window of the cabin, and they were riding up on it when Morg Long's voice surprised them, sounding from the obscurity of a lean-to off to their left: "Sing out! Who is it?"

Crosley answered, and the gaunt homesteader walked up out of the shadows as they swung around, a carbine slanted in the crook of his arm. "Somethin' wrong, Sheriff?"

"Rush got away," Crosley told him.

Enough lamplight shone from the window to let the lawman catch the slow, pleased smile that came to Long's thin face. "Now that's nice," the homesteader drawled. "Real nice."

"He had help," Crosley said tartly. "The idea was that someone from up here did it."

It was a moment before the homesteader replied. "No one that I know of, Sheriff. Not that we didn't think of it. Tom come down all redheaded after you left this evenin', sayin' we ought to do something about Idaho. But I talked him out of it."

"How about the others?" Cass Waite asked.

Morg Long wheeled around, peering intently into the blackness in Cass's direction. "Who's that?"

"Cass Waite," the lawman put in hurriedly. "Along with Ralph Molders and John Higgins."

Long didn't say anything, but Crosley saw his face set doggedly as he stood there, not asking them in. And only then did the lawman realize that an unexpected complication had developed. He had ridden up here to ask Long to let him and his possemen throw their blankets under the lean-to or on the cabin's wide porch. Now it was obvious that the homesteader wasn't going to invite a Bell man into his cabin.

George Crosley did some quick thinking then, saying shortly: "Cass is on the way over to stir up Mark Ames's crew at the Springs and get them out on this. You want to rest a spell or go right on, Cass?"

It was a long moment before Cass said tonelessly: "Guess I'll go on."

Crosley could hear the Bell man climb into his saddle, and then Cass was asking: "Anything special you want me to tell the boss, Sheriff?"

"No. Only Buford might send a man up to look over the line shacks. Idaho might not be leavin' the country as quick as we think."

"Why would he be stickin' around?"

"No telling," Crosley answered, and then heard Cass's horse going slowly away.

"Come on in and have some coffee, gents," Morg Long said, once the sound of Cass's horse had died out against the murmur of the creek. "The missus will want you to bed down inside. It's turned chill for sleepin' out."

They went into the cabin and found Mrs. Long at the stove end of the single room, and Crosley said apologetically: "Didn't know when I left this evenin' I was to be your star boarder, ma'am."

"You're welcome just any time, Sheriff," she told him, and presently they sat down to a supper of hot biscuits and honey and coffee.

A strange annoyance blended with the sheriff's gratefulness to her and Long. Despite his prejudices and his ingrained dislike for these poor nester families, George Crosley couldn't help liking Long and his wife.

When they finished eating, Crosley and his possemen insisted on spreading their bedrolls on the porch. It didn't take them long to drop off to sleep.

Much later Crosley was awakened by a sound he couldn't immediately identify. He lay there, looking at the stars from under the porch's shake roof, listening at first, then beginning to drowse once more. Abruptly he caught another sound and came wide awake. He thought he heard a horse moving quietly away from the cabin in the direction of the creek. And then a shadow moved far off to the left. He turned his head and saw Morgan Long's gaunt shape disappearing into the

blackness of the alders, growing close to the stream's edge on the far side.

Crosley lay as he was for several seconds, until his curiosity became too strong. Finally he threw the blankets aside, thought of putting on his boots but rejected the notion. Then he moved out past the sleeping figures of his two possemen, the gravelly roughness of the ground biting into his stockinged feet.

He circled the far side of the cabin and into the trees behind it. Passing the ruin of the barn, he could make out the charred and twisted timbers strewn across the ground, and anger hit him at sight of that wanton destruction. He reached the creek and waded in, his spindly legs going numb to the knees at the water's coldness. Once on the stream's far bank he moved cautiously, scanning the shadows ahead and the spaces behind the thickets. Presently he saw them—two men, standing not thirty feet away, one of them leaning against the horizontal waist-high pole of a rotting windfall. The starlight wasn't strong enough for him to be sure, but he guessed that heavy-bodied, short man with Morg Long must be Stoneman.

He stood for a full quarter minute, once catching the low run of a voice, another answering. He was puzzled now and feeling a little ridiculous with his eavesdropping, yet still curious about Morg Long's furtive manner. He had a vague and irritating hunch that their meeting concerned Idaho's escape tonight and wished he could move closer to overhear what was being said. Suddenly a hard object pressed into the middle of his spine. His slight frame went rigid and instinctively his hands lifted to the level of his shoulders. He wanted to look around, but didn't dare. Then a hand ran over his waist and whatever prodded him in the back wasn't there any more. A voice behind him drawled pleasantly: "Go on over and join the palaver, Sheriff."

It was Jim Rush who had spoken. Irritation and a feeling of sheepishness gripped the lawman as he slowly turned about. There, standing within arm's reach of him, stood his escaped prisoner, tall and straight, a broad grin on his lean face as he dropped a Colt back into a holster riding his thigh.

The other two had heard Jim speak and now walked in on the lawman, Morg Long saying as he approached: "Nice work, Idaho. Damned if you aren't part Indian."

"Just what is this?" Crosley asked, embarrassed and halfway angry.

"Idaho's made some good use of his time since he broke out of your lockup, Sheriff. He's run onto something. Came to Bob with it, and Bob brought him down to me. We were tryin' to think up a way of waking you without rousing the others, when Idaho saw you headed across here. Now you can come with us to give this thing a look-see."

"What is it?" Crosley's tone held more interest than anger now.

"Something up Echo," Stoneman said. "And from what Idaho says, all three of us had better wait and see for ourselves."

"Want to bring the horses across, Long?" Jim asked. "Make sure the sheriff's two sidekicks don't follow you."

"And you could bring my boots," Crosley put in.

Morg Long at once disappeared into the heavy obscurity of the nearby thicket, and Crosley, more puzzled than ever, asked: "What's the game, Idaho?"

"The same one we talked about this morning. By the way, what did you run into at Arrow Springs?"

"What you said I would." Crosley qualified his answer by adding: "But it doesn't have to mean what you think."

"Maybe not." There was a light touch of mockery to Jim's words.

"So your bunch busted him out of the lockup, after all," Crosley said, turning to the bearded Stoneman.

"Not us."

"It was Cass and Whipple, Sheriff."

Crosley's glance swung sharply around at Jim. He laughed dryly. "Talk sense, Idaho. Cass and Whipple were the ones that found out about it. With Carson's help."

"That's the way they'd play it. So you'd never tag them with it."

The lawman stood a moment, trying to get his thinking straight. He couldn't and finally said: "First, you want me to believe that Ames rustled his own beef. Now I'm to swallow it that he had you broke out of jail and hung the blame on Stoneman and his friends here."

"That's right. Only it didn't come off the way Cass planned it. I got away, and he didn't blow in the back of my head like he wanted to. But even if it had gone the way he wanted, he'd have saddled the blame for the break on these men. It all fits in with Ames's pushing them out of the country."

"You've been eatin' loco weed, son."

Jim smiled. "Maybe you'll be changing your mind on that in a couple of hours."

"And maybe I won't!"

It was a good bit more than two hours before George Crosley had the chance to change his mind. After Morgan Long led a pair of horses across the creek, Stoneman and Jim brought theirs down out of the timber while Crosley was pulling on his boots. Directly all four men headed up the wide cañon, climbing an off-shoot out of it six miles above, and then riding a ridge that angled obliquely to the deep tangle of Echo. Along toward three o'clock a waning moon rose over the peaks to shed a wan and thin light over the timber and high meadows. At the end of this long interval George Crosley, tired and sleepy and confused, had to admit that this was a strange experience. He had set out tonight to hunt down an escaped prisoner. Instead, his prisoner had hunted him down and was now trying to prove something that would blast the foundations of his upbringing as a cattleman. The further he went into this thing, the less sense it made.

Jim found a trail halfway up Echo that led down off the rim into the black depths of the cañon, and for a quarter hour they rode a tricky, narrow ledge where the horses turned nervous at the unsure footing of loose rock and talus. They were no sooner in the bed of the cañon than Jim turned down along it, snaking his way through the boulders that occasionally choked the bottom.

"Where's this getting us?" Crosley wanted to know after they had covered the better part of a mile. He hadn't been this tired in years, and now he was beginning to resent knowing so little about why he was taking this grueling ride.

"You know how this cut got its name, don't you, Sheriff?" Jim turned in the saddle to look back at the lawman.

Crosley nodded. "There's an overhang where the rock almost closes out the sky. Throws back a strong echo."

"That's where we're headed."

Jim said no more than that. They had reached a stretch now where piles of brush choked the bed of the chasm, and presently the lawman asked dryly: "This where you got your skull dented?"

"Right here." Jim had come to a gap in the brush barricade and lifted a hand, pointing to a dark shadow on the ground beyond the line of brush that Crosley guessed might be the ashes of a fire. Nearby, the lawman could make out the square shape of a tarpaulin, one of its corners still propped up by the forked branch of a pine. Jim went on: "Cass and I made our gather from below, pushin' the critters this far. The crew had cut this brush a week ago. Cass and I finished the job, and he left right after supper. The rannies that rustled the herd pushed it up the cañon. You'd think they were headed for one of the passes and down the far side of the hills, wouldn't you, Sheriff?"

Crosley tilted his head. "Probably over into the next county. There are a couple of men across there that don't ask questions when they buy cattle."

"That's the way you were supposed to figure it."

George Crosley mulled that over in his mind as Jim led the way onward. Presently he was asking: "How else could a man figure it?"

"You'll see."

Jim didn't speak again for the better part of another mile, until they were riding in a deeper blackness where the high rims drew close together overhead. The bottom of the cañon had narrowed somewhat, but not in proportion to the meeting of the rims. Finally, looking straight above, Crosley could see no more than a slit of star-dusted sky showing. Almost immediately Jim was reining in, and the others were closing in on him.

Jim's high shape swung aground, and, squatting on his heels, he flicked a match alight. "Take a look, Sheriff."

Crosley got out of his saddle and, followed by the other two, walked over to Jim and studied the moist, sandy ground by the match's flickering light. It wasn't until Jim had lit the second match that Crosley noticed anything and said: "All right, I see tracks."

"Pointed which way?"

Crosley hunkered down, looking closer. "Both ways."

Jim got up and moved out toward a thin trickle of water

running along the center of the open space between the sheer walls. He repeated the procedure, lighting another match. "Here they're thicker," he said. "Goin' both ways again. But mostly down."

"Get on with it, Idaho," Crosley said irritably. "What're you proving?"

"That whoever did this slipped up on something," Jim told him. "He counted on that storm to wash out sign. He didn't think of this spot, didn't remember that not enough water drops in here to fill a fry pan during a hard rain. You wanted proof. Here it is, Sheriff."

George Crosley knew that something was escaping him, but, try as he would, he couldn't see it. "Proof of what?"

"The herd was being pushed upcañon from the brush when I made my run for it and got away. That's what everyone was supposed to think, that those steers were headed up."

"And weren't they?"

Jim shook his head, pointing to the ground. "Take a good look. These tracks pointin' down are on top of the ones headed up. They were made last. Sheriff, that herd came back down through here during the storm."

Crosley had it now, and a quick excitement ran through him, only to die the next moment. "Couldn't be, Idaho. Someone would have spotted the herd if it had come out into that country below."

"It never did come out. I'll lay you ten to one that the main herd at Arrow Springs was moved south late yesterday afternoon or during the night. Maybe they're on the move now. And this other bunch has already been thrown in with 'em."

"How?"

"That's where the crew was when you were huntin' 'em today. Workin' these critters over through a side cañon, deep onto Bell range. By mornin' every last animal will be with the main bunch."

"While we're saddled with rustling a herd that was never run off." Morgan Long's low-drawled words added a final touch of irony.

IV

They cooked a meal shortly before sunup in a coulée deep in a timber spur jutting southward into Bell grass. Crosley had packed enough grub along to last him during the hunt for Jim, and the lawman, after his fourth cup of scalding coffee, began to look more like himself.

Jim was thinking as he said: "You'll have to do it on your own, Sheriff. They'd like nothing better than to throw lead at me. And if Morg or Bob go with you, they'll know something's up."

Crosley nodded. "Wish you could give me more to go on, Idaho. There are one hell of a lot of animals in that bunch." He was remembering how big Bell's herd had looked out there on the slope above the timber just at daybreak. As Idaho had predicted, the herd had been moved south from Arrow Springs.

"That's all I can give you to go on," Jim said now. "Just take your time. We've got the rest of the day."

Crosley sighed deeply, then repeated what Jim had told him several minutes ago: "A whiteface minus a left horn and eye, two steers branded Circle Dot under the Bell and with slit ears. Where do you reckon they had their ears doctored?"

"Must've belonged to somebody before Circle Dot got 'em," Morg Long put in. "And, of course, Ames bought 'em from Circle Dot."

The lawman nodded, frowning as he went on: "And a mangy bull with blow sores on his hump. Idaho, I'll be a week lookin' for those lost critters."

"Find just one, Sheriff. Just one. They were all in that cañon two days ago. If they're with the big bunch now, you've got your answer."

Crosley stretched and yawned before he walked stiffly to his horse, staked out with the others on the grass along the bottom of the coulée. He stopped momentarily to call back: "Better pick me up along the town road."

"We'll keep an eye on you," Jim answered.

He and Morg and Stoneman filled their cups once more and rolled fresh smokes as the sheriff rode out of the depression and disappeared through the pines on the far side. None of them had anything to say for a time, knowing how much depended on the lawman's errand. None of them wanted to make their guesses on how it would turn out, but finally Stoneman became impatient and broke the silence.

"When do we move?"

"Not yet," Jim told him. "Give Crosley time to get there."

Morg Long was frowning as he looked down at the smoldering ashes of the fire. Abruptly he asked: "Idaho, how's all this comin' out? Even supposing Crosley gets what he's after, how do we make Mark Ames eat crow?"

"That's what I'd like to know," Bob Stoneman said.

"Crosley's a good man," Jim told them.

"But not that good," Long insisted. "Ames has this country by the tail. He put George Crosley in office."

"And he may be regrettin' that," Jim drawled, trying not to let them see how near his own feeling was to theirs. Then, to hide his uncertainty, he added: "We might mosey along and see what Crosley's doing."

They saddled and left the coulée, striking farther toward the south than the line the lawman had taken, and presently they could look down through the trees across a sweep of tawny grass, Bell's upper range. Far to the north, just below the wavy horizon, they made out a dark blotch that was the shipping herd. They tied their horses back in the trees, made themselves comfortable, and settled down to wait, watching the herd draw nearer.

It was close to half an hour later—and the herd was near enough for them to distinguish individual animals—when Jim saw a pair of riders leave the near swing and cut across into the pines possibly two miles above. The biggest of the two looked like Ed Buford.

"See that?" he asked.

"Doesn't mean anything," Morg Long answered. "They'll show in a minute."

But as the time dragged on—a quarter hour, then thirty minutes—neither of the riders appeared. And presently Jim drawled: "I don't like it."

"Couldn't have anything to do with us," Bob Stoneman said.

Jim decided the homesteader was right. Still, a feeling of restlessness grew stronger in him as the minutes went by. Finally he could sit still no longer. He stood up and turned, looking back through the trees, back the way they had come.

Across the stillness he could faintly catch the bawling of the cattle. But that sound only heightened the quietness. The small sounds a man hears in timber—the scolding of a jay, the rustle of a squirrel, the whisper of a breeze through the tops of the pines—were all stilled now. And that unaccountable feeling of restlessness, of something being not quite right, heightened in Jim.

Suddenly a flash of movement far back through the pines caught his attention. He hadn't been looking squarely in that direction, and he could see nothing now, yet his nerves were enough on edge to make him breathe softly: "Heads up."

He started walking back toward the horses, his glance still

probing the depths of the timber. He had taken three slow strides when the brittle *crack* of a rifle slapped across the stillness, coming out of the direction in which he was looking.

A streak of fire stabbed through his left shoulder. A heavy blow spun him halfway around. He let himself fall, rolling to the right, seeing Long and Stoneman already on their feet. As he came belly down, he reached for his Colt and was lining it when a voice hard to his right spoke sharply: "Drop it!"

Jim opened his hand and let the .44 he had last night borrowed from Stoneman slip from his grasp. He looked back over his right shoulder and saw Morg Long and Bob Stoneman standing rigidly several paces behind him, their hands raised.

Then Ed Buford edged into sight from behind a thicket of oak barely fifty yards away. He held a carbine slacked from his shoulder. He looked at Jim and drawled: "Stay set." Then he whistled shrilly.

He was walking in on the two homesteaders and Jim when Cass Waite rode in on them, relieving them of their weapons. Then he came over to Jim, who was sitting now, and kicked the .44 beyond his reach, looking down at him with a broad grin. "Played you for suckers, didn't we? Thought we'd backtrack Crosley when he showed up so sudden. Guess you'd say it paid off." His glance went to Jim's shoulder. "Better wind something around that before you bleed yourself dry, Idaho." He looked at the others. "You two can get ready to move."

Jim was beginning to feel a smarting pain in his shoulder. While Cass watched the two homesteaders walk to their horses, Jim unknotted the bandanna at his throat, pulled off his jumper, and, making a pad of the bandanna, pressed it against the deep channel Cass's bullet had cut into the heavy muscle capping his left shoulder. The wound was bleeding freely, had already stained his sleeve a bright crimson halfway to the elbow.

"You were lucky, Idaho," Cass drawled, following Long who was leading Jim's horse across. "My sights must've been off."

Ed waited until Jim was in the saddle before he spoke again, reining alongside to say tonelessly: "This ought to give the boss something to think about. We not only run onto three rustlers, but a lawman that ate his breakfast with 'em. Wonder how Crosley's going to like bein' locked in his own jail?"

They didn't have a chance to see George Crosley. Once they reached the edge of the timber, Ed nodded out toward the herd. "Go get Crosley, Cass. Just tell him the boss would like to see him at the layout. And you don't know where I've gone. Me and you took that sashay into the timber, thinkin' we saw a three-prong buck. For all you know that was me shootin' at it. No sense tipping our hand."

After Cass left them, Buford pointed the way south through the trees until they reached a shallow wash that angled out across the open ground to a scattered growth of jack pine a quarter mile away. Beyond that, a fold of the hills put the herd out of sight, and they jogged steadily on in the direction of Bell's headquarters.

Once Morg started to say something to Jim, only to have Ed warn him to silence. When Morg ignored him and went on talking, Ed spurred up to the homesteader and belted him across the mouth. From then on not a word was said by any of them.

Having this strong sample of Ed's brutality to add to his own experience with the man, Jim had no illusions about what was to come. Until now he had halfway believed that Ed was entirely responsible for this play of Bell's against the homesteaders, that Mark Ames might have no knowledge of it, but the fact that Ed was taking them to Bell to see Ames, rather than heading for town, hinted strongly that the rancher had, after all, directed the maneuver.

Jim saw his own involvement as the only factor that was not foreseen. Cass had really shot to kill him, and Ed hadn't seemed to care. So now he realized for the first time that he counted for little or nothing in the intrigue Bell was using to clear its range. To Ames, even to Ed, he was a nonentity who had by accident survived the Echo Cañon incident only to perform the added service of shifting the blame for the jail-break onto the homesteaders. Reasoning this way, Jim could also figure that they would never let him ride clear of this range now, knowing as much as he did.

He was nursing these bleak thoughts, holding his good hand to his hurt shoulder, as they dipped down across the wide basin and rode in on the cottonwoods shading the ranch headquarters. They were turning up past the corral toward the big log and rock house when Mark Ames stepped out of his office onto the porch.

As they breasted the tie rail under a huge cottonwood thirty feet short of the house, Ed told them—"You can wait here."—and went on, dismounting at the foot of the porch steps.

He towered a full head over Ames when they stood together. After the pair of them had talked, low-voiced, for several minutes, Morg Long drawled to Jim: "You wouldn't think a runt like that could raise so much hell, would you?"

His question didn't need answering, and Jim offered none. Stoneman was asking: "Hurt bad, Idaho?"

"Not bad."

"Why the hell do we have to sit here?" Morg Long muttered, then deliberately swung aground.

Ed's glance swung quickly out to him, but he went on talking to Ames, and shortly Jim and Bob followed Morg's example, dropping their reins to ground-halter their animals and to step deeper into the shade of the cottonwood.

"What comes next, Idaho?" Long asked. He didn't wait for an answer but went on: "What he said about Crosley havin' breakfast with us didn't sound so good."

"You two and Crosley tracked me down in the hills last night. You were bringing me across here this morning. The sheriff rode out to let the crew know he'd found me."

Jim had to grin at his feeble attempt while Morg Long kept a straight face, adding: "Sure. Right after Crosley pulled out, you grabbed Bob's iron and. . . ."

"And it won't do," Stoneman growled through his beard.

"I'd play along with the sheriff," Jim said seriously. "He may have all the answers he needs by now."

"We'll damn' soon find out." Long nodded out across the basin. Looking off there, they saw Cass and the sheriff headed up toward the corral.

They stood watching as Ed and Mark Ames came down off the porch and sauntered out to stand beyond the tie rail nearby. Mark Ames gave them a look, saying flatly: "You three keep quiet. And I mean that."

George Crosley was talking to Cass and evidently didn't see them until he was halfway between the nearest shed and the big cottonwood. His glance swung around to them then, and his expression was one of momentary disbelief. Then a studied impassiveness settled quietly over his face.

"'Mornin', George." Ames's voice was too casual as Crosley reined in some thirty feet short of the tie rail.

Crosley only nodded. He stayed in the saddle as he asked: "What've we got here?"

"That's what I was going to ask you," Ames answered.

"Get down and help us figure it out."

Crosley sat unmoving a long moment, then finally decided there was no point in staying in the saddle. He swung stiffly aground and left his horse near the rail, dropping the reins a few feet short of it. His animal stood on the far side of Morg Long's roan mare, a stride or two from Jim. Cass stayed back where he had reined in behind the sheriff, folding his arms and leaning against the horn, the faintest of smiles on his narrow face.

George Crosley must have weighed his chances of bluffing it through and decided they were slim. For now his glance came around from Mark Ames to Jim and Long, standing close to him. "You told him what we found last night?"

"They haven't told me anything," Ames interrupted. "Haven't had the chance to, yet. Thought we might get it from you, George."

The lawman's eyes were flinty as they shuttled back to Ames. "Maybe you better speak your piece first, Mark."

"About what?"

"How these deputies of mine, along with our prisoner, come to be here."

Ames frowned at that. But his puzzlement was put on and soon faded before a tight smile. "Prisoner? Ed took a gun away from Idaho."

"I gave it to him."

"Why?"

"Because he showed me some things last night that let me know how wrong you were in all those things you said about him."

Ames studied the sheriff a moment. "That'll take some explaining, George."

"So will some other things." Crosley's look now went to Bell's ramrod. "Buford, I'm putting you under arrest." He had no sooner spoken than slowly, deliberately, he brought his hand along his thigh to his holster.

Behind the sheriff, Cass went stiff in the saddle. His hand streaked to his Colt, and Jim called stridently: "Don't, Sheriff!"

The hammer click of Cass's weapon told the lawman why Jim had spoken. Crosley lifted his hand away from his holster and turned slowly to look at Cass, at the .45 lined at him. Then he glanced back at Ames. "Mark, are you buckin' the law?"

"Yes, until I know why the law's bucking me," Ames said. "You can take off that belt and hand it over while we talk this out. You'll notice I'm not armed. There's no call for a man wearin' an iron while he talks to a friend."

Crosley made no immediate move to do as Ames had said, and the rancher nodded to Cass. Cass came aground and walked in behind the lawman, unbuckling his shell belt. After Cass had hung the weapon from Crosley's saddle, he holstered his own and sauntered across to join Ames and Buford.

"Now we can sort this out, George. On a friendly basis." Crosley's face went pale with anger as Mark Ames continued. "Just what did Idaho show you last night that makes you think I was wrong about him?"

The sheriff made a visible effort at controlling his temper now, doubtless realizing what delicate handling this situation called for. Jim, watching him, guessed that he must be weighing what he suspected against his friendship for Mark Ames. Crosley said bluntly: "Mark, either you've got a head hard as rimrock, or you've turned crooked as a dog's hind leg. That herd of yours up Echo was driven back down again and thrown in with the main bunch. None of the Flint Creek men had anything to do with it. Neither did Idaho."

When the sheriff hesitated, Mark Ames drawled: "Go on."

A flinty look had come to his face. There was no trace of surprise in him, nor in Ed or Cass.

Crosley saw that and said quietly: "So it wasn't just Ed's idea. I'd hoped it was. For your sake, Mark, I'd hoped it was."

"Go on. How much more do you know?"

"Enough to take you in, along with Ed," the sheriff said. "It was you that had Idaho busted out of jail. You had Cass do it, so you could wish the job off on these neighbors you're trying to push around."

Abruptly Mark Ames's soberness vanished, and he smiled. "George, tell this to a jury and they'd laugh you out of court."

"Then it's been you all along? Not Ed or anyone else?"

"Be your age," Ames drawled mildly. "I've run cattle on this range for twenty years. Along comes this bunch of sodbusters and moves in on me. What would you have done?"

"I'd have got along with them."

Ames gave a slow shake of the head. "No. You'd have done just what I did. Tried to run 'em off without anyone getting hurt. That's what would have happened, if you hadn't horned in. Now someone will get hurt."

Jim felt a tightness running along his nerves. Ames's meaning was plain. The gravity that settled over Crosley's hawkish face was evidence that he, too, realized it. There was no pretense in Mark Ames now. He hadn't denied anything, and this fact Jim saw as the most ominous of all.

"Mark, you can't play with the law like this. Maybe there are plenty of folks think the way you do. But they won't stand for the thing you're talkin' about." Crosley spoke quietly, eyeing the rancher oddly, as though surprised at never really having known him.

Tension mounted in Jim. He was taking out tobacco, rolling a smoke as Ames queried blandly: "Won't they?" The rancher laughed softly. "People will believe almost anything if you make it look right, George. For instance. Suppose you and Idaho and these two others don't show up in a day or two. They'll start lookin' for you. They could find you and Idaho, lyin' up there in the rocks at the head of Echo, nothin' but coyote bait, your guns in your hands. They might never find Long and Stoneman."

Morg Long breathed: "You blood-thirsty devil."

The rancher's glance settled on him coldly. "Long, your hide isn't worth as much to me as a wolf's. They don't pay a bounty on homesteaders. You're like wolves, the whole pack of you."

"You're breaking the law," Crosley said.

"If the law's wrong, the hell with it!"

Jim picked this moment to light his smoke. The match wouldn't flame as he flicked it with a thumbnail. He looked down at it, saw that its head was chipped.

Two strides away and in toward Crosley stood Morg Long's roan mare. Immediately beyond was the sheriff's gray horse, down-headed and nibbling at a tuft of grass. Just short of the roan a rock lay half-buried in the dirt.

Deliberately, moving slowly so that they wouldn't misread what he was doing, Jim stepped over and leaned down to strike his match against the rock. As he straightened, cupping the flame to his cigarette, he saw that Ed Buford's hand had started lifting to his holster. But after a careful look at Jim, the big man straightened his arm, and his eyes moved to the sheriff again.

Jim stayed where he was as Crosley spoke once more. "Mark, you've still got a chance of clearin' yourself. The only law you've broken so far is stealing cattle. Since they were your own cattle, no one gives a damn. A lot of folks might even respect you for what you tried to do."

Jim took a deep drag on his smoke and idly reached over to stab his cigarette into the roan's rump. The animal lunged ahead, hitting Crosley with his shoulder and knocking him off balance. For a full second, as the lawman went sprawling and Jim wheeled in at the gray, Morg Long's mare was between Jim and the trio beyond the rail. Jim reached for the sheriff's Colt, hanging on the saddle horn.

A shot blasted the stillness, and Jim felt the air-whip of the bullet as he rocked the Colt down. The blast of the .45 seemed to push Cass backward in an ungainly lurch. The man's gun hand clawed open, his weapon spun into the gravel, and he was falling.

The next instant Jim could see both Ames and Ed. He found himself staring down the bore of Ed's leveled gun. He timed his shot without hurrying it, tightening his finger about the trigger as Ed's gun settled into line. The weapon slammed back against his wrist, and he breathed the acrid flames of powder smoke, seeing flame stab from Ed's .45. But that wink of flame was thrown off-line by the impact of Jim's bullet. He saw it strike, saw the big man's right shoulder jerk back, and a flash of surprise cross Ed's face.

George Crosley moved fast for a man of his years. He was a split second late in trying to snatch the weapon before Ames could get it, but then he clamped a tight hold on the rancher's wrist, twisting it. For a moment Mark Ames stood rigid, trying to turn the gun in at the sheriff. Then, slowly, Crosley twisted the rancher's arm back, and quite suddenly Ames let out a hoarse cry and went to his knees.

Crosley said: "Morg, bring me a rope."

It wasn't until they were riding away from the house some five minutes later that any of them spoke. Then Morg Long said: "Idaho, you've got my thanks."

"Mine, too," said Crosley. "Last night and this mornin' has proved something to me. I'm not the man I was. Too old for the job, they been sayin'. Well, maybe I am."

"That's fool talk you're makin', Sheriff."

"No, it's the truth. Without all the help I got, I'd be layin' back there now instead of Ed and Cass." Crosley was still looking at Jim. "Idaho, will you stay on here?"

"Doing what?"

"Law work, son. In sixty days we elect a new sheriff. The job's yours for the askin'. People are going to hear about this. No man's goin' to be fool enough to vote against you."

Gunpowder Campaign

"Gunpowder Campaign" was completed and sent to Jon Glidden's agent on February 19, 1939. After reading the story, Marguerite E. Harper sent it to David Manners, editor at the time of Popular Publications' *10 Story Western*. Street & Smith Publications paid for stories upon publication. Popular Publications, although usually paying less, paid upon acceptance. Manners bought the story on March 19, 1939, paying the author $63.00. When it appeared in *10 Story Western* (8/39), the text was abridged for reasons of space and the story retitled "Charge of the Cowtown Brigade." For its appearance here the text has been restored according to the author's typescript.

I

Thirty seconds after the fight started, Paul Baker ran into the blacksmith shop, saw that no one was there, and bellowed breathlessly: "Amos!"

No answer.

"Amos!" roared Baker again. Then, flashing a last look along the street to where the yelling crowd was gathered across from the courthouse, he ran on into the shop and to the stall to one side of the rear door. There, as he'd halfway expected, he found Amos Short.

Amos was lying in the straw at the head of the stall, his thin arms and bandy legs spread-eagled, the mouth under his grizzled mustache hanging open. One hand clasped the neck of an empty quart bottle of whiskey. As Baker hesitated, Amos's mustache quivered under a rasping snore.

Baker dipped half a bucket of water from the barrel by the forge and threw it in Amos's face. Amos sat up, clawing and gasping for breath. But his eyes were still closed. All at once he shouted in a stentorian voice: "Charge, men! Give 'em the bayonet!"

With that he sank slowly back again, turned on his side, and curled up. Before Baker had come back with the second bucket of water, he was snoring peacefully once more. The water didn't even cause him to stir this time, so Baker took him by the shoulders and shook him, dodging as Amos came awake and swung a fist at him.

"Get the hell out o' here!" Amos said. "Lemme alone. I . . . !"

"Bruce is in a fight," Baker cut in.

"And what if he is?" Amos queried belligerently, wiping the water from his mustache. "He's paid to fight, ain't he?"

"Not to fight Walt Kief, he ain't!"

"Kief," Amos croaked. "Walt Kief. Why the hell didn't you say that the first time?" He struggled uncertainly to his feet and bolted for the door, Baker at his heels. "Where?" he yelled.

"Hotel," Baker said as they turned down the walk. He ran alongside Amos with a hold on one arm to steady his friend, remembering the empty bottle back there and knowing the usual effects of a quart of whiskey on Amos's leg muscles.

"How'd it start?" Amos asked.

"Don't know."

Old Amos ran past the bank alongside his shop, then past a vacant lot, the Silver Dollar Saloon, another vacant lot, and into the crowd in front of the hotel steps. He wasn't the only one running. Men cut across the courthouse square opposite the hotel; more were running from upstreet. Amos clawed his way through the shouting throng, wound up inside the close-packed circle, and finally saw the fighters.

"Beat hell out of him, Bruce," he croaked, and watched his son, Bruce Short, town marshal, take the full crushing weight of Walt Kief's fist along his jaw. Amos winced as Bruce went down, sitting hard in the dust. But he was cheering, when Bruce rolled onto his feet and came at Kief again.

Town Marshal Bruce Short stood two inches short of six feet. Walt Kief was six-one without his boots and thirty pounds heavier than the lawman. He was dark-skinned, brown-eyed, and handsome. Bruce Short was light, with blue eyes that matched his father's, a thatch of unruly blond hair, and his square face was freckled and now contorted in ugliness. He had a cut beneath one eye, a lump along his jaw, and his shirt was torn with his five-pointed star flopping at the end of a long streamer.

"Use your spurs, Bruce!" Amos yelled. "Knee him!"

Bruce Short heard his parent. He had been wild-eyed until now, plainly getting the worst of it. But a quality in Amos's voice seemed all at once to steady him. Instead of rushing Kief, as he'd done before, he brought up his guard and waited.

Kief frowned, said: "Come on. You yellow?"

And still Bruce waited. Kief's temper mounted in a wave. He came at Bruce, arms shielding his face, and, when he got within reach, his two fists lashed out.

Bruce side-stepped, ducked a wild swing, then stepped in to pump two pile-driver blows into Kief's middle. Bruce danced back on the toes of his boots, cocked his arms, and, when he lunged in again, his knotted fists had the tough drive of his hundred and sixty pounds behind them. Kief's head tilted back with the first blow, farther back as the second caught him on the point of the chin. The roar of the onlookers punctuated the exact instant Kief's knees went loose. He fell forward, still gazing skyward, and, when he sprawled his full length on the walk to lie face up, his eyes were vacant in the glassy stare of unconsciousness.

Bruce Short rubbed his sore knuckles, looked at the circle of faces around him, and said: "Break it up, gents. The fun's over."

A few heard him. Those at the fringes of the crowd didn't. They were looking downstreet to where old Tom Kief was just stepping through the doors of the bank. Someone said—"The fun ain't over, not by a damn' sight!"—and there were a few laughs and then an expectant hush settled over the crowd.

Tom Kief's rangy stride covered plenty of ground even though he didn't seem to be in a hurry. He was as tall as his nephew, Walt, and heavier. His black broadcloth suit and his white hair and bushy white eyebrows gave him dignity and lent weight to his reputation for being the biggest man in the Wild Horse country.

He didn't have to push through the crowd. It gave way respectfully before him so that it wasn't necessary for him to break his stride until he stood squarely in front of Bruce Short and looked past the law officer to where his nephew lay sprawled on the walk.

"Well, Marshal," he drawled. "What's the trouble? A bit of campaign strategy?"

He, like everyone else, was amazed to see that it was Bruce and Walt who were fighting. They were both running for town marshal. With election day only a week off, the implications of this knock-down-and drag-out were ominous.

Someone in the crowd said: "Somebody called somebody's old man a souse!"

Walt Kief stirred weakly and elbowed up to a sitting position. He must have heard this last, for he growled: "You're damned right I did. The old buzzard lyin' down there in a horse stall all mornin'. Len Reed came in to get a piece of iron welded and couldn't even wake the old goat."

Amos had slipped back into the crowd at Tom Kief's appearance, for the banker didn't approve of him. But now he stepped into the inner circle again, advancing on Walt Kief with a belligerent: "Who's an old goat?"

Tom Kief reached out and barred Amos's way. Walt came to his feet with a scowl on his face. "You are," he told Amos. "What I said about you still goes."

Bruce faced about and made one wild swing at Walt that Tom Kief knocked aside. Then the banker was between the two men, shouting angrily: "Lay off or I'll take you both on! Walt, get away from here! And from now on bridle your tongue! Bruce, you hold your temper or I'll have you thrown in your own jail."

Walt Kief picked up his crushed Stetson off the hotel steps and sullenly pushed his way out through the crowd. Amos, a little of last night's whiskey still working in his guts and giving him courage, set his face in an ugly grimace and started after Walt. "No sidewinder's goin' to call me a name," he began. "No yellow. . . ."

"Pa!" Bruce snapped. "Get back here." He was cool now. He said to Tom Kief: "I'm sorry this happened. If I'd kept my head, we. . . ."

"Sorry, hell!" Amos sputtered. He didn't see the mounting flush on Tom Kief's face, or he would have had his warning. "It's no one's damn' business how I spend my money. That. . . ."

Tom Kief exploded: "Shut up, Amos! You're the cause of this! You and your bottle. All you can think about is whiskey and that hunk of iron in the courtyard." He gestured toward the lawn under the cottonwoods in front of the courthouse. A six-pounder Civil War cannon sat across there, a monument to the Confederate soldiers slain during Colonel Bruce Fowler's campaign through this country. Bruce Fowler had been Amos's commanding officer through the war. Amos had named his only son after him.

"Amos, you've got to straighten out," Kief went on, calmer now. "We don't mind hearing how you were the best gunner in the Confederate Army, but we do mind the way you hit the bottle. You don't drink like other men. Two nights ago you sobered up around two in the morning and started banging that anvil and woke up the whole town. You. . . ."

"I had a job to get out by mornin'," Amos cut in, glowering stubbornly at the banker. "It's my affair, how I run my business."

"When you disturb the peace, it ceases to be your own business. And speaking of elections, Walt may not be so far wrong. I want this to be a fair fight. You keep on like this and there won't be a woman in the county who'll let her husband vote for Bruce."

"Psalm singin' again, eh?" Amos mumbled. "I can't. . . ."

His words trailed off weakly as Tom Kief turned, shrugged helplessly, and strode off down the walk. A few onlookers dared to laugh right then. Those closest didn't, knowing Amos. He had their sympathy and a lot more of their pity than he wanted. He saw it in their faces as they turned and walked away. In ten seconds he and Bruce had the walk before the hotel steps pretty much to themselves.

Amos was always sorry after those too frequent exposures of his one vice. He looked shamefacedly at his son, said: "I reckon I shouldn't have butted in."

Bruce brushed the dust from his shirt and vest, clamped his Stetson on his head. He understood the workings of Amos's mind perfectly. Just now his freckled face broke into a wide smile; he slapped his father on the back. "Forget it. I wouldn't take six months' pay for what just happened."

"You sure cleaned him, son." Amos said proudly. He felt a little better as they headed upstreet and turned at right angles toward the jail, facing the courthouse from the leg of the square obliquely across from the hotel.

They made most of the walk in silence. Only when they were in the privacy of Bruce's office did Amos get out what was on his mind. He muttered: "I'm the only thing people got ag'in' you on this election. I'm a souse. I run off at the mouth. I ought to go stick my head in a barrel and take a deep breath."

Bruce looked serious, hurt. "Don't say that, Pa. What about your game leg?" Rumor had it that two musket balls were lodged in Amos's right thigh, his souvenirs of a week's running battle with two companies of Union cavalry. His excuse for drinking was always that he'd go crazy from pain if it weren't for the whiskey. "Don't you pay no attention to what people say. They're a damned ungrateful lot. If the drinkin' helps, go to it. I may take to drink myself after this election's over."

Amos said brusquely: "The hell you will! You're goin' to win."

"I'm not so sure."

"Why shouldn't you? Walt Kief's a ladies' man, lazy. He ain't built for the job. He can't get out and sit a week in the saddle, eatin' dust and wind, chasin' to hell and gone after a horse thief. All he's got is a loud mouth and a pretty gun he ain't too good with. You're different. You're a born law-dog. There ain't no one you won't tackle with guns or without. You're the man for marshal, and people know it."

Amos was about to add that people knew it, but that lately he'd made such a nuisance of himself, people were getting tired of it, wondering why his son didn't jail him and put him through the cure. That business Tom Kief had mentioned about his blacksmithing in the middle of the night, waking the whole town, was merely one of a dozen offenses he'd unintentionally committed. He'd have to go easier on the whiskey. Cut down to, say, a quart a day.

Thinking this, he was staring across at the hotel. The noon stage had just pulled in. The driver was handing down baggage to three nicely dressed strangers in city clothes. Amos said: "You'd better go over there and give them fellers a look-see. There might be a gambler among 'em."

Bruce nodded. He went to a trunk alongside his desk and

took out a clean shirt and put it on, transferring his badge, and then throwing his torn shirt into the stove, ready to kindle next fall's first fire. Then he went out and across the square toward the hotel. This business of inspecting new arrivals in town was part of his duty. Gambling in Prairie City had been outlawed for ten years. A few itinerant gamblers hadn't heard the news.

Amos was glum and feeling sour inside, so he walked back to his shop, using the opposite side of the square out of habit because it led past two saloons. A feeling of righteousness hit him as he was turning in at the swing doors of the first. He backed away and went on, his mouth dry and his uneasy stomach begging for just one drink. But to hell with whiskey from now on! The two chunks of lead in his thigh had never hurt him. He'd played up that story since the war simply because there was no other way of his commanding the hero-worship of the kids and the ladies about town. Now the kids were grown up and the ladies were onto him and it didn't matter any more.

He cut across the square on purpose, so that the second saloon wouldn't tempt him, and, trudging beneath the heat-relieving shade of the cottonwoods, he paused a moment before the six-pounder cannon that was the Confederate memorial. He'd never shot this particular fieldpiece, but one like it had been his main concern through two and half years of the war. He knew every fitting on it, earplates, sponge and rammer, elevating-screw, handspike, and linstock. The carriage was now paintless and weathered a dull gray, the fellies and spokes of the wheels dry and shrunken loose.

It made Amos boil inside to think of the way people had allowed the old fieldpiece to weather into disrepair. Half a dozen of the cannon balls from the neat pile alongside the left wheel were gone; probably the kids had swiped them to use in some makeshift bowling alley, the one in Kale's barn, for instance. But strangely enough two canisters—looking like two brass quart cans, filled with half-inch lead balls—had remained untouched through the years. They sat beneath the cannon's thick timber stock. Old Amos smiled wryly at the thought of the deadly destruction contained in each canister. Those brass containers with their lead pellets, shot from the cannon instead of the regular six-pounder ball, would spread and cut a twenty-yard swath through advancing troops at close range. He'd used them many times.

He trudged on across the courtyard, managed to get past the Silver Dollar Saloon between the two vacant lots two buildings short of his shop, and met Paul Baker in front of the bank. Paul fell in alongside without a word, and they turned out of the sun's hot glare at the open maw of the blacksmith shop door.

Paul said: "I'm thirsty as hell. You got a bottle, Amos?"

Amos shook his head seriously. "I'm layin' off the drink."

Paul guffawed. "Wait a minute," he said, and went out the door.

Five minutes later he was back with a quart bottle of rye. Amos eyed it with a lowering scowl. "Take it away. I'm reformin'."

"Why?"

"My drinkin' don't help Bruce none."

"Get out! What's your drinkin' got to do with Bruce?"

"Who's goin' to vote for a marshal that's got a souse for an old man?"

"Me, for one. There ain't no one goin' to vote for Walt Kief." Paul Baker had uncorked the bottle, and now he tilted it to his lips. He took two long pulls at it, made a wry face, then breathed contentedly: "Ah-h-h!"

Amos's mouth was full of cotton, and he eyed the bottle

hungrily. Baker corked it, said: "The stage brought in a whiskey drummer, a corset salesman, and a cattle buyer." He uncorked the bottle again and took another pull at it, saying when he'd finished: "They're agin' this stuff more these days. This goes down good."

Amos reached out and snatched the bottle from Baker's hand. He tilted it in under his grizzled mustache and held it there a good ten seconds, the bubbles running up from his mouth along the neck of the bottle.

"Here! What the hell, you old fool," Baker growled, jerking the bottle away. He looked at it ruefully. It was half empty. Then, peering up at Amos with a guileful smile on his face, he said: "Ain't so bad, is it?"

Amos growled, "If you'd've let me taste it, maybe I'd know."

Sighing, Baker passed it across again.

II

Paul Baker could, on occasion, put down a quart of whiskey and stay on his feet. No one knew how much Amos could carry inside his shad-belly. But at eight that night there were three empty bottles sitting on the anvil close to the forge. Baker was asleep back in the hay, and Amos was still going strong. Dusk was thickening outside. Amos, staring out at the treetops across the street and trying to squint them out of their fuzzy indistinctness, realized all at once that he was hungry.

Habit took him to the rear alley door of his shop to lock up. Pulling the door closed, he happened to glance down the alley and see three saddles horses tied to his hitch rail. They stood at the end nearest the bank, which was the building alongside. He saw a tall man, one he recognized in a moment as Walt Kief, tie the last set of reins to the rail and walk away in the gathering darkness.

Amos was puzzled. He didn't call out to Kief simply because he was stubborn. Then, after Kief had disappeared, he laughed. Jeff Williams, owner of the only other blacksmith shop in town, closed promptly at six. Kief ran a livery service and probably wanted these horses shod and was too damned proud to come in and tell Amos to do the job. He'd tied his horses out there, expecting that Amos would discover them and go about his work.

"Damned if I will!" Amos bridled. "Let him come ask me, if he wants work done." He walked out, untied the three sets of reins, and led the horses in through his barn and out the front door to the hitch rail there, where he tied them. They were in plain sight now. Walt Kief would see them, and, if he was in such a hell of a hurry to have them shod, let him come and ask like a gentleman.

He went on up the walk, stopped in at the Silver Dollar for a drink, and then crossed the square to Miley's Eat House, where he ordered soup, a steak with potatoes, a piece of pie, and coffee. When Amos drank, he was hungry.

He was halfway finished with his soup when an earth-jarring thud ran through the timbers of Miley's one-room shack. A fraction of a second later an explosion sounded, in a prolonged, muffled *Bo-o-om!* The front window shook from the concussion of air outside. Miley, behind the counter, dropped a stack of saucers and stared wide-eyed out the window.

There was an interval of tense expectancy. Then Amos saw it, the cloud of dust that boiled out along the street off one corner of the square. "The bank!" he shouted. Miley vaulted his counter and raced out the door. Amos followed. From across the square two gunshots sounded above the shouts of the men running along the street.

Amos called—"Someone get Bruce!"—and bolted across the street.

Five staccato-spaced shots exploded from behind the hotel. Then Amos happened to glance across at the Silver Dollar in time to see the swing doors burst open and a swarm of men pour out onto the walk. Two muffled shots came from inside the saloon, and suddenly the lights shining through the windows went out.

Amos gained the walk in front of the hotel, started following the men who were running along the walk past the vacant lot toward the saloon, when from up ahead he heard Bruce's voice call stridently: "Get back! Everyone stay back! They're forted up in there."

As if in answer to his words a volley of shots rang out of a side window of the saloon—the one facing the vacant lot on this near side—and a man ten feet from Amos screamed, coughed pulpily, and sprawled face down on the walk. Someone picked him up and carried him back to cover, following Amos and the rest, who were hurrying in behind the protection of the hotel.

A man brought a lantern after a minute or two, pushing his way through the sober-faced knot of men standing around the outstretched figure on the walk. "He's dead . . . shot through the lungs," one of the onlookers said. "Blow out that damned light, will you? You want us all to get it?"

The lantern was extinguished. Bruce Short made his appearance a moment later. They made way for him, and he looked down at the dead man. Someone said—"Bill Medell . . . dead."—and the sober look on Bruce's face hardened.

He looked around to see who was present. More men were coming each second. Another group stood a hundred yards beyond, in front of the bank and beyond the vacant lot below the Silver Dollar. An occasional rifle shot cracked from the front of the saloon. A bullet ricocheted off a tie rail twenty feet away and droned overhead.

The marshal said: "Half a dozen of you get rifles and take to the windows upstairs in the hotel. Watch the alley. They may try to break out that way. Then. . . ."

"Who are they? What happened?" asked someone as ignorant of the circumstances as Amos.

"Those three strangers that came by stage this noon," Bruce answered. "They blew out the vault in the bank. I was next door, looking for Amos, and managed to turn them up this way when they made a break out the back door of the bank. Someone above in the alley stopped them from heading that way, so they went into the saloon. You know the rest."

"You're damned right," another man said. "I was there. They got one man, I think it was Fogarty, before we could get through them doors."

Bruce said: "Tom Kief's in the bank now, checking the loss in the vault. You, Sam, take a bunch up into the hotel and cover the alley. I want those men, alive if possible."

"And how are you going to take them?" came a bland query from the edge of the circle. It was Walt Kief who had spoken.

Bruce turned slowly to face him. He knew what Walt meant, without looking. The Silver Dollar was an old, sturdy building—its walls were of two-foot-thick adobe, the windows small, the roof of sheet tin. Neither fire nor bullets could damage the place. But Bruce had his answer ready. He said: "Walt, you're to hunt Len Sweetser, get his key to the powder house, and go out there and bring back a case of dynamite. Better take one man along to help."

Walt Kief laughed dryly. "And who's goin' to toss a bundle of dynamite across that vacant lot and onto the roof?"

"I'm carrying it across," Bruce answered, and turned his back on Kief, who walked away with another man a moment later.

Bruce was busy for the next three minutes, giving directions to the men he wanted in the second-story hotel windows. While he talked, the crowd in front of the bank below the Silver Dollar scattered. Bruce saw that and quit talking. The men down there spread out across the street and in beneath the shadows under the cottonwoods around the courthouse. The firing from the saloon was still desultory, aimed at nothing in particular but serving the purpose of keeping the walks ahead of the saloon clear.

Suddenly a dozen guns opened up from beneath the cottonwoods. Then men were rushing across the street and into the hail of bullets coming from the three guns in the saloon. One man went down, another, then a third, who crawled feebly back toward the square and was finally hit by a second bullet to fall flat and lie unmoving. The men were halfway across the street before they hesitated. They finally broke and ran, and two of them fell before the cottonwoods hid them once more.

Bruce snapped out: "Not a man's to move out from this cover." A moment later he was running across the street. Amos followed him, not minding that on the way a bullet from one of the Winchesters in the saloon flicked a strip of felt from his hat. The lights along the square danced fuzzily in a whiskey fog before his eyes. But the whiskey in his guts made him unafraid, and he was thankful for that.

He caught up with Bruce halfway through the trees in the courthouse yard. Bruce was headed down toward the bank, walking parallel with the street. Amos caught his arm and stopped him.

"Bruce," he said, breathing hard. "You can't do it! They'll cut you to ribbons."

"Can't do what?"

"Get across either of them vacant lots with dynamite. Damn it, you'll be blown to doll rags! There's windows on all four sides of the Silver Dollar."

"You know a better way?" Bruce asked.

Amos didn't and admitted it.

Bruce shook his arm free, starting on. "Then keep out of it," he told his father curtly.

Amos knew then that Bruce had smelled the whiskey on his breath, knew that he'd found Paul Baker passed out in the stall at the blacksmith shop.

Amos stood there, for the first time in all these years seeing himself as he was, a sodden drunk, a worthless tramp compared to this son who was doing his best to fill a job with the handicap of a father who made his gestures at keeping the law seem ridiculous. Amos turned off across the square, wishing he could do something. His legs were unsteady; he had to squint to see clearly. And, to bring home his utter worthlessness, a man hurrying across the square saw him and called good-naturedly: "How're them pink dragons tonight, Amos?"

It made Amos mad, not at the speaker, but at himself. He stood there alone, mumbling every curse word in his extensive vocabulary. He thought of getting the horse pistol from the tool shed in his shop and making a try at the Silver Dollar on his own, recognizing immediately that it would be plain suicide and do no one any good.

He was tired, and the whiskey in his guts had set up a nausea in him these last few minutes. He looked for a place to sit down. The nearest object was the Confederate memorial, the old six-pounder cannon. He walked across to it, sat down on its thick stock. His hand ran idly over a brass earplate, then along the hasp of the sponge-chain. He was remembering his days with Colonel Fowler, the way he'd sighted his own cannon with one eye squinted along the special sights he'd rigged along the barrel.

Suddenly something inside him tightened at the beginning of an idea. That thought brought him to his feet a moment later, sent him running awkwardly across the square. At the hitch rail in front of the restaurant he found a saddled horse. He untied the reins and climbed clumsily up and into the saddle, finding the stirrups too long. That didn't matter. He used the end of the reins to whip the horse, and, when the animal lunged into a run, he had to grip the saddle horn to keep from falling off. As he rode, he was thinking that here was a way of answering Tom Kief's argument. Maybe he wasn't so worthless, after all.

He turned into the first street along the east side of the square and rode along its length. Beyond the last houses, he cut off the road and across a fenceless pasture, smiling once as he saw a light wagon, two men on the seat, coming along the road. That would be Walt Kief and the man who had come along to help him get the dynamite from Ben Sweetser's powder magazine.

He rode up on Sweetser's small, isolated frame shack two minutes later. Sweetser did quite a business with the mines back in the hills and kept his powder and dynamite and fuses stored out here, away from town. The door was locked. But after half a dozen attempts, even Amos's puny weight pulled loose the hasp, and the door banged open. He didn't dare light a match, so he felt around in the dark until he got what he wanted.

He rode away with a keg half full of powder balanced on the saddle ahead of him. Amos had to walk the horse back to town, and the time seemed endless. Once on the square again, he reined the animal up over the walk and in under the trees, not lighting until he was alongside the six-pounder.

He left the powder keg there, took the horse back to its place at the hitch rail, and then went into the restaurant, finding it deserted. His glance ran over the place, finally settling on the oil-cloth counter. He took a knife from his pocket and made a slit in the oil cloth low enough to get his fingers into. Then, with one sweep of his arm, he ripped a ten-foot length of the oil cloth from the counter. He went behind the counter and searched through the drawers and amid the silverware until he found an ice pick. He was folding the oil cloth, as he went out the door.

He worked in feverish haste for better than five minutes alongside the cannon in the square. He cut the oil cloth into squares, dumped powder from the stove-in butt of the keg, and then wrapped each load of powder. He tied the bundles with narrow strips of oil cloth. He tried the fit of each deadly package in the mouth of the cannon and had to re-wrap two of the half dozen he had made. As he worked, he eyed the group of men in front of the hotel. In the light shining from the lobby window he could see Bruce and Walt Kief. Bruce and one other man were on their knees on the walk, working at something and with the dynamite case sitting on the walk close by. Amos knew that they were doing a job similar to his, rigging a bundle of dynamite-sticks to a cap and a fuse. He intended to finish his work before they did theirs, before Bruce could start his suicidal run across to plant the dynamite along the saloon wall.

Men were shooting from the hotel windows now, and answering shots racketed from the side window of the saloon. There were a few rifles on the roof of the bank, too, and these were also being answered.

Amos stood on his feet a few seconds after he'd seen Bruce come to a stand on the walk opposite. Bruce held a package in his hand, and the look of that bundle made Amos's heart skip a beat. What if Bruce should get started before he, Amos, could?

He didn't waste any more time with the powder charges then, but shoved one into the mouth of the cannon. He took the ramming rod from its hooks under the barrel, until the feel of the rod told him that the powder fit snugly against the solid breach. Looking for some wadding, he decided on his shirt. He took it off and tore it up and rammed a wad of shirting close down onto the powder.

As he dropped the first cannon ball into the mouth of the barrel, he heard a shout coming from the saloon. "Sheriff!" a voice called. "Sheriff, we've got a proposition to make you."

Amos turned and listened. Of course, there wasn't any sheriff present. But in a moment Bruce's voice answered: "What is it?"

"We'll turn over the money, if you'll let us go."

A chorus of shouts answered the words, some angry, others pleading. Amos looked through the trees and saw Bruce lay down the bundle of dynamite. Men ringed him, and he heard their voices raised in argument.

Amos dropped the rammer and ran across the square. He crossed the street, shouldered into the group surrounding Bruce. Walt Kief was doing the talking as he stepped close enough to listen.

". . . give into 'em, we'll have every hardcase in this country on our necks. No, sir. Bruce, it's your job to go get these men. Either that or you don't deserve to wear your badge."

"Why don't you carry that dynamite across there, Walt?" someone asked.

Walt Kief turned to face the speaker with a leering smile on his handsome dark face. "Because, Gus, it ain't my job. Short's gettin' paid a hundred and a quarter a month to take care of just this sort of trouble. Now let's see him do it. When it comes my turn, after I'm elected, I'll do it. Not until then."

The mutter of voices that greeted his words was mixed in feeling. Kief plainly had backers in the crowd, and Bruce had his. Amos put in his own feeble word: "Bruce, don't you go across there. Let 'em go."

Bruce said soberly: "Four men dead. It won't hurt to have one more to bury with 'em, if this works." He raised his voice, shouted: "It's no deal, gents. Either throw down your guns and come out with your hands up, or we come after you."

"Come ahead!" was the shouted answer, accompanied by

a raucous laugh. "We got plenty of food and drink in here. We can last a week."

Bruce turned to a man alongside him. "Where's the dynamite?" he asked.

Amos didn't wait for more. He ran back across the street again, on into the square and alongside the six-pounder. He picked up the ice pick, rammed it down into the firing hole, and worked it around until he knew he had a large hole punctured through the oil cloth. Then, taking up a handful of powder from the keg, he let it sift through his fingers and into the hole until the hole was full.

The barrel of the cannon was pointing upward. Amos turned the elevating-screw by the handles, sweat beading his high forehead before he found that the screw was corroded and didn't work freely. But he worked it down finally until he could squint along the line of the barrel at the proper elevation. Then he found the cannon was pointed wrong.

He put his shoulder to the wheels three different times, throwing all his weight against the iron tires. Finally he had it lined true, squarely at the front window of the Silver Dollar to the left of the swing doors. He chocked the wheels with cannon balls. Reaching into his pocket for a match, he looked across the square to see Bruce run suddenly from behind the protection of the hotel. Bruce carried the bundle of dynamite.

A paralysis of fear gripped Amos, held him for a long second. A rifle cracked out from the saloon. Bruce stumbled, went down.

Then, hand steady, Amos wiped the match alight along the seat of his pants. He touched the flame to a trailing smudge of powder to one side of the fuse hole. It flared alight.

The cannon's earth-shaking explosion smote out against the stillness, the concussion rattling the leaves of the cottonwoods. The orange burst of powder flame lit up half the square. Through the billowing smoke, Amos saw one front window of the Silver Dollar spray inward. A split second later the thud of a falling wall was plainly heard, and a cloud of dust rose up from the alley behind the Silver Dollar.

The rifles stopped their racketing fire inside the saloon. Amos, using the dry sponge of the rammer to swab out the barrel, looked back over his shoulder and saw Bruce crawling back into the protection of the hotel foundation. He felt a sudden excitement well up through him. Bruce was alive and safe.

A shot rang out from the saloon, and a bullet cut into the cottonwood branches over Amos's head. He laughed drunkenly, ramming home oil-cloth packing, wadding, and then dropping in the solid shot. He aimed the fieldpiece again, this time at the wall to the right of the saloon's swing doors.

The six-pounder exploded again. The wall beside the doors went in as though a giant's hands had pushed it. A twenty-foot length of the wide *portal* over the walk suddenly let go and crashed to the planks in a burst of falling timbers and adobe rubble. Before the dust had cleared, Amos had loaded again, this time using one of the canisters instead of the solid shot.

He aimed at the hole in the wall. A second after the fieldpiece blasted its throaty roar, the front wall of the Silver Dollar was sprinkled with live puffs of dust, where the lead balls of the canister struck. From inside came the crash of falling glass.

A man in there screamed, staggered out of the opening and into view. He was riddled with bullets as he took his second step into the clear. Then all at once the other two broke out from the shadows at the hole in the wall at a stiff run, firing as they came.

The first went down in a skidding lunge. The second came

on across the street, ignoring the fire from the hotel and bank, and emptying his six-gun across the courtyard in the direction of the six-pounder.

Amos felt a blow hit him high on one thigh. Its force spun him around, and he fell back against a wheel and then slowly sagged to a sitting position, eyeing the oncoming bandit. Suddenly, when the man had almost gained the shelter of the trees, he clutched his stomach and took two staggering, slow steps, then fell headlong, his body jerking as more bullets cut into him.

They found Amos a half minute later. The men of both crowds, the one in front of the bank and the one before the hotel, had the same idea at the same instant and ran out into the square and toward the Confederate memorial. Half a dozen lanterns lighted the scene as Bruce, the first to arrive, knelt beside his father. Amos was sitting with his back to one wheel of the carriage. His left hand was clamped about his thigh. He blinked into the lantern glare, saw the blood showing on Bruce's shirt at his right shoulder, and a look of alarm came into his eyes.

"Bruce, you're hit." He raised his voice. "Where the hell's a doctor?"

Bruce said: "It's only a scratch, Pa. Let's have a look at you."

Amos pushed him away, got a hold on the wheel, and pulled himself erect. "Let me have your cutter, Bruce," he said mysteriously, as the crowd pushed in closer.

Bruce frowned, looking at his father as though he hadn't heard right. So Amos reached out and lifted his son's six-gun from its holster. He said to Bruce: "Now get back."

Bruce took a backward step out of sheer instinct against having a gun pointed at him. Amos swung the weapon in a tight arc, and the crowd gave way behind another man as it settled into line with him. The man was Walt Kief.

"Walt," Amos drawled. "Step out here."

Kief's face gathered in a scowl. "Why should I?"

"Because Bruce is arrestin' you," Amos said. "I reckon if those three had found the three horses out behind the bank where you tied 'em tonight at dark, they'd have been long gone by now. Gone with the bank's money."

To one side of Amos, Tom Kief's voice boomed: "Amos, you're a liar! You're drunk!"

"Sure I'm drunk," Amos agreed. "But I got them horses to prove it. They're. . . ."

Suddenly Walt Kief whirled into the crowd behind him. His right hand palmed a .45 from the waistband of his trousers. He clubbed one man who tried to stop him.

Bruce snatched his weapon from his father's hand. He stepped up onto a wheel hub of the gun-carriage, looked out over the heads of the crowd. He brought his weapon up, lined it. "Walt!" he shouted. "I'm going to shoot!"

Walt Kief must have stopped moving and turned and faced Bruce. For his gun spoke twice, and Amos later remembered seeing the twig of a branch within six inches of Bruce's head break off and fall to the ground. Bruce fired once, and then slowly holstered his weapon. He climbed down and stood alongside his father, his face drained of color.

They carried Amos to the doctor's house. He was there an hour before the physician had a chance to look at him. Even then Amos made the doctor dress Bruce's shoulder first. The reason the medical man took so long in arriving was that Tom Kief made him stay with Walt, working out there under the cottonwoods, trying to save his nephew's life.

But when it was all over, as the doctor later bandaged Amos's leg, he told Bruce and his father: "No one knows this for sure, but me and Tom Kief, Bruce. Walt came to before he died, long enough to let Tom pry the truth out of him. He made a deal with them three to come in here and make a fool of you, Bruce. Their share was to be what came out of the vault. His was to have been winnin' the election."

The next morning old Tom Kief was at the doctor's house before breakfast, looking haggard and in need of sleep. He didn't come in, but asked the medical man's wife about the patient and seemed relieved when he was told that Amos would be well in a few days.

He handed the doctor's wife a package. "Give Amos this," he said. "Tell him who sent it."

It was a quart bottle of whiskey, finer than any Amos had ever tasted. He killed the whole bottle that day.

Angel Peak

In the last half of the 1940s at Popular Publications, Mike Tilden was the general editor for *Dime Western*, *Star Western*, *Big-Book Western*, *.44 Western*, *Ace-High Western Stories*, and *New Western*. Harry Widmer was the editor for *10 Story Western*. Alden Norton was editor for *Fifteen Western Tales*. It was not unusual for Mike Tilden to buy a story for one of the magazines he oversaw only for it to appear in another because a story of that length was needed to complete a particular issue. "The Echo Herd" was bought for *Fifteen Western Tales*, but in the event Tilden needed it for *New Western* (11/47), and for that issue it was emblazoned on the cover as the lead story. Alden Norton bought five other Peter Dawson stories in late 1946 and early 1947, all of which did appear in various issues of *Fifteen Western Tales* in 1947, with their titles and the author's name showcased on the covers. "Angel Peak," as Jon Glidden titled this story, was purchased in October, 1946 and appeared under the title "The Devil on Angel Peak" in *Fifteen Western Tales* (3/47). The author was paid $90.00. Jon Glidden tended to avoid dealing with the Indian wars in his fiction because he firmly believed there were two sides to the conflict and most stories tended to be one-sided. On those rare occasions, when he did deal with the Indian wars, as here, he was balanced in his approach

This post was just another of those god-forsaken places the Army built in the West during the Indian troubles. It was miles from nowhere, and so little happened that a man's roots were liable to turn around and start growing right back into him. Accordingly, it was mighty natural that the officers and their few wives—even the enlisted men—took an uncommon interest in the courtship of Arabella Evans.

In the first place, Clee Towers was something of a man. His arrival from the Academy in the summer of '83 had caused quite a flurry, chiefly with the remount man down in Deming who looked around hard for a month before he could find a pair of geldings big enough to carry the new lieutenant any distance. Clee was six-foot-five and weighed a lot more than you would have guessed from his rangy build. These two geldings both stood over seventeen hands. It was maybe a year before Major Evans got out of the habit of seeing that visiting officers had a good look at Clee on one of them. Clee had been born and raised in Kentucky, and working with horses came as naturally to him as fooling with firearms. His riding was such a pretty thing to watch that Dr. Martin, of all people, wrote a young artist he knew up in Wyoming, trying to get him to make a trip down here. This fellow liked to draw soldiers and cowboys and such. Dr. Martin didn't come right out and tell him he'd like to see him do a painting of Mr. Towers on the chestnut. Instead, he praised New Mexico's sunshine and the color of the land and spoke of the fierce, proud Indians. The artist's name was Frederic Remington.

Dr. Martin never received a response from him.

Getting back to the courtship, Clee and Arabella hit it off right from the first. The feeling about Arabella had been that she belonged at some big post, say in the East or at Leavenworth, where she would have the pick of fine men. But Arabella made liars out of those who blamed the major for bringing her out here into these mountains, away from all the things such a downright beautiful and alive girl needed, for she thrived on the life, loved it. She rode as much as anyone on the post and was so free and easy that the men worshipped her. They even got to using her instead of the adjutant in dealing with her old man, whose disposition needed an overhauling and would never get one.

So, in that first excitement over the match, it was decided that, after all, here was Arabella's chance to lay hands on as fine a man as walked the earth. Everyone thought Clee was just that. Everyone. For weeks there was a sight more talk about those two than about the silver strike at Kingston, or about the Apaches busting off their reservation—or even about George Adams's try at making pets of two motherless silver-tip cubs.

Then, finally, Arabella went along with Clee's detail, guarding the paymaster's Daugherty wagon as far as Deming, and the word got around that they were to be married down there. But when the detail got back, all Arabella had to show for the trip was a batch of dresses and no ring. Everyone was disappointed but still hopeful. Then things went wrong, but not so's you could tell it for a time, either.

Clee didn't change from his easygoing ways, and Arabella would laugh just as much as ever and still play tomboy. But after the Deming trip you didn't see them together often. And by the time winter set in, it was usually George Adams who took her to the Saturday night dances. Around Christmas it was pretty plain that George was serious about her, and only Clee's closest friends were still curious over what had happened.

By the next spring Clee, young as he was, was shaping up as a sure-fire bachelor, still eligible but likely to remain one. This was partly because he looked older than he was, and he had an older man's ways, like being able to hold a lot of whiskey, yet leaving the poison alone when he wanted. Then he and Earl Hamilton—captain and adjutant—and Dr. Martin were the "steadies" of the poker crowd that sat most every night except Sundays in the medical man's cabin. If Clee ever thought of Arabella in a serious way these days, none of his close friends knew it.

As an officer, there were some who were ahead of Clee any way you looked at it. He wasn't out for anything, never pushing for a soft detail, or, for that matter, ducking a hard one. There didn't seem to be a grain of ambition in him those days. Which may have been one reason he was so generally well liked. Maybe it was just the spring, or maybe the lonely life had put him off his feed, but on one particular night Clee was on edge. Finally it got so bad that he left the game and went outside, regardless of leaving a good run of cards.

He stood for a long time in front of his cabin, half of a mind to go to bed. Yet something held him where he was, staring across the parade at the barracks windows glowing against the black backdrop of the pines. He heard the sentry at post number four dragging his feet along the gravel, and then a coyote's howl cut loose from deep in the cañon beyond the mesa's edge, that mournful sound nagging at his nerves until he wondered if he was getting liverish. He was fond of tobacco, but tonight it tasted awful, and he tossed away his half-smoked cigar and drew in a deep lungful of the cedar-sweet air, thinking maybe he ought to give up the weed.

Then, oddly, his glance went down along the plank walk to a light in the side window of the cabin next to headquarters. And before he knew it, he was headed that way.

He was darned sure he was going to keep walking right on past the cabin, but, when he was even with the porch, he saw a pale shadow there against the blackness, and some devilish instinct he had no control over made him call softly: "Arab?"

"Yes?" came Arabella's cool answer.

He was tingling all over as he sauntered across there. He leaned against the porch railing in that way he always had of putting his big frame at ease when he wasn't in motion. And his excitement didn't show as he drawled: "Like to take a walk, Arab? We could go out on the point and watch the moon come up."

"You know it's against orders to go beyond the gate, now that the Apaches are off the reservation," she told him.

He laughed softly, delightedly, remembering how easy she was to tease. "Afraid?" he asked.

"Of what?" she wanted to know. Then, typically, she rose from the chair and came down the step to join him, saying: "You overestimate your capabilities, Mister Towers."

He took her arm, and she moved away from him, shrugging his hand aside as they started across the parade.

After a few moments, she announced: "George told me about your performance last night. About Doc Martin having to help you to bed."

"George didn't approve?"

"Should he?"

"This time, yes. It was a wager, Arab. Major Robey challenged me in a way I could hardly turn down."

"To get drunk?" she asked, plainly disbelieving him.

"What amounted to as much. You see, the old man. . . ."

"Clee, I've told you before that I won't have you calling

Dad that. After all, he's not old, and he's your commanding officer."

He nodded and, with a chuckle, went on: "Never had so much fun in all my life. Your father had asked us all to go out of our way to please Robey, what with his inspection coming off today. Last night it came out that Robey likes mescal. He laid a twenty-dollar bet that none of us could drink a bowl full of the stuff and stay on our feet. To prove it could be done, he did it himself. Then. . . ."

"Then you covered his bet," she cut in dryly. "Clee Towers would never let a chance like that pass."

"Now wait, Arab. Your dad didn't object. And I saw that Robey would be disappointed unless someone took him up. So I covered his twenty, drank the mescal, and a couple minutes later fell on my face like I meant it. Robey was so pleased he roared. And today inspection went off fine. He didn't even look at the arms stores, and I understand George hasn't had those twelve-pounders cleaned in over two months."

"That's not the truth, Clee Towers!" Arabella's head tilted up and around.

She caught his grin then and knew he was guying her. She stamped her foot, angry-like, and she was standing there so tall and pretty and everything that he just reached out and gathered her in his arms and kissed her like he used to. She tried to push away and clenched her fists and beat at his arms a time or two. Then her hands opened, and her arms went around him, and, if a man ever got a kiss, he got one right then.

When he let her go, he told her: "That's the medicine I've been needing."

She reached up and straightened her hair and then let him have it the same way she'd have yanked the spade bit on a mean horse. "It's the last you'll ever get! That was a very ungentlemanly thing to do, Clee."

"You didn't seem to mind too much."

"For a moment I forgot. We're finished, Clee. Remember? The Deming trip?"

"That was a long time ago."

"You're still the same," she said. "And I'm just as sure about you as I was then. Besides, George and I are going to be married. Probably before the month is out."

He laughed the same way he would at a poor joke, drawling: "Try something else, Arab. That's no good."

But all at once he knew it was good, real good. She meant it. He fumbled around, trying to get a hold on himself, and, when he did, all he could think of to say was: "You can't do that, Arab. George is ten years older than you. He's nice. But, my God, you want a man who'll more than hold your hand."

"You leave that to me, Clee Towers! George is fine, he's good to me, and there isn't a better officer on the post."

"You're not in love with him. You love me."

"Yes, once I was fool enough to think I did love you. But now I won't let myself. You know the reasons."

"What are they?"

"Let's not talk about it, Clee."

"Let's do talk about it." He felt the sweat breaking across his forehead, the way it used to back in school when he was wrestling with a gunnery problem. "What's wrong, Arab?"

"We talked about it once, Clee."

"I've forgotten what you said. Say it again."

"All right," she said, deciding to use the spur on him now. "It's because you have the makings of a fine officer, yet you do nothing about it. You simply drift along, not caring about anything."

"I care about you, Arab."

That rubbed her the wrong way, and she burst out: "I'm

disappointed in you. For generations it's been bred into my family that the only soldier worth his rations is the one who does a little more than he's asked to. Your soldiering just isn't good enough."

"Has your father any complaints against me?" he asked.

"No. Probably no one will ever complain about you. Can't you see it, Clee? Our whole life would be like that. We'd get by because things come to you naturally. I'm not ambitious, but I'd always be wondering how much more you could have made of yourself, if you really tried."

He asked: "What more could I be doing?"

"Lots of things." She tried to think of them and finally said, lame-like: "You . . . you could get Doc Martin to teach you better care of the wounded. Or . . . well . . . for instance, do you know how to work the heliograph?"

"No. I knew Morse code once. But I've forgotten it."

"I know how to use the heliograph," she said, a proud edge to her voice. "I've had Sergeant O'Rourke teach me to use it. Then. . . ." She was looking up at him and broke off as she saw his face set hard as a brick wall. She knew then that she had hurt him, and she reached out and laid a hand on his arm and said, ever so gently: "I didn't want to say these things, Clee. But it's the way I feel. I . . . I hope we can be friends."

He managed a smile. "Sure, we'll be friends, Arab."

She turned and left him, and he watched her slim shape, so tall and straight, until it had faded in the darkness. And he was thinking: *This time she means it.* Now he was no longer restless. Something else was wrong. He felt like maybe he hadn't eaten for two or three days, like the chill air was so thin his lungs couldn't get enough out of it to keep him going. He was sort of faint, and that made him sore because he had never fainted.

He finally walked over to Dr. Martin's cabin and cashed in

his winnings. He was too busy thinking about Arab to pay much attention to what they said. He even turned down the offer of a bottle.

After he had gone, Bob Lacey, the new lieutenant, asked: "Is Mister Towers usually this restless?"

"No." Dr. Martin slid a glance at Earl Hamilton. "No, he hasn't been for seven or eight months now. I wonder if it's his old ailment come back again."

Clee always slept light as a feather, and, when the horse kicked up all the racket slogging up out of the cañon at four the next morning, he came awake in a hurry. He heard the sentry give his challenge and was pulling on his boots as the horse galloped across the parade. Voices started talking down there, and then someone bawled—"Mister Towers! Will someone awaken Mister Towers!"—and he grabbed up his hat and holster and bolted out of his cabin.

He met O'Rourke, his sergeant, halfway to headquarters, and O'Rourke told him: "Mister Adams wants you right away, sir."

"What's up, Tim?"

"Them bloody red devils has busted loose again," the Irishman told him. "They took a few scalps at the placers above Kingston, and this sodbuster killed a horse gettin' here to tell us. He's up there now."

"Have the troop ready to move out in ten minutes," Clee cut him short. "Rations for six days. Issue twenty extra rounds apiece for carbines and a spare canteen for every other man. Off you go."

"Will this be what the major calls a show of force, sir? Or maybe we do get some time in town?"

"We'll make our guesses later, Sergeant."

"Very good, sir." O'Rourke wheeled away and set off

across the parade like something was after him.

The sky off the peak to the east was dirty gray with the first dawn, and it was so cold Clee's face felt raw, when the air hit it, as he ran to headquarters. He found four men in the major's office. There was the major himself, flannel nightgown showing over the top of his open shirt and his big paunch folded over the edge of the desk as he sat, leaning against it. George Adams, acting as officer of the guard, looked just as calm and dignified as usual. Ben Hiatt, the scout, sat with his moccasins propped up on the edge of the desk in his usual don't-give-a-damn way. His derby was slanted down over his gray eyes that were heavily lidded but at the same time taking in everything. The fourth man Clee had never seen before. He wasn't a sodbuster. His overalls were bleached and stained with adobe along the thighs, and he wore heavy brogans. He was a gold hunter if Clee ever saw one.

The major answered Clee's salute with his usual scowl and he started right off, without preliminaries. "Mister Towers, it seems Victorio's on the loose again. You will take J Troop down to Kingston as a show of force. Pick up as many of those settlers and miners as you can on the way down. You'll organize any defense of Kingston that's needed and patrol around there until relieved. Doctor Martin will accompany you. I should also like the new lieutenant, Mister . . . ah . . . Mister . . . ?"

"Lacey," Clee said.

"Take Mister Lacey along and get him acquainted with a routine patrol." Quick-like, the major shot Ben Hiatt a glance, growling: "Damn it, Ben, that's no place for your feet! You'll also go with Mister Towers."

Hiatt tongued his tobacco to the other cheek, then eased his extremities to the floor, asking: "Is this just what you call another show of force, Major? Or do we have a go at Victorio?"

"You'll let Victorio strictly alone," the major said. "These sniveling civilians and all their talk of our treatment of the downtrodden redskins have changed things. Now we need Washington's permission before we can even fire a shot at one of the plaguey devils."

Clee was standing there, thinking about the things Arabella had said last night. They brought something to mind just now, and, before he'd halfway thought it through, he was saying: "Sir, mightn't Victorio have swung west around the end of the hills and be coming back along the far side? He could cross over and raise Cain with those other camps. With your permission, I'd like to anticipate such a move."

"Mister Towers, it's perhaps a little early in the morning for you to be completely awake," said the major in a voice dry as leaf dust. "I have just explained to Mister Hiatt that Washington won't any longer let us hunt Indians."

Clee could be stubborn, too, although it wasn't many but the poker crowd that had sampled his bullheadedness. Right now he was half sore at the way Arab had rubbed it in last night. So he spoke right back at her father. "Have I your permission to order my troops to defend themselves, if attacked, sir?"

"That goes without saying, Mister Towers. Now let's waste no more time quibbling."

It was a sight longer than Clee had counted on before the troop moved out. Dr. Martin took more time than necessary with his pack animal. Then, with J Troop beyond the gate, there came another delay when Clee had his brainstorm. He signaled a halt and turned to Tim O'Rourke, asking: "Sergeant, do we have a heliograph?"

"No, sir."

So he had O'Rourke send Corporal Beskins back for one.

The corporal was hardly through the gate when Clee was asking another question. "How many men can operate the heliograph, Sergeant?"

"Just me and Beskins, Lieutenant."

Lieutenant Bob Lacey, who had been sticking close to Clee, spoke up: "I know how to use one, sir."

"Good!" Clee's glum look went away, and he said: "Hold the men here, Sergeant."

He wheeled the big chestnut around and went back through the gate at a hard run. He was dismounting before headquarters when he saw Arabella standing there on her porch next door with a dark robe wrapped around her. He didn't let on like he saw her and was headed up the steps, when she called: "Clee, please be careful!"

He still didn't let on that he knew she was there, so she called a lot louder: "Clee, aren't you going to say good bye?"

He looked around, and then stopped in the doorway and touched the brim of his wide hat as he told her: "Good bye."

Her head cocked up the way it always did when she bridled, and she called across: "I almost wish it was a real good bye."

"When I get back, maybe something can be done to make it a real one, Arab," he told her. He got out of her sight as quickly as he could then.

George Adams was alone in the office, and Clee told him: "George, I'd like to sign out for two spare heliographs. There may be news to send back here, and, if the weather closes, we'll have to relay."

George was willing enough, so they headed off across the parade to the quartermaster cabin. On the way, Clee said: "Arab gave me the good news last night, George. Congratulations. You're a lucky man."

George looked up, puzzled as all get out. "What news, Clee?"

"That you're going to marry Arabella."

"Me? Get married?" George asked in his slow way. His face got red as he took Clee's hand and shook it. Afterward, he still looked like he couldn't quite take it all in.

By sunrise, J Troop was well down in the yellow pine belt around the waist of Bald Mountain, and a little later they came across a mud-chinked shack and warned two homesteaders about Victorio's raid. The pair thought it would be quite a lark to go along and draw government pay, so Clee swore them in as militiamen. Around ten o'clock, at the head of Lost Man Creek, they routed three men, two women, and six kids out of another cabin. Clee left four of his men to guard them on their way down to Kingston by wagon.

By three that afternoon, because of several more things like this, Clee had only sixteen men following him when they sighted Kingston, lying far below in a loose fold of the hill. He stopped the troop along a stream, and, while the men watered their animals and filled canteens, Clee called a get-together that included Ben Hiatt, Dr. Martin, Bob Lacey, and Tim O'Rourke.

"Sergeant," he began, "you're to send Corporal Olds on down to Kingston alone. He'll have plenty of men by the time they get all these people herded down there. He'll help the settlement every way he can. He's to keep a man ready at all times to ride up the Angel Peak trail with any news for the fort. I'm putting Beskins up there on that shoulder at the trail-end with a heliograph. Now go get him started."

Tim O'Rourke was walking away, when Ben Hiatt asked: "And what'll we be doin' meanwhile, Mister Towers?"

"Tell you in a minute," Clee said. He looked at Dr. Martin. "Doc, you can have your choice. You can go on down with Olds. Or you can stick with us."

"I'll tag along with you," Dr. Martin said in a hurry. "There's a horse doctor down there. Besides, the scare's over."

"Fair enough," Clee said. "Now, Ben, you ask what we'll be doing. The major said we were to patrol, which is what I intend doing. To start with, I seem to remember a cañon that cuts through to the far slope of Angel Peak right below the pass. Can you take us through there?"

Ben gave a start, like a horse shying at the rustling of a sidewinder. He looked at Dr. Martin like he was asking if he'd heard right, before he said: "Maybe I can. But if we got through to the west side, we'd be thirty or forty miles from Kingston. The old man said to patrol around it . . . *around* . . . Mister Towers."

"He didn't say how far, did he?"

"No," Ben admitted, like it was hurting him. "I reckon he didn't."

"Then I'll be within my orders."

"You got somethin' in your craw?" Ben eyed Clee, sideways and sharply, with the same sort of a first-off look he'd give a draw hand at poker before he ruffled out the cards.

"Nothing yet," Clee said, innocent as anything.

"Then why don't we take the pass straight across to the far side?"

"We might be seen by hostiles, Ben. You heard what the old man said. We're not to invite trouble. If the Apaches can't see us, they can't attack."

One of his rare smiles cracked the set of Ben Hiatt's leather face. "I'm damned," he said. "Well, I'll put on my thinkin' cap." And he gave Dr. Martin a broad wink.

While the old scout tussled with the problem Clee had put him, Clee sent Corporal Beskins and three other men on up the Angel Peak trail with a heliograph. As the small detail moved out, the remaining troop was tightening cinches, getting ready to ride.

This cañon Clee had picked to travel was a jumble of big boulders and scrub oak thickets and alder and willow all tangled together. There were ledges where the troopers had to get aground and drag their animals up across tricky footing, and it was no wonder it took until sundown to cover those six miles. A funny thing, though. No one complained a bit. O'Rourke didn't, and he was wondering why they were taking two extra heliographs on instead of using them for relay to the fort in case of bad weather, like the lieutenant had said. Even Dr. Martin didn't complain, and he hated saddle work like all get-out.

They made a cold camp in the pines at twilight, washing down canned beef and cold biscuits with water, when their stomachs were gnawing for a tin of hot coffee. An hour after dark they were in the saddle again, Clee telling them before they started: "No more rest this trip, boys. We'll be at it all night."

Young Bob Lacey had all this day ridden close as a pup on Clee's heels. Just short of eleven, when the moon lifted up over Angel Peak—miles behind and above now—he ventured his first comment in hours, saying: "No one could possibly have seen us working across here, could they, Mister Towers?"

"Hope not, Bob."

"You have some plan in mind, sir?"

"Not much of a one yet."

Now Clee called another halt, resting the horses and letting the men eat more of that cold food that tasted like so much sawdust and sand. And he sent Tim O'Rourke and three more men off with a second heliograph. There was a big hill close by—what looked like the highest anywhere around

—and O'Rourke headed off through the trees toward the crest of it.

When they went on again, they swung north and rode for two solid hours with only one ten-minute halt. Then, studying his landmarks, Clee finally turned east and rode for the higher country. They wondered what he was doing, and Ben Hiatt began feeling like the fifth wheel on a cart, for this was his job and Clee wasn't asking him anything.

Shortly after three they rode into a ravine and kept on a good mile before Clee called a halt. He had the picket-line placed well above camp, and he was particular to warn the men against fires, even against smoking.

"This cut," he told Ben, Dr. Martin, and Lacey, "runs on through and empties into Lost Man Creek on the far side. Farther up, you run onto a deer trail that takes you all the way. It and that cañon below Angel are the only easy ways across the hills without being seen."

"And how does it happen you know about it, and I don't?" asked Ben. After all, he had a right to feel huffy, with Clee doing all the scouting.

"Last fall we tracked a wounded deer through here, Ben. I was. . . ."

"The time you were out that extra day and the old man combed you over for missing the wood detail?" Dr. Martin put in.

"The same," Clee answered.

Dr. Martin walked away, chuckling, to find a place to throw his blanket.

Clee saw that guards were posted, and then he took Bob Lacey aside. He told him he was awfully sorry, but there was still work to do. Then he asked Bob if he'd mind helping him get the heliograph up onto the south rim of the ravine. You'd think Lacey might have minded after something like twenty-two hours in the saddle, off and on. But he didn't.

So they took the ungainly instrument with its legs and mirrors wrapped in gunny sacking and started the climb. Forty minutes later, heaving like their ribs would bust loose, they were sitting on the rim right above the camp. The minute they stopped moving, the cold cut into them like a dull knife. Clee was dog-tired, and all he could tell Bob Lacey was: "We just sit tight and wait."

It was a pretty poor thing to have to admit, but he'd told Bob just about everything he knew about what to expect. Now, for the first time since he'd left the fort, it struck him that the whole thing was pretty addlebrained. He'd been a fool to take Arab so seriously, and he asked himself: *What are you proving, Mister Towers? You've lost her regardless.* It hurt him deep down inside, when he thought of her, of her cornsilk hair shining so golden in the sunlight, and the way her deep brown eyes used to laugh at him.

He must have dozed off then, for, when the uncoiled pin of the heliograph's reflector started squeaking, he opened his eyes to the bright light of day. Bob Lacey was kneeling down behind the instrument, working the thing with fast jerks as he flashed in Morse code.

"Anything happening?" Clee asked, yawning.

"Oh, you're awake," Bob said. "Didn't want to bother you till I'd got it straightened out, sir. They can't see me, can't understand that I'm getting their signal. It's the sun, Mister Towers. It hasn't reached us yet."

"What do they say?"

"Beskins up there on Angel Peak reported to O'Rourke an hour ago that at dawn he saw a dust boil down along the flats close to these hills. Of course, he had the sun first. Now O'Rourke keeps flashing that he's spotted a band of forty or fifty Indians, passing within a mile of him, headed this way."

"How long ago did he first start saying all this?" Clee got to his feet in a hurry. He looked mad.

"Just now, sir. I was about to wake you. You see, he's just got the sun."

Now Clee wasn't mad. "Take care of things," he said, and ran for the edge of the rim, thankful for the timber that hid him from below.

He took chances only a fool or a man in love would take, covering those two hundred straight down feet. He slid across talus slopes that wouldn't have held a burro, and the jumps he made got Dr. Martin's stomach all knotted up as he and several others watched from below. He tore his uniform and gouged his hands so that they left red stains wherever he touched. Finally he took a man-size spill and rolled head over boots and wound up against the gnarled branches of a piñon that grew within a foot of a fifty-foot drop right down to the camp.

He lay up there on his belly and called down, soft as he could and yet make them hear: "Indians. Get in those rocks and behind the trees there below. Don't a man of you fire a shot until I do." He opened the flap of his holster and drew out the big .45 single-action Colt and waved it.

He saw them scatter like a covey of quail, Ben Hiatt moving like a Mescalero, Dr. Martin waddling off into the brush clumsy as a bear, the blue-clad troopers bent low as they trotted off with carbines. In ten seconds there wasn't a man in sight.

It was a long wait for Clee. He was well hidden up there, and he could see a good way through the pines down the ravine. But damned if that first buck, big and shiny with his war paint and forking a roan horse, didn't get up to within a hundred yards of him before he ever knew he was there. That sort of jolted him, and then he got to worrying that maybe this was just a scout sent on ahead, that the main band might be miles below. But just then this big buck rode out of the trees and turned and lifted his head. And two more Apaches sort of rose up out of the ground and rode into sight, coming in on the first. The three came on then, and Clee waited until it was getting to be a bad straight down shot before he squeezed the trigger.

Lightning couldn't have kicked up thunder more suddenly than the Colt. The big buck rocked back over the roan's rump like a boulder had hit him. Then the carbines cut loose.

Clee got a fair shot at one of the other pair as he was going away. His lead must have caught the buck in the shoulder, because he twisted sharply and then grabbed his horse's mane, and, the last Clee saw of him, it looked like he wasn't sure whether he would stay on or off. There was some more ragged firing, and then it was over, all in less than half a minute by the clock.

Clee lay there, watching the troops move out of the brush. He saw Ben Hiatt go over to the buck he'd knocked down and run a big knife around the dark head and then pull off the scalp. Ben looked up at him and waved, calling: "Savin' it for you, Mister Towers."

Pretty soon a corporal stood below and called up the score, and it wasn't bad. Two troopers had been wounded. Dr. Martin was working on them, and so far a busted leg looked like the worst there was. Nine dead Apaches had already been counted, with more to come. They had taken four hostiles prisoner. One of these they thought might be Nana, who cast a wide shadow and was one of Victorio's best hole cards.

It was a long hard climb back to the rim where Bob Lacey waited beside the heliograph, his eyes all red from lost sleep.

"I've just got through to O'Rourke, sir."

Clee took his time making his report, which he told O'Rourke to relay on to the fort. He stretched a point or two. In one place he used the words—"defending myself"—and in another he mentioned that "the hostiles rode off unmolested." Finally it was finished.

So Clee chose a spot of shade under a cedar, and it took him until he let his head fall back to drop off to sleep.

It was ninety minutes later, when Bob shook his arm and handed him a signal pad, telling him: "It looks bad, sir. Major Evans wants a full explanation as to why you opened fire on the hostiles. Then there's this other I can't make head or tail of. It came later."

"What other?"

"What I've written there."

Clee read what was written on the pad:

That was a mean trick to play on George. Stop. After all will want him as our friend.

Clee was grinning, and Bob didn't know what to make of it and said: "It looks like the stop is in the wrong place. Or is it some new code I'm not familiar with?"

Clee laughed out loud. "You might call it a new code, Bob."

"Would you like me to send an answer, sir?"

Clee scowled, looking at the heliograph. "No, I'll send it," he said after a minute.

Then he got up and walked over to the heliograph and hunkered down behind it. He was gritting his teeth and glaring like he was mad, as he asked: "How do you work this fool thing?"

Showdown in Shadow

This was Jon Glidden's original title for this story. He sent it off to his agent on May 25, 1938. Marguerite E. Harper sent it on to John Burr who edited Street & Smith's *Western Story Magazine*, and Burr bought the story on July 10, 1938, paying the author $135.00 for it. Burr changed the title of the story to "Boothill Challenge" when it appeared in the issue of *Western Story Magazine* for 12/24/38. It was the thirtieth Peter Dawson story to be published, and another story in which a frontier physician is a principal character. In 1929 at the University of Illinois, Jon Glidden met Dorothy Steele, and they were married the next year. She was the model for several of his heroines, including Mary Clemens in this story.

Showdown in Shadow

[illegible]

I

It was after office hours, nearly nine. Dr. Porter sat well out of the light, tilted back in his swivel chair against the wall. He had placed the only other chair in the office directly in front of his desk, fully in the glare of the lamp, so that he could study his visitor.

Fred Scull didn't have a bad face. With eyes a clear blue even if they were a trifle cold, a well-shaped, though thin-lipped, mouth, Scull was rightly called a handsome man. Porter was dispassionately trying to discover his reasons for disliking that face, and not making much headway, when Scull said: "Is it because I'm not known here? If it is, I can. . . ."

"It don't amount to a tinker's damn with me where a man came from or who raised him," the physician interrupted. "All I said was that Mary'd have to decide. That's the way you'd want it, isn't it?"

Scull stirred a little uneasily at the bluntness of these words, shifting his broad shoulders in the nervous gesture Dr. Porter knew so well. "Of course, that's the way I'd want it, Doc," he said, pausing a moment to study the medical man openly and deliberately before he added, "I had the idea you weren't with me."

Porter chuckled guilefully in his old man's way of hiding his true feelings. "What could I have against you, Scull? You've got a good job at the bank. You could give Mary a comfortable home. But it's up to her."

"You're not thinking of Bill Spence?" Fred Scull asked warily, trying to catch the expression on the medical man's grizzled face and not succeeding because of the glare of light in his eyes.

Porter shook his head in great deliberation. "No, I'm not thinking of Bill Spence." He knew all at once what it was he disliked about this man. Scull was suspicious, distrustful. That was it. "But I can't speak for Mary. I never figured it was any of my business whom she loved until she chose to tell me."

"I'll be able to give her a lot more than Bill ever could," Scull persisted. "He draws sixty-five a month as deputy. That ranch of his is a lonely place, no place for a woman. And he's got that mortgage. It'll take him ten years to crawl out from under. . . ."

"Bill Spence doesn't crawl," Porter put in gruffly. He got up out of his chair, hooked his thumbs in his suspenders, and added: "You get your answer from Mary. If you hurry and go up there now, you can see her before I get home."

It was a plain dismissal. Sensing that further talk was futile, Scull rose from his chair, a genial smile on his lean face as he said: "Wish me luck, Doc."

"Sure, sure," Porter agreed, crossing the room to open the door.

He slammed it savagely behind the younger man's departing back, and, even before the sound of Scull's boot tread had died on the wooden stairway outside, he was swearing softly, viciously. He crossed to his desk, opened a drawer, and took out a bottle of whiskey and gulped down three full swallows. When the edge had worn off his temper, he muttered derisively: "Bill Spence crawling out from under!"

He gathered his instruments and tossed them fiercely into his black bag. The heavy handle of a pair of surgical scissors hit a bottle of pink pills and broke it, and the physician spent two minutes picking out the broken glass and the pills and replacing them with a freshly filled bottle from the cabinet behind his desk, more amused than angry now. Then he pulled on his coat, clamped his Stetson onto his grizzled head, and blew out the lamp. He locked the door as he left.

He was three steps from the bottom of the open stairway outside when he all at once saw below the two indistinct shapes in the cobalt shadows of the passageway alongside the adjoining building. As he hesitated, a hushed voice spoke out: "Hold on, Doc!"

Porter was surprised to see the blunt outline of a six-gun in the fist of the man nearest, the one who had spoken. Once over his surprise, sight of that leveled weapon brought on a quick rise of anger, and he asked sharply: "Well?"

"We've got a job for you, Doc," the same voice intoned. "It'll take most of the night."

"Why the plow handle?" Porter asked, his voice sharp-edged.

There was a moment's silence, then awkwardly: "No special reason, only we don't want any trouble."

"And who the hell told you you'd have to use a gun to get me to treat a patient?" Porter exploded. His words carried weight, for he saw the gun slowly arc down to settle into the holster at the man's thigh. Then he queried: "Is it bullet trouble?"

The man nearest nodded and jerked a thumb back toward the mouth of the alley. "We brought an extra bronc'. You'd better come along *pronto*. There ain't much time." And the speaker started back along the passageway.

Porter followed reluctantly, for the prospect of a sleepless night wasn't anything to look forward to. Yet he sensed that this pair was in deadly earnest, that they would take him whether or not he wanted to come. So he gave in and followed them into the alley and along it to the far edge of town. There, hidden behind an unused shed with a caved-in roof, were tied three horses. The man ahead pointed to the bay, and, as

Porter climbed into the saddle, he queried: "Anyone I know?"

"No, I reckon not," was the noncommittal answer.

They rode west from Rawhide at a fast, mile-eating trot, which told Porter that plenty of distance lay ahead. Cyrus Porter had been a medical doctor for thirty-four years, and his profession had taken him into strange places. His hunch tonight was that he was riding into trouble.

He acted on that hunch four miles beyond town, abruptly pulling in on the bay and growling at the riders who flanked him. "These stirrups'll kill me in another quarter mile." Without a word from them he got down and unlaced the rawhide thongs that tied the latigos. The strangers, obviously impatient to be under way again, paid him little attention.

When he was sure they weren't looking, his thin, spatulate-fingered hands snapped open the lock of his medicine bag and snatched out a short-barreled Smith & Wesson .38. When they rode on once more, the solid bulk of the weapon under his belt was reassuring. He had relaced the latigo strings in the same holes he found them; the stirrups had been exactly the right length all along.

It was a two-hour ride, ending at a slab-sided shack the medical man knew well—an abandoned Three Star line cabin. One of his companions rode straight to the door of the shack and swung to the ground, calling back: "I'll have a look inside first."

When Porter moved to follow, the second said quickly: "Wait'll Hank gives us the word."

This time Porter's curiosity was aroused, not his anger. He waited patiently near his horse, striding slowly up and down the hard-packed yard to take the cramp from his short legs. Finally the door opened, and Hank called out: "Bring him in." There was a light inside now, where before there had been darkness.

11

The physician stepped into the single room and found it bare of all furnishings but a poorly mended, sheet-iron stove, a stack of wood alongside, and a pile of blankets in the far corner by a shiny new lamp. On the blankets, his back to the wall and a gun in his lap, sat a tall-framed man whose lean, unshaven face was twisted in pain. He looked across at the medical man and tried to smile and said in a drawling, almost gentle voice: "I'm sure glad you got here."

It was that voice, not the face, that Porter recognized. The knowledge that he knew this man hit him like a sudden plunge in icy water. Unbelieving, he strode closer and into the light, so stunned he couldn't speak.

At sight of Porter, the gray eyes of the wounded man opened wide in a look of utter astonishment and disbelief, and he breathed hoarsely: "Hell, I'm dreamin'!"

"No, you're not, Trig," Porter said, and held out his hand.

The wounded man took it, and for a moment the lines of pain were almost erased by his glad smile. He glanced beyond Porter at the pair by the door and said evenly: "I'll be all right now, Hank. You and Quinn wait outside." Then his eyes dropped to the six-gun lying in his lap, and he picked it up and tossed it to one side, adding sheepishly as he once more regarded the medical man: "I was a bit spooky, Doc."

As the door creaked shut behind the other two, Porter reached in under his coat and lifted out the .38 he had rammed in his belt on the way out. "So was I," he said. He laid his weapon alongside the wounded man's and added: "In the old days Trig Clemens wouldn't have sided a pair that'd let a stranger tote a cutter into his camp."

Clemens swore softly, still smiling. "I've come a long way since then, Doc. Mostly down."

There was nothing Porter could say. He took off his coat and opened his bag. "Let's have a look at that bullet." And he knelt alongside Clemens. When he lifted a corner of the blanket off Trig's right shoulder, it was to reveal a blood-soaked shirt sleeve.

Porter cut the sleeve and lay bare an ugly wound at the point of the shoulder. He was busy for ten minutes, rising once to go to the stove and set a half-filled lard pail of water on it and add wood to the fire.

When he came back, he stood unmoving before Clemens. "It's going to hurt. The bullet's still in there, against the bone. Whoever threw the slug shot from behind." Porter was silent a moment, regarding his friend. Then he said levelly: "They say the sheriff down at Socorro scared off three men tryin' to bust into the bank four nights ago. They claim he winged one before he quit shootin'."

Trig Clemens nodded, making no pretense at a smile now.

The physician waited for him to speak, to explain. He didn't, and, when the silence had dragged out awkwardly, Porter finally said: "Years back, I heard that you'd been cleared of that murder, Trig. I thought you'd go back and maybe you'd write. When you didn't, I figured you'd cashed in."

Clemens shook his head. "It came too late, Doc. A man can hold out so long and no longer. I was starvin', afraid to show my face within a hundred miles of the law. A month before they cleared me of the frame-up that sent me on my high lonesome, I fell in with a wild bunch. We held up a stage and one gent with a quick trigger finger cut down on a passenger. That made me an outlaw for sure. I couldn't come back."

"So you've been . . . ?"

"I'm in pretty deep now," Clemens said dispassionately.

They didn't talk for long minutes. Finally Porter saw that the water was boiling and began his work on the shoulder. As his probe drove into the open flesh of the wound, Trig winced, then asked abruptly: "What about the girl, Doc?"

It was a question Dr. Porter had been expecting, dreading a little. But when he realized that somehow time hadn't much changed Trig Clemens, he was relieved. Trig was still all man, as in the old days, and Porter was now no longer afraid to tell him the truth. "She's the finest thing that ever grew up, Trig. Pretty, with your hair and her mother's eyes. . . ." Porter paused as he felt Clemens's frame go rigid under the thrust of the probe, then added quickly: "You heard about your wife, didn't you? How she died?"

Trig nodded. "I heard it a month too late. When they told me you'd taken the baby, I decided to play dead. It wouldn't have done her much good to grow up knowin' who her father was."

"She knows," Porter said. "I told her."

His probe had closed on the bullet, and his words were calculated to rouse the outlaw to violent anger. They did. As Trig's face swung around to regard him, the gray eyes stony, Porter pulled viciously at the probe.

The sudden pain drained the color from Trig's face, and for a moment Porter thought the man would faint. But that sudden flare of passion had dulled the agony, accomplished its purpose, and Porter now added: "She's damned proud of her father. Thinks he's dead, like I did."

All the flaring hostility drained from Trig Clemens's eyes, and now small beads of perspiration stood out on his forehead as the pain hit him. He forced that same smile again and drawled: "You had me riled there for a minute, Doc." Suddenly he understood, and his smile broadened. "You're still the same old fox."

Porter made short work of bandaging the wound. When he was finished, he washed his instruments and returned them to his black bag. As he worked, he was thinking. And when his thoughts had taken on some semblance of meaning, he stood before the wounded man and said bluntly: "You'll have to come home with me, Trig."

The outlaw's expression was one of momentary panic. "I can't," he breathed. "She'd see me. It'd be hell, Doc."

"But you'll have to," Porter lied. "You'll have gangrene in that shoulder inside twenty-four hours unless you have constant medical attention. And I won't see you cash in out here at the end of nowhere like a stray wolf."

Trig shook his head stubbornly. "I couldn't run that chance. . . ."

"Mary won't need to know," the medical man cut in. "I can say you're a friend. You aren't known around here, and people won't be curious, so long as you stay at my place. When you're mended, you can ride away."

Studying the outlaw's expressive gray eyes, Porter could see the change his words worked. The trace of panic faded from Trig's glance, to be replaced by an eagerness that was somehow pitiful in so strong a man. Finally the outlaw said: "You'll promise not to tell her . . . no matter what happens?"

"I promise."

"Then I'll come." The outlaw struggled weakly to his feet as Porter was putting on his coat. But all at once some inner thought made Trig frown. "What'll I do about Hank and Quinn?"

The physician shrugged, growling: "Get rid of them. I said

once before they're a poor pair for you to be siding."

Trig Clemens stood in obvious thought for a long ten seconds, then called: "Hank!"

Boots moved along the gravel outside, and the door opened. Hank and Quinn stepped in. "Feelin' better?" Hank asked.

"Some," Trig said. "But I'll be laid up for a while. The sawbones is puttin' me up in town. You two had better high-tail out of the country. It'll be a few days before I can ride. If you run onto anything good, forget about me. If you don't, I'll see you at the hide-out."

It was as simple as that, Trig's dismissal of the two. In five minutes they had rolled their blankets and were riding away from the shack, headed into the north. And in as many more minutes Porter and the outlaw were in the saddle and riding back toward Rawhide. Porter wanted to ask where they had found the fourth horse and saddle but told himself that the horse he was riding wouldn't be a stolen one. Either Hank or Quinn would be forking that one.

Trig Clemens was a sicker man than Porter realized. Once the physician rode alongside barely in time to keep his friend from falling from the saddle. Trig was feverish, thirsty, and Porter was thankful when they finally rode down Rawhide's main street in the gray, false dawn and directly to his white frame house at the far edge of town.

Trig insisted on riding back to the barn and helping the medical man unsaddle. Porter understood, realizing that the outlaw didn't want to be left alone in the house. Now that he was faced with meeting a grown daughter he had never seen, Trig was half afraid, half shy.

They were on their way from the barn to the house, when Mary opened the door and stood looking out at them. Trig's step was uncertain, and, as Porter reached out to steady his friend, Mary saw that something was wrong and stepped down off the porch to help. She wore a quilted robe over her nightgown, and her taffy-colored hair was down, flowing in loose waves over her shoulders. Without a word, she stepped in beside Trig and put an arm about his waist to help steady him, her clear blue eyes wide and full of concern.

That look of hers was haunting, calling up the memory of another woman. It staggered Trig, and his steps became more halting. This girl was overpoweringly beautiful in his eyes; it was hard for him to believe that she was his.

She said comfortably: "You'll be all right."

Her voice was low and rich. Trig, weighing its every intonation, was repaid for all the torture of sixteen long years of hell. He felt the urge to bend and touch his lips to his girl's smooth, high forehead. Instead, he swallowed thickly and muttered: "I think I will . . . if you're goin' to be part o' my cure."

For three days Trig Clemens lay in a half-conscious stupor. Nightmares haunted him, when he slept, so that he tried his best to stay awake and listen to the sounds that came from the street and from the back part of the house, where Mary worked. The few glimpses he had of the girl eased the throbbing pain of his shoulder, erased the memory of his nightmares. He gradually lost his awe of her and even let her feed him food he didn't want.

On the fourth day, after a long, wakeful night, he slept from sunup to dark. And when he awakened, his shoulder was stiff but no longer throbbing; the fever was gone, and he was really hungry.

Dr. Porter was in the kitchen and heard the creak of bedsprings as his patient stirred. He came into Trig's room, carrying a lamp, and set it down on the washstand. "Better, eh?" he asked. And while Trig was wondering how his friend had known he would be better, the physician removed the bandages and inspected the wound. At length, after he had put on fresh bandages, Porter stood up and said: "You're on the way to being a well man, Trig."

The outlaw only half heard him, for he was listening to Mary's voice coming from the kitchen, and to another voice, a man's. He heard Mary laugh, and Porter, listening too, abruptly said: "I want you to meet that man, Trig. I'll bring him in." The physician stepped to the door and called: "Bill, come here a minute."

Bill Spence came down the short hallway and into the room, Mary a step or two behind him. Trig's first glance took in the deputy's badge pinned on Spence's vest, and he felt his pulse weaken and knew that his face drained of color.

Spence, seeing that look and thinking that the patient was still a mighty sick man, tiptoed across the room a little awkwardly in his high-heeled boots. He had a rugged, square-jawed face and brown eyes that were honest and guileless. He wasn't a tall man, but his every move gave a subtle hint of sureness. He held out his hand to Trig, smiling broadly, and said: "Doc tells me you're hard to kill, Jones. Is the shoulder better?"

All Trig could do was move his head in a feeble nod. He was wishing that he had a gun at his side, wondering what this deputy's presence here meant.

Dr. Porter looked intently at Trig and said: "Jones, this is Bill Spence. He's deputy under the sheriff. I've had him out on the Lode City road for the last two days hunting that bushwhacker. But the road's so littered with sign he couldn't find a thing."

The deputy frowned, agreeing. "Not a thing. Doc, you're sure it happened up by Table Rock?"

"That's where I found him," Porter said. "This friend of his . . . the one who came in after me . . . claimed he and Jones had business in Lode City and said he wanted to go on up there if Jones was all right. So I let him go. You might send a man to Lode City to see him. Said his name was Adams."

Bill Spence shrugged and looked down at Trig again. "It'd probably be a waste of time. But I'll see your friend Adams, if you want."

"Let it go," Trig said. He was quickly making sense out of this, realizing that Porter had invented a story as a means of protecting him. So he added convincingly: "They must have been after Adams's money. We were on our way to close a deal on some cattle."

This seemed to satisfy Bill Spence. Mary came to stand between him and the physician, and, seeing the look she gave the deputy, Trig felt a faint spark of jealousy glow within him. Yet he put it down immediately, realizing that he liked Spence. Mary was choosing a good man.

As if to echo his thoughts, Porter said: "Jones, Mary and Bill are taking up a small ranch one day soon. If you're ever through here again, you might try and sell Bill some of your critters."

Mary's face flushed, and her eyes shone with a mixture of surprise and gratitude. She looked up at the physician. "You really mean that, Dad?"

The way she spoke, the look in her eyes, told Trig that this was the first time the subject had been mentioned openly. Porter had taken this occasion to bring it up, realizing what it would mean to the real father of the girl.

Now Porter put his hands on Mary's shoulders and said: "Bill wouldn't come to me and ask it. I thought he needed some help." He glanced across at Spence with a look of mingled shrewdness and respect.

Bill Spence didn't know what to say. He was embarrassed and at the same time so overcome with a deeper emotion that it was mirrored plainly on his face. He took Mary gently in his arms, holding her close a moment, then looked at Porter and said: "Thanks, Doc. I . . . I didn't think it was quite time yet. I'm a poor man and. . . ."

"And you'll be happy, even if you are poor," the physician said. "When a man and a woman feel the way you two do, why put it off?"

"But there's Fred Scull." Bill was looking down at Mary now.

She shook her head. "No, Bill. There isn't any Fred Scull." Then, remembering Trig's presence, she looked at him with a blush of confusion and said quickly—"I'll get your supper."—and went out the door. Bill Spence followed.

Porter looked across at Trig, his eyes lighted with amusement. "He's a good man, even if he is a badge-toter."

"He is," Trig solemnly agreed. "You've done a fine job with her, Doc. I hardly know how to thank. . . ."

"Thanks be damned!" Porter growled. "You think I haven't liked every minute of it?"

Later, after Bill Spence and Porter had left the house on some errand and Mary was doing the dishes in the kitchen, Trig heard a knock at the front door in the hallway outside his room. He had a glimpse of Mary, going past his door, drying her hands on her apron.

Then, from out in the hallway, a voice said: "Hello, Mary. Can I come in?"

A sudden foreboding flowed through Trig Clemens. That voice was hauntingly familiar. He caught Mary's answer, then heard the door close, and another open. After that Mary's voice and the other sounded from another part of the house, the living room, Trig guessed. He couldn't make out what they were saying, but time and again the deep-throated tones of that man's voice came to him. He knew it and couldn't place it, nor could he define his feeling of fear at the sound of it. Fear was there, a stark and real fear that tormented him. Somewhere, far along his back trail, he had known this man. And the fragmentary memory was somehow coupled with danger.

The more he thought of it the more certain Trig became that he would have to see this man. He pushed himself up onto one elbow and threw back the covers. When he sat up, his feet on the floor, a sudden nausea of faintness took all his strength away. He sat there until the spasm had passed, then, taking a hold on the bedpost, he pulled himself erect. Half standing, half sitting, the faintness hit him again, this time so hard that it took all his strength to pull himself back so that he could fall onto the bed.

He lay there for minutes, too weak to move. And it was then that he heard those voices once more, Mary's and the other. They were louder now, in the hallway again, and Trig heard the man say: "I hope it isn't final, Mary."

"It is, Fred. I like you. But I love Bill. I guess that's the answer."

"Then I'll hope you change your mind," came that voice again. Trig drew his legs up onto the bed and pulled up the covers just as he heard the door close. Mary was coming back along the hallway toward the kitchen.

"Mary," he called, as she passed his door. She stopped and came in, and he asked: "Who was it?"

"Fred Scull," she told him, her look faintly puzzled. Then she went on to explain. "He's the one we talked about when Bill was here. He wants me to marry him."

"Known him long?"

For some strange reason she saw nothing peculiar in his curiosity. "For three or four years. He's nice, but not like Bill. He has a good job in the bank and ought to make any girl think twice before she refused him." She smiled, and added: "But I've already done my thinking."

"The right kind, too," Trig said. Then, seeing that she waited, expecting some explanation, he went on: "From the sound of his voice I thought I knew him. But the name isn't familiar."

"You can see him any day at the bank when you're well," Mary said, and went back to the kitchen.

IV

During the days that followed, Trig's thoughts centered on meeting Scull. He was impatient, worried. He talked a lot with Mary and bit by bit drew from her the story of Bill Spence and Fred Scull, of Bill's struggle to get his small ranch, and of the money he had borrowed to do it.

Trig was out of bed a day before Porter wanted him on his feet, and the two days of rest the physician insisted he take before he went outside were the longest Trig remembered having lived through. He couldn't explain his feelings or the vague premonition that Scull was in some ominous way associated with his past.

On the afternoon that Porter gave in and let him take his first walk down the street, Trig went to the center of town, found the bank, and entered, stepping to one side of the plate-glass doors and out of the closing-hour traffic. His glance searched the faces behind the counters, in the cages, yet he saw none that was familiar. So he waited, hoping to see someone he recognized come out of the two private offices at the back of the room.

It was while he was standing there that Fred Scull stepped alongside him and said quietly: "Howdy, Trig."

For the space of two long seconds the nearness of that voice held the outlaw in a numbed paralysis. Even before he turned to look squarely into Scull's wryly smiling face, he remembered the man. All the training of his trouble-dogged years went toward making up the set inscrutability that took possession of his lean face as he drawled: "It could be Slim Waters."

"It is," Scull said. "Only I'm usin' my right handle these days. Slim's dead . . . with a three-thousand-dollar reward collected on him. I collected it. Call me Fred Scull."

Eight years ago, a thousand miles to the north, Trig Clemens had last seen a much younger Fred Scull through a haze of powder smoke. Remembering that, Trig thought of the gun riding at his hip and let his hand settle nearer his holster. "You've changed a bit," he said.

Scull thumbed the lapels of his black broadcloth coat and conceded: "Times are better." Then his look took on a cunning, and he queried: "How about you?"

"The same."

"On your own?"

Trig nodded, and turned his attention to the rolling of a cigarette.

After a moment, Scull edged in closer and asked in a low voice: "Are you open for a job . . . one that'll pay plenty?" He hesitated, then went on "Or are you rememberin' that the last time I saw you was over the sights of a Winchester?"

Trig forced a chuckle. "We were hired for our guns, weren't we? It wasn't your fault you chose the other bunch to run with."

Scull was plainly relieved. "Then we can make a play here that'll stake us both."

"What kind?"

Scull's brows came up in a meaningful expression, and he glanced pointedly toward the open vault door at the rear of the crowded room.

Trig understood. "Count me out," he said. "I'm safe in this state, and I aim to stay that way."

Scull started to say something but checked himself as he glanced beyond Trig. All at once he smiled affably at someone behind Trig and said: "Howdy, Doc."

Trig turned to see Dr. Porter, a bankbook in his hand, come across from the nearest teller's cage. When the medical man stood before them, he looked quizzically from one to the other and asked: "So you know Jones, Fred?"

"We hadn't gotten down to names yet, but he's a new customer," Scull answered suavely.

"He's one of mine, too." The suspicion that had first edged into the medical man's glance faded as he explained: "Some jasper out on the Lode City road took a shot at him one night last week. When I found him, he had a bullet in his shoulder and was missing a couple quarts of blood. He's damned lucky to be anybody's customer." He took out his watch and looked at it and said to Trig: "You'd better tell Mary I'll be late for supper. I'm driving out into the country to see a patient."

When the medical man had gone out into the street, Scull looked at Trig in a calculating way and said: "Let's have a drink and we'll make medicine, Trig."

The outlaw shook his head. "I tell you I'll pass this hand. I'll forget you ever mentioned it. Find someone else."

"Think again," Scull breathed, then queried intently: "How long have you known Doctor Porter?"

His question changed things. There was an edge to his words that carried a subtle warning of some hidden meaning. A moment ago Fred Scull had been an unpleasant, but impotent, reminder of the past. Suddenly he was a dangerous man, and Trig was no longer safe until he knew the reason for that question.

"I met Porter a week ago tonight," Trig answered.

Scull's narrow-lidded expression changed abruptly to one of surprise at some inner thought. He smiled wickedly and shook his head. "It's a good story, Trig, but not good enough. Maybe I'd swallow it, if I hadn't met a friend of yours a year or two ago. He called himself Saunders. Remember him?"

Trig remembered Al Saunders and dreaded what was coming.

"Saunders claimed he knew you well," Scull went on. "He told me a lot of things. For instance, that you had a youngster, a girl, and had to leave her when the law got after you. He knew a Doctor Porter too, only the Porter he knew was a bachelor." Scull paused and regarded Trig with a mocking, devilish smile. "Now will you let me buy you that drink?"

In the sudden realization that Fred Scull knew his secret, that he might know enough to change the lives of Mary and the physician, Trig Clemens for the first time in his life felt the overpowering urge to kill. He had killed before, but not willfully; the men who had fallen before his gun had forced him to fight. This was different. Hatred was a passion that rarely guided the outlaw, yet now his hatred for this man took deep root in his being. He was cold, calculating, and his gray eyes met Scull's squarely as he drawled: "I could use a drink."

"Then come across to the Paradise in ten minutes. I'll be upstairs, in that first room beyond the landing." As an afterthought, he explained: "We shouldn't be seen together."

V

As Scull turned away and went behind the nearby counter to get his flat-crowned Stetson, Trig was tempted to lift his Colt from its holster and empty it into the man's back. His curiosity checked the impulse, that, and his instinct for self-preservation. He would willingly murder this man, yet it would give the law one more reason for hunting him, and he couldn't risk it.

So he watched Scull go out the doors and across the street. He took out his tobacco and papers and carefully rolled a cigarette. When he had lit it, he went across to the saloon. Unhurried, he walked to the bar and had a drink of straight bourbon. The raw warmth of the whiskey in his stomach felt good after all these days on an invalid's diet. Sickness and emotion had left him weak, and now he found that the liquor wiped away a measure of that weakness. He had another drink, and walked to the rear of the room and up the steps that led to the balcony.

He opened the first door beyond the head of the landing and stepped into the small cubbyhole of a room. Fred Scull stood beyond the green-felt card table, to one side of the single window that looked out into the alley. Half a dozen chairs ringed the table, and an unopened bottle with glasses on a tray stood in its center.

"Have a chair," Scull said.

Trig took the nearest chair. He was barely seated when Scull moved. It was lightning fast, so sudden that Trig had no chance to move his hands from the chair arms. Scull's blunt-nosed .38 flashed out from under his coat lapel and swung down with practiced swiftness. Trig tensed, expecting each instant to see a flash of powder flame and feel the slam of a bullet in his chest.

It didn't come. Scull laughed softly, menacingly. He came across to the table and took a chair opposite, laying the weapon at his elbow as he said: "That's so you'll be careful, Trig. I haven't lost the feel of a hog-leg."

He reached for the whiskey bottle and opened it, pouring two drinks into the glasses on the tray. Pushing one across to the outlaw, he said: "Trig, I'm goin' to marry your daughter."

Trig was unimpressed. "I've known that for the last hour," was the level answer.

"And you'll not stand in my way."

For a long moment Trig was silent. Then: "Sixteen years is a long time. I'd forgotten I had a daughter. She isn't mine."

"I was hopin' you'd see it that way," Scull said. "Doc won't stop me, either. Now about this other. I want. . . ."

"You want the bank robbed so they'll call in their loans. You want Bill Spence out of the way . . . ruined, since he can't settle that mortgage. Have I got it straight?" Trig didn't wait for Scull's momentary surprise to leave him but went on: "That's all right with me. What happens to you, to Mary or Porter, doesn't make much difference. But if I come in on the deal, I'll want plenty." He had spoken dispassionately, hiding the smoldering emotion that burned within him behind a shell of time-hardened unconcern.

But Fred Scull was a shrewd man. He shook his head and grinned. "I don't trust you, Trig. Not after the way you shied at the idea across the street. But I've done business before with men I don't trust. Maybe you don't care about the girl and Porter. Whether you do or not won't count. I'll fix it so you can't double-cross me. If you're really serious about wantin' to ride out of here with a lot of money, we'll get along fine. If you run a sandy, you'll end up with your neck in a noose."

Trig Clemens's hopes faded. Scull was a hard man; what he was saying was true. Trig was suddenly taken with an overpowering anger. "I could let the law know who you really are," he said.

Scull again shook his head. "You could try, but it wouldn't work. The man you knew . . . Slim Waters . . . is legally dead and buried. I can get at least a dozen people in Wyoming, including one honest sheriff, to swear that they saw him put in his grave. I'm the only one who knows that saddle tramp, with his face smashed in, wasn't Slim Waters. It doesn't matter to you who he was. All that matters is that I have an honest name here. You haven't."

Fighting this man with words was as futile as using a clasp knife to cut through solid granite. Trig saw that, and his look must have betrayed it, for Scull laughed softly, and went on: "Play along with me and we'll both win." He edged forward in his chair and leaned across the table. "You can do the job tonight. That vault in the bank is old. A month ago I spent three hours late one night learnin' it. We'll get it over with in a hurry, and you can head out of here."

"Write down the combination and let me have it. I'll be clear of town by midnight," Trig said.

Scull shook his head. "I don't put anything on paper, brother. I'll tell you the combination, and you'll remember it. And if you're smart, you'll be across the state line before morning."

Porter wasn't back from his call in the country, when Trig returned to the house for supper. Mary, when she heard that the physician would be late, heaped his plate with food, put it in the oven, and said: "We won't wait for him."

Several times during the meal she noticed that Trig was unusually silent, and once, as she saw that he had barely tasted his food, she asked: "Is that shoulder hurting again?"

He tried to be off-handed in his answer. "Not a bit. I got so hungry this afternoon I stopped in at the Chinaman's for a piece of pie and a cup o' coffee. I should have had more sense."

His explanation satisfied the girl. A minute or two later Porter climbed the rear porch steps and came in, grumbling about the patient he'd driven eight miles to see. "She wasn't sick," he muttered while he washed his hands at the sink. "She had a big wash piled up on her this mornin' and came down with a headache so her old man would haul the wash water and hang her clothes on the line. He's the one that sent for me."

The medical man ate his meal hungrily, and, if he noticed that Trig was more quiet than usual, he didn't let on. Trig, through with his meal long before the physician, got up from the table, took his Stetson from the peg on the back of the door, and announced: "That walk did me good. Think I'll take another."

"Wait for me," Porter said. "I've got to go to the office tonight."

Ten minutes later, as they went through the front gate, Porter slowed his stride and said abruptly: "Tell me where you met Fred Scull, Trig."

The outlaw hesitated too long in his answer only to say lamely: "It was up in Center City six or eight years ago."

Porter snorted. "Damn it, man, I want the truth!"

"You've got it."

"No, I haven't. By the look on your face when I met you and Scull this afternoon, I could see plenty was wrong. Hell, I've known you too long for you to be able to hide things,

Trig. If you're in trouble, I aim to know about it."

"What trouble could I be in?"

"This Fred Scull's a queer man," the physician went on, as though Trig hadn't spoken. "He is dead set on having Mary, and, if I know his kind, he won't give her up. He hates Bill Spence. Trig, was Scull one of the wild bunch?"

They were facing each other now, and, as the physician shot his question, he had his answer in the momentary confusion that changed his friend's expression.

"Tell me about it, Trig," he said. "Maybe I could help."

Trig Clemens's quiet laughter was mirthless, lacking life. "There isn't a thing on earth that'd help, Doc, outside of a bullet. And I won't shoot a man in the back."

"I said to tell me about it."

Trig was remembering that in the old days, when he had known Porter better, the medical man's rugged character, his honesty and fairness, were things to be depended on. And tonight he felt a need for confiding in Dr. Porter, for asking his help. So he told the physician.

"When I knew Fred Scull, he was wearin' another handle. That was in Wyoming, in the Jackson Hole country. He had hired out his guns, the same as I had mine, and had a price on his head." He went on, speaking calmly and dispassionately, telling the physician his story from beginning to end. And when he had finished, he felt years younger, as though he had suddenly been relieved of a weight too heavy to carry.

Porter stood, silent, for a long interval, before muttering: "We'd all be ruined . . . not only Bill Spence, but me and the whole town. That bank never has been any too steady. I doubt if old Harris even carries insurance." He paused an instant. "Trig, I've got it."

The outlaw's fading hopes flamed alive once more at those words. Porter reached out and took him by the arm and said quickly: "You go back and get your horse out of the stable. Saddle him and ride straight down the alley to the bank. Go in, just like Scull said, and open that vault. Drag a couple of money sacks out and leave the vault door open and then ride away from here. Ride hard and don't come back."

"And what'll Scull say when nothin' happens?" Trig shook his head. "I'll stick until this thing's settled."

"Why the hell do you think I'm havin' you go to the bank?" Porter bridled. "It'll be all settled by morning. There's a thing or two I can do."

"What, for instance?"

"I don't know for sure yet. But you get clear of this. You have my promise that Fred Scull won't dare breathe a word about Mary . . . and the bank'll be safe."

"How?" Trig was not convinced.

Porter held his excitement down and spoke now in the same manner he would have used in pleading with a youngster too young to grasp a meaning. "Trig, I tell you everything'll be all right. I want you out of here, miles away, before this happens. I've got an idea, but it's only the beginning. Now, if you think anything at all of Mary, do as I say. The longer you stay, the more danger there is for her."

It was a brutal thing, using Mary's name to carry his point, but he had no choice. He knew exactly what he would do, how he would do it, and the main thing now was to make certain that Trig would in no way be involved.

With that subtle threat of his bringing danger to Mary, all of Trig's stubbornness left him. "I'm to open the vault and ride away. Is that straight?"

"You can leave the back door of the bank open. If Mary hears you at the stable and wants to know what you're doing, tell her you've decided to work some of the fat off your broncho. He hasn't had a hull on his back for a week now. I'll give you half an hour to do the job and get clear of town. Make it across the state line by morning, Trig. Something might go wrong, and I'd hate to have them catch you."

Trig held out a hand. "Then I won't see you again?"

Porter gave him a firm grasp, smiled. "Sure you will. In a month or two, after they've forgotten who Jones was, write me a letter and let me know where you are. Maybe you can come back one of these days. Mary and I will always be glad to see you."

Trig had known for days that this moment was inevitable. It wasn't in the cards for him, an outlaw, to enjoy the friendship of a man like Porter for long, nor had he expected to have many more days with Mary. He was thankful for this one week of knowing her.

He turned and left the medical man abruptly, sensing that there was nothing more to say. Mary didn't hear him at the stable, and he rode off into the alley entrance not trusting himself for even a last glance back at the lighted kitchen window.

VI

Scull had said that the bank's alley door would be unlocked. It was. Trig carried his .45 in his hand as he pushed the panel open and entered the cobalt emptiness of the single big room. His pulse quickened, and once more he felt that time-mellowed wariness surge up within him. Scull might have set a trap, and now was no time to let him spring it.

Trig had discovered long ago that patience is one of man's strongest weapons. He used it now, standing for a full two minutes, letting his glance search out every detail of the shadowed room. The lights from the saloon across the street shone dimly through the big window up front, and he could see fairly well.

When he was certain that he was alone in the room, he worked swiftly. Several times these past few years he had worked a safe's combination. He turned this one surely, swiftly, even lighting a match and holding it cupped in his left hand so that he could be sure of the markings on the dial. The light from that match flared for a bare five seconds. When he flicked it out, the vault door was open and he was stepping inside.

On the floor at the back of the vault he found two partly filled money sacks. He carried them out and laid them on the plank floor alongside the door. He remembered Porter's instructions to leave the back door open. He swung it wide as he went out, and half a minute later he was in the saddle and angling off from the alley and into open country.

He held his gelding to a walk, wondering at his feeling that he had left something back there undone. Porter had said to ride hard, to be across the state line before morning. But just now his own safety seemed unimportant. For the first time in his life, Trig Clemens was letting another man do his work for him.

He had gone less than a mile, when he suddenly knew that this was all wrong. He couldn't go through with it. As he wheeled the gelding about, spurring him to a stiff run back toward town, he left behind all the vague doubts and uncertainties of the past few hours.

Riding down Rawhide's street, past the lights of the Paradise, he saw Bill Spence come out of his jail office and saunter toward him along the walk. Bill happened to look up and see him. The deputy lifted a hand in greeting.

"Howdy, Bill." Trig was surprised at the evenness of his own voice, since only an instant before he spoke he had drawn abreast of the bank and looked in through the front windows and glimpsed the flickering light of a match in there. It was a signal to him. He turned in at the nearest hitch rail and swung out of the saddle. Directly ahead, on the other side of the walk, a narrow passageway between two buildings ran back to the alley.

At the moment Trig's fingers had spun the dial of the vault's combination, Dr. Porter had been knocking on a door in the hotel down the street. He'd come into the hotel by way of the back door. No one had seen him.

When Scull swung open the door and saw who was standing in the hall, he made a poor effort at hiding his surprise. "Come in, Doc," he said. Then, when the medical man had stepped in, he closed the door. "You're out late."

"Don't I know it?" Porter said. "Fred Amby's wife took me all the way out there this afternoon with nothing more than a headache." His look narrowed, and he studied Scull intently. "You were working late yourself?"

Scull shook his head. "Not since closin' time."

Porter frowned. "Funny," he mused. "It was a tall man because he could reach that blind on the front window. I could have sworn it was you, working late. Well, it might have been Baker." The physician shrugged, as though dismissing the thought. "About Mary, Fred, I was sorry she feels the way she. . . ."

"Hold on a minute!" Scull interrupted. "Who did you see in the bank pulling down that blind on the front window? Baker drove over to Cañon City this afternoon."

The physician shrugged. "I thought it was you. It was ten, fifteen minutes ago, as I was driving past in my buggy on the way home."

A light of cunning flared into Scull's glance. He reached for his Stetson and put it on, then thrust his hand under his coat and took out his .38 and spun the cylinder, making sure that it was loaded. As he rammed it back in the shoulder holster again and stepped toward the door, he breathed: "Let's get Bill Spence to go over with us and take a look."

"Bill's not in his office. I stopped there on the way up here."

"Then let's have a look for ourselves," Scull said. "Ten to one someone's broken in and is bustin' open that vault. It wouldn't take a man long. Let's hurry."

Scull led the way to the back stairs, explaining: "We'll go out into the alley. If someone's in there, he went in the back way."

As the medical man followed, he was remembering Scull's inspection of his six-gun, wishing he'd had a look at his own a few minutes before as he had taken it out of his bag and thrust it in his belt. That old Smith & Wesson hadn't been fired for years. The shells might be worthless after all that time.

But now was no time to think of a thing like that, so Porter put all his attention in keeping close behind Scull. They walked quickly along the alley, until Scull slowed as they came within sight of the bank's brick wall.

He stopped abruptly, saying in a low voice: "The back door's open."

"It sure as hell is," Porter agreed. "I don't like this, Fred."

"You come along with me," Scull said urgently. "If someone's in there, we'll get the drop on him."

Scull walked ahead now, on his toes, soundlessly. Porter, a grim smile on his grizzled face, played his part and followed. Scull stood for a moment flattened against the rear wall alongside the door, listening. His .38 was in his fist now, held hip-high. He jerked it suddenly, motioning the physician to follow as he rapidly stepped in through the door.

Porter, through the door a second later, stepped in close and stood there, waiting, letting his eyes search the darkness of the room. Scull was rigid, tense, as his glance traveled to one side and took in the open vault door. Cupping a hand to his mouth and leaning close to Porter, he whispered: "He's either in the vault, or we're too late. I'm going to light a match."

As the match flared brightly and Scull stood staring out across the room, the medical man's fist was closed tightly on the weapon at his belt. He drew it out slowly, surely, as the match flickered out. As Scull dropped the matchstick to the floor, Porter swung the gun to one side, ramming it in Scull's ribs.

"Too bad Trig wasn't here so you could cut him down," he said. "But he's gone . . . without the money."

With the snout of his weapon, he could feel Fred Scull's quick intake of breath.

Scull said in a hollow voice: "I don't know what you're talkin' about, Porter."

"You will in a minute," the physician replied. He stepped around in back of Scull and added: "Hand me your cutter. Make it. . . ."

Afterward, Porter couldn't quite remember what happened. He felt Scull's body move slightly, and suddenly the man had whirled from in front of him, striking out with a booted heel that connected in blinding pain with his shin. He tried to thumb back the hammer of his Smith & Wesson, but the action was stiff, rusty, and, before he could swing it around and fire, Scull's down-flashing palm had numbed his wrist and the gun was spinning from his hand to the floor.

It was over in a second, Porter standing numbed with the pain in his leg, staring into the blunt snout of Scull's weapon.

"A double-cross," Scull breathed, his thin lips curled down in a brutal sneer. "I told Trig what would happen, if he tried a play like this." He took a step backward and stood there, spraddle-legged, regarding the medical man. "To-morrow mornin' every lawman in the state will be on the trail. . . ."

He bit off his words abruptly, and Porter, half facing the open back door, saw what took his eye. A tall shape had stepped into the opening and was moving through it.

Suddenly the thunder of Scull's gun cut loose, and the room was momentarily lit by the light of a powder flash. By that light, Porter saw Trig's weaving frame dodge through the door, his hand leveling a six-gun. The next split second the snout of that .45 lanced fingers of orange flame to meet the echo of Scull's shot.

But Scull had whirled in behind the physician, and now Porter felt his arm taken in a vise-like grip. Trig's bullets had missed the mark. Realizing this, Porter was seized with a sudden panic. His own ruse had failed, and now Trig was losing.

Suddenly he saw Scull's arm flash upward at his side, aiming the .38 at Trig's indistinct shape. Porter went berserk then. His two hands clawed at Scull's arm, got a hold, and he let his knees go out from under him. He was a slight man, but the fierceness of his lunge made his weight enough to carry Scull's arm down. The medical man fell to the floor, still clutching that arm.

He lit on one shoulder, rolling onto his back, feeling Scull's arm tear itself loose. But Scull's weight was overbalanced, and he fell awkwardly on top of the medical man and with a force that drove Porter's breath from his lungs.

Scull rolled away, came to his knees, and struck a vicious blow at Porter's head. The physician moved barely in time, but the down-swinging gun crashed into his shoulder, setting up a torment of pain. It was then that Porter felt the bulk of his fallen gun under his thigh. His right hand slid down and closed on the butt of the weapon at the precise instant he saw Scull lunge to his feet.

Somewhere off to his left, Trig called out: "Get clear, Doc!" The words were ominous, for they told Porter that Trig was afraid to shoot, that he hadn't seen Scull come to his feet again.

In the panic of that moment, knowing that Trig couldn't see but that Scull could and was now leveling his .38, Porter's thin-fingered hands moved with long-trained precision. As he pulled his gun free, he rolled onto his back. Then, taking the weapon in both hands so that both his thumbs could pull back the stubborn hammer this time, the physician raised his weapon and leveled it true. He squeezed the trigger a brief instant before he saw the winking flame strike out from the snout of Scull's .38.

Porter lay paralyzed after his two wrists had taken up the buck of that gun. Was it his imagination, or had Scull's six-gun wavered as it threw that shot?

Suddenly the room was lit with brilliant flashes and filled with an inferno of sound as Trig's weapon spoke time and again. Punctuating each blast of that gun, Scull's body jerked backward. His arm fell abruptly to his side, the gun dropped from his fingers, and his head onto his chest. Then, rigidly, his long frame fell forward with a force that made it skid sideways as it struck the boards.

In the utter silence of the next two seconds, Porter heard the shouting on the street, the pound of running feet.

Trig's voice suddenly spoke out: "You all right, Doc?"

Porter got painfully to his feet, feeling a surge of relief that for a moment made it impossible for him to answer. Trig wasn't hurt or his voice wouldn't have been so steady. The physician reached down and rubbed his bruised shin, muttering: "A man who kicks another ain't worth a damn. Scull kicked me so hard I can't think."

"Fred Scull!" the deputy breathed, in an awed voice. "How in the . . . ?"

Porter gestured toward the open vault, indicating the two money sacks lying near it on the floor. "I caught Scull right in the middle of things. He'd have got away in another minute or two. I was walking past the bank here a few minutes ago and happened to look in. This white wall is lighted up pretty well by the saloon lights from across the street. I saw someone moving around back here by the vault. So I came back to the alley to have a better look."

"Why didn't you give a yell?" Spence asked.

Porter snorted. "And let whoever it was get away?" He shook his head. "I found the back door open and came in. Scull must have heard me. He was waiting, and rammed a gun in my ribs. The first thing I knew, Jones was in here, and they were shooting it out."

Bill Spence looked at Trig. "How come you were in on this? I saw you out in the street a minute ago."

"You saw me just before it happened," Trig said. "I was lookin' for Doc and spied him walkin' along in front of the bank just before you came out of your office. It looked a little queer to me, when he cut back between those buildings toward the alley, runnin'." His gaunt face took on a smile. "Doc doesn't often run. So I left my horse out front and came back to have a look. This is what I found."

The deputy was convinced, yet still held by the same astonishment that had taken hold of him at his first sight of Fred Scull's body. "Robbin' his own bank," he breathed.

"Bill, for a gent who's worn a law badge as long as you, anyone'd think this was the first dead man you ever saw," Porter growled. "Get a couple of gents to carry Fred over to the undertaker's. Friend Jones, here, can sure make a gun talk."

Skull Creek Double-Cross

This story was completed in April, 1939, and submitted by Jon Glidden's agent on April 26, 1939 to Robert O. Erisman who edited *Western Novel and Short Stories* for Newsstand Publications. This magazine purchased the story on August 27, 1940, paying $67.50 for it upon acceptance. It was not published until the November, 1940 issue with the title changed to "The Man Who Hired His Own Guns." Erisman also edited for Newsstand Publications *Western Short Stories* and *Best Western*, both monthly pulp magazines as was *Western Novel and Short Stories*. Newsstand was a market that Marguerite E. Harper cultivated for the author, and numerous Peter Dawson Western stories appeared in one or another of these magazines in the late 1930s, until Jon's first novel, THE CRIMSON HORSESHOE, won the Dodd, Mead prize for 1941 and was serialized in Street & Smith's *Western Story Magazine*. Four of his subsequent novels were similarly serialized in *Western Story Magazine* prior to book publication by Dodd, Mead, and from 1941 until he entered military service *Western Story Magazine* was the foremost market for Jon Glidden's Western stories.

I

At two that afternoon, George Beeson happened to look out from the corral and down across the pasture and see the rider cutting out from the timber a full mile away. "Visitor, Bob," he remarked to his companion, a slight-framed man who was busy filing down the hind hoof of a hogtied broncho nearby. "Looks like she's in a hurry."

Bob Phelan laid aside his rasp and got up off his knees, pounding the dust from his Levi's as he squinted into the sun glare and down the lower valley trail. When he saw the rider on the fast-running claybank horse, his freckled face turned serious.

Seeing that look, George Beeson said in slight embarrassment: "I'll wait up at the cabin." He started for the corral gate.

"You'll wait right here, George," Bob Phelan told him.

"But she'll want to see you alone."

Bob Phelan said dryly: "It's been three months since Chris Nichols has laid eyes on me. If she's managed to stand it that long, I reckon your bein' here now won't matter."

When the dark-haired girl riding the claybank rode in past the woodshed, Bob Phelan was sitting on the top pole of the corral, and Beeson was trying to make himself inconspicuous by resuming the job his friend had left unfinished. There was a mixture of confusion and alarm written on Christine Nichol's face as she drew rein a few feet out from the corral. She said hurriedly: "Bob, you'll have to leave right away. Dad and the sheriff and Ed Kemp are coming up after you."

The intentness of her tone had more effect on George Beeson than on Bob. He came to his feet and wheeled around and said: "Sheriff? What's Bob done?"

The girl's pretty oval face took on a tide of color at Bob's indifference. "George," she said urgently, "you make him see it! He has to get out of here . . . to hide. Two days ago our north fence was cut and better than a hundred steers driven off. They think Bob did it." Her manner was plainly nervous, and she tried not to look at Bob Phelan.

He drawled: "You're a little late, Chris. Here they are."

She turned and looked down the valley to see three horsemen leaving the margin of the trees below, and breathed quickly: "Take my horse, Bob. Please." She started down out of the saddle but hesitated when she saw that he hadn't moved. Sudden anger rode into her brown eyes. "Bob Phelan, do you know what you're doing? They'll arrest you. Dad will make it the excuse he's been looking for. You. . . ." Her words broke off in the face of her helplessness.

"Nothin' to run from I know of," Bob said. His glance clung to the oncoming riders. He smiled briefly and added: "Besides, I'd hate to disappoint John Nichols."

"Don't be a damn' fool," Beeson growled. "You ain't got a chance. Take her horse and high-tail."

"No."

That single word was so definite that it left the girl and Beeson no opening. All they could do was to stare dully at the trio turning in toward the pasture gate. John Nichols, cattle king of this broad range, was first through the gate, a man well on in years, yet with his solid frame still holding a disciplined erectness. He was grizzled, with a lean, weathered face that set bleakly as he sighted his daughter. Behind him rode his ramrod, Ed Kemp, a tall, sure man whose careless slouch was backed by his fitness for his job. Kemp wore a low-slung holster, and a Winchester in a saddle scabbard nudged the inside of his right thigh. Last of all came Sheriff Tom Ward, a mild-mannered oldster who made it plain by bringing up the rear that he didn't relish this job.

John Nichols stopped twenty feet out from the corral, his glance first taking in Phelan, and then going on to his daughter. He said tersely: "I thought you were told never to come here, Chris. Why did you disobey?"

"Because I don't believe it of Bob!" the girl flared. "Because you. . . ."

"What you believe doesn't matter," the rancher interrupted. He added curtly: "Get on home."

The girl's eyes flashed in anger, and she seemed about to protest. But her father's uncompromising look carried a definite command to back his words, and she reluctantly reined the claybank around and rode away. Bob called out after her—"Thanks, anyway, Chris."—and received no answer.

John Nichols waited until she was out of hearing, then said: "Phelan, I've sworn out a warrant on you for murder. We're taking you to jail."

"Murder?" Bob drawled. "I thought all I'd done was try to get away with some Anchor critters?"

"Barney Drew died last night," Nichols said. "One of your bunch shot him." His glance took in George Beeson, then whipped back to Bob. "You're the only one we have proof against. That gray. . . ."

"Better start at the beginnin'," Bob cut in on him. "I'd like to know what I'm supposed to have done besides killin' a man I bunked with for a year."

Ed Kemp's darkly handsome face shaped a wry smile. He said tonelessly: "Why waste time at this horse play, boss? He ain't packin' an iron. Let's take him."

"He's entitled to an explanation," Sheriff Ward put in testily, for once breaking out from under Nichols's authority that had for years kept him in office. He looked at Bob: "Phelan, two nights ago a piece of Anchor's north fence was pulled down and better than a hundred head of steers driven up into the hills. A line rider found out about it next mornin', yesterday. Nichols and his men followed the sign all day. At dark they headed for Eagle Pass on the hunch the herd was headed across the peaks. They were forted up below the pass, when four men started pushin' the herd on across. Someone lost his head and opened up too soon and the rustlers got away, minus one horse. That lughead was your gray gelding, Phelan. Barney Drew stopped some rustler's lead. We buried him this mornin'."

George Beeson flared softly. "Me and Bob have been two days buildin' this corral and cold-shoein' a few bronc's. We ain't been off the place."

Sheriff Ward gave Nichols a questioning glance: "Hear that, John? What'd I tell you?"

"I'd have a story thought up by now, too," Kemp said suavely. He shrugged his wide shoulders, added: "But suit yourself, boss. Only if they didn't do it, who did?"

Bob sat listening to this exchange of words with the hint of a smile turning his face to its habitual good humor; his eyes, however, failed to show any amusement as he regarded the Anchor ramrod. He said in open sarcasm: "That's right, Nichols. If we didn't do it, who did?"

George Beeson, older, not so level-headed, let his temper get away with him. He said savagely: "Kemp, you'll one day prod us too far! Someone's goin' to whittle you down to size. You want proof. Here it is. That gray gelding of Bob's was. . . ."

"Hold it, George!" Bob cut in, breaking short the information his neighbor was about to impart. He climbed down off the corral and faced Nichols. "All right, I'll go in with you."

Beeson gasped incredulously. "You're goin' to let 'em take you in?"

"Know a better way, George? Didn't they come up here to start something and make an excuse for clearin' this valley? Take it easy. No jury's goin' to convict me."

There was a quality of warning in his tone, in the look he gave Beeson, that commanded a grudging agreement. Ten minutes later he rode out the pasture gate with Nichols, Kemp, and the sheriff, leaving Beeson at the corral helpless in his anger. Bob, forking a sleek roan, rode alongside Ed Kemp across the pasture, Nichols and the sheriff coming along behind. They entered the timber below in that order, and took the trail that twisted sharply along an aisle between tall stands of yellow pine and thickets of scrub oak and low-growing cedar. To Bob's left, on the side where Kemp rode, the ground climbed sharply toward the crests of a series of timbered hills that closed in to form this narrow neck of the valley. To the right, Skull Creek followed the line of the trail, its waters flowing swiftly over the downgrade rock shelves and forming pools where trout lay motionless against the current in the shadows. Bob reined in a trifle, letting Nichols and the lawman draw closer behind.

Without turning his head, he drawled in calculated slowness: "A year ago, when I worked for Anchor, I had you pegged as a white man, Nichols. What's got into you? Why do you want this Skull Creek range so bad? Isn't your thirty sections enough to move around in?"

"Any man that says I want this graze is a damned liar!" Nichols exploded from behind. "For three months now I've seen water holes fouled, my line shacks burned, and now this rustlin'. I aim to stop it for good and all."

"You aren't by any chance riled because a forty-a-month

cowpoke once had it in his head to marry into the family, are you, Nichols?"

Alongside, Ed Kemp's glance whipped across in a hostile stare, and the ramrod's hand settled to the butt of the Colt he wore thonged low on his flat thigh. "Any more o' that and we'll have to lay you across your hull to get you to town," he grated flatly.

Nichols, out of Bob's line of vision, was apparently willing to let this sentiment be his, for he said nothing.

"That was the first mistake I made," Bob went on, ignoring Kemp, "thinkin' I had a right to look twice at Chris. The second was comin' up here, takin' out a homestead with three others, and goin' to the trouble of throwin' up that earth dam and diggin' all these ditches. This valley's worth ten times what it was. It'd be easy for you to frame something like this on us, kick us out, and then move your fence a couple of miles east to take in this strip, Nichols."

Sheriff Ward's voice sounded a brief warning—"Hold your tongue, Phelan!"—as Ed Kemp turned in the saddle and flashed a look behind at Nichols. He evidently caught a signal from the rancher, for his right hand started up, fisting his six-gun. For the last few seconds, Bob's undersized frame had been cocked and ready for such a move. As Kemp's weapon rose, Bob gouged his roan with his spurs and reined sharply over toward Kemp.

The ramrod was too sure of himself and was caught by surprise. The roan struck his horse with a lunge that jarred his off boot from the stirrup. Then, as he breathed a savage oath and instinctively reached with his right hand for the saddle horn to steady himself, he took a down-slashing blow on the wrist and felt his Colt wrenched from his grasp. Bob reined away, wheeled his pony around, and let the weapon he had taken from Kemp fall into line with the two behind. His move was quick enough to stop the sheriff's reach for his six-gun. Nichols was unarmed.

The Colt at his hip, its sights on Nichols, Bob began: "It's time we laid our cards on the. . . ."

A furtive move of Ed Kemp's brought the .45 in Bob's hand arcing around. It exploded in a flat welling of sound that racketed up through the trees. Kemp gave a choked cry and clenched his numbed right hand, letting the Winchester, half drawn from its leather sheath, thump to the ground. The rifle's walnut stock was splintered where the six-gun bullet was embedded in it.

Nichols had caught the swift timing of Bob's hand as it threw that shot. The rancher's eyes widened in surprise. The sheriff, too, had seen it and now swallowed thickly over his astonishment and raised his hand clear of holster.

Bob said—"Better shed your belt, Ward."—and waited until the lawman had unbuckled his heavy shell belt and swung it outward onto the turf. Then, glancing across at Kemp whose face was twisted in a grimace half of pain and half of surliness, he went on: "Ed, when this is over, you and me are goin' to tangle." He hefted the Colt. "You can have your choice, either guns or fists. I'll take on some of the whittlin' George mentioned."

"When this is over?" Nichols scoffed, letting out a harsh, sneering laugh. "Hell, it's over now, Phelan. You're through here. You. . . ."

Bob's hand whipped around and once again the .45 exploded in a burst of sound. Nichols's head jerked sideways as the air-rush of the bullet fanned his cheek. "It's my turn to talk," Bob drawled, smiling thinly to see that the color had drained from the rancher's face to leave it a sickly yellow. "Nichols, you're either blind or a fool, and I'm guessin' it's blind. First, ask yourself why our bunch of ten-cow outfits would go out of the way to make trouble for you. We don't want anything we haven't got, except to be let alone. If you get that far, start lookin' for the jasper that gets the most out of this once you've crowded us out. If you aren't him, then take off the blinders and find out who it is. It isn't me, or any man along Skull Creek." He nodded down the trail. "Now tuck your tails and ride out o' here."

He wheeled the roan off the trail. Ward came on past him, saying tersely—"Better come along, Ed."—as Kemp hesitated. When Ward and the Anchor ramrod had gone on, Nichols drew abreast of Bob and stopped. He had regained a little of his composure now, and his brown eyes, so much like his daughter's, blazed in a defiant look.

"You've made a hell of a good start down the wrong trail, Phelan," he intoned bluntly. "Today you've asked to be sent the rest of the way. We'll be back . . . with a posse."

Bob's smile broadened. Abruptly he asked: "Want to make a bet, Nichols?"

The rancher scowled and made no answer.

"For high stakes," Bob went on. "If you lose, give Chris her head and let her choose her man, either me or Ed Kemp."

"Chris has a mind of her own. She's already chosen Ed."

"Because you made her. But we'll forget that. If I win, you're to lift the ban on me, let Chris and me thrash out what's between us. If I lose, I'll have to pull out for good anyway."

"Name the bet."

"That I'll bring you the jasper that ran off your herd the other night."

Nichols's manner turned strangely sober. After a moment he muttered: "Phelan, you're either playin' me for a fool or. . . ." Some inner thought made him hesitate there, before he added: "I'll take your bet, and give you fair warnin'.

You've resisted arrest. You're buckin' the law. I'll back the law to the limit, and that means you're fair game for the first man that can throw his sights on you and bring you down."

Bob nodded, and pointed along the trail with his six-gun. "Better get goin'. And be careful how you come back, Nichols. This isn't Anchor range. They don't waste much love on you up here."

11

Bob waited until Nichols was out of sight around a lower turning and then picked up the guns—the sheriff's .45 in its belt and the bullet-damaged Winchester—and reined the roan across to the creekbank and down into the stream. Keeping to the gravelly bed of the creek, he started upvalley, trying to think out an idea that had struck him a few minutes ago. The idea was elusive, hard to fit in with what he knew.

He had gone less than half a mile and was almost within sight of his own pasture when he heard the quick hoof drum of a pony, coming toward him along the trail. It was George Beeson, riding one of Bob's bronchos bareback. Beeson carried a Winchester, and there was an ugly, wary look on his face as he scanned the trail ahead. Bob hailed him.

Beeson's look was one of plain relief as he rode across to the creekbank. "That shootin'? What was it?" he asked.

Bob held up the Winchester and the sheriff's gun belt. It was answer enough, for Beeson breathed an oath and his eyes widened and he said in sarcasm: "That's all right for now. But what about later, when they get a posse up here and start pushin' the rest of us around? This'll bust it wide open, Bob. We'd have stood a better chance if you'd gone on trial."

Bob gravely shook his head. "They'd have framed the rest of you along with me. George, you damn' near let it slip about that gray horse of mine."

Beeson frowned. "I don't get it," he said. "There was your proof. Why didn't you let me tell it? Nichols wouldn't have had a leg to stand on."

"Neither would we."

Beeson was plainly puzzled. "You're talkin' around it. What's on your mind?"

"Plenty, George. If you'd traded a horse to a strange wrangler outfit, and if that horse turned up a few days later shot from under a rustler, what would you think?"

"I'd think the sheriff ought to know about it. I'd think maybe the horse trader crew had run off that herd."

"That's one answer. Only you're forgettin' that they were still camped on the flats below here last night when we rode down to your place after that keg of nails. Remember, we saw their fire and the chuck wagon. If they were the ones that did the job, they'd be makin' themselves plenty scarce around here."

Beeson nodded an agreement but complained: "We ain't any further than when we started."

"We will be. And here's why. One of that horse trader crew hired out to Nichols last week, breakin' bronc's at ten dollars a head. He's stayin' in the Anchor bunkhouse while the rest of the outfit works the spreads south of Anchor. We don't know who did this, who tried to frame it on us. But we do know that gray horse of mine . . . the one they bought . . . was mixed up in this. Now, if I pay that wrangler a visit and make him a certain proposition, it's goin' to get back to Nichols damned quick if they had anything to do with this."

"What sort of a proposition?"

"Leave that to me. Here's a job for you, George. Get the rest. . . ."

Beeson cut in: "You can't ride out there on the flats to see that horse trader! Every jasper within fifty miles will be on the lookout for you. You don't think Nichols and the sheriff are forgettin' this, do you?"

"I'll go after dark," Bob told him. "Meantime, you've got

work to do. Nichols and Kemp and Ward will be back here within two hours with a posse. They won't expect to find me, but they'll lay down the law and warn the others to keep their heads, not to talk back. Let Nichols get it off his chest. After he's gone, every man is to start gatherin' his pasture herds. I want every steer on Skull Creek bunched in Lost Cañon by sunup tomorrow mornin'."

Beeson's glance sharpened. "That's a hell of a lot of work to do in one night!"

"I know, but it can be done. It has to be. Leave one man to see that the herd doesn't drift and tell the rest to meet me at that big, dead cottonwood along Anchor's east fence an hour before dark tomorrow night."

"Why? What's all this gettin' us?"

"I'll tell you along with the rest, tomorrow night."

"How about Ormsby and Getchell and the rest? They're family men. If you're buyin' into a fight with Anchor, they'll pull out."

Bob said intently: "Don't let 'em back out. Tell them there won't be any fight. They won't even need their guns."

"You sure o' that?" Beeson asked. Then he saw that his doubts were out of place, and added: "It ain't that I don't trust you, Bob. You brought us up here in the first place, showed us how to ditch our fields, and build something from nothin'. But I'm plain scared, and I don't give a damn who knows it! Nichols is a range hog, and our buckin' him is like a few flies tryin' to pester a steer."

"You've got it wrong, George. Nichols isn't a range hog. I think he's honest. Ten to one he doesn't know any more about this than we do."

"Then who the hell does?"

"That's what we're goin' to all this trouble to find out."

Beeson let out a gusty sigh of helplessness. "I'll do my

best," he said soberly. "Only I hope you know what you're lettin' us in for."

"I will before the night's over," Bob told him.

A studied gravity was written on Beeson's face long after he watched Bob ride off through the timber that climbed the slope of a low hill to the west of the creek. Then, with a feeling of foreboding too strong in him to be ignored, Beeson rode slowly back to Bob's cabin and saddled his horse and started up the valley to spread the word to his homesteader neighbors.

At eight that night, with the faint light of the myriad stars winking down out of the black void of the sky to show him his way, Bob rode in toward the fire near the horse trader's chuck wagon far out on the flats below the foot of the valley. Close in, he made out four figures hunkered down near the fire, two others moving about in the shadows beyond. When he had ridden the roan well into the circle of firelight to bring their glances swinging around to him, he reined in and said: "'Evenin'. Is the boss around?"

A burly, thick-shouldered man with a ragged beard stubble on his face came slowly to his feet: "I'm Jacobs. What can I do for you?" The horse trader's glance narrowed in recognition, and he added: "Ain't the sheriff lookin' for you?"

Bob's freckled face took on a good-natured grin. "So they tell me. Can I have a private talk with you, Jacobs?"

The horse trader's glance took in the low-hanging .45 strapped to Bob's waist, the .32-20 Winchester he held cradled across the swell of his saddle. "Not while you pack all that artillery, you can't," he drawled.

Bob swung the Winchester out and dropped it to the ground. He unbuckled the sheriff's belt and gun and tossed it across to where the Winchester lay.

A down-lipped smile took possession of Jacobs's face. Lazily, he thrust a hand in under his loose-hanging coat and brought it out, fisting a six-gun. The weapon fell into line with Bob. "They didn't tell me you was this much of a sucker, Phelan," his grating voice intoned. He laughed mockingly. "That five hundred reward is goin' to come in mighty handy." He called loudly: "Sid, bring across a rope, and we'll tie him!"

Bob drawled: "I still want that talk with you, Jacobs."

"What good's a talk goin' to do you now?" Jacobs asked.

"Because what I'm goin' to put you next to will make Nichols's five hundred look like bean money." Bob saw Jacobs's expression gradually change, and a greediness come to his eyes. He drove home his point by adding: "You've got nothin' to lose by listenin'. Only our talk has to be alone."

Jacobs's three companions had risen to their feet. A fourth man came across from the chuck wagon, carrying a coil of rope. Jacobs motioned him to stay where he was, finally said: "Clear out. I'll hear what he has to say."

They drifted into the shadows beyond the fire. Bob swung his short frame down out of the saddle and sauntered across to where Jacobs stood. He looked down at the six-gun in the horse trader's hand and said caustically: "You still need that?"

Suspicion lurked in Jacob's eyes as he thrust the .45 back into his belt. He took a step backward that put him well out of reach. "What's the play?" he asked warily.

"First, what happened to that gray gelding I traded you last week?"

Jacobs said: "I heard about that. I sold that jughead to a stranger headed through here the day I got it from you. I've got his horse to prove it."

Bob nodded off-handedly: "I figured something like that

must have happened. It doesn't matter." He fixed Jacobs with a level stare and asked with abruptness: "Could you use a couple of thousand for three days' work?"

"Who the hell couldn't?"

"This John Nichols is tryin' to run the small outfits out of the Skull Creek graze," Bob went on. "I've found a way to frame him like he did me. Only you'll be the one to cash in."

Jacobs's manner underwent a subtle change, one that erased his suspicion and put in its place a studied belligerence. "Sounds forked to me," he flared. "I'm an honest man in an honest business."

Bob's brows raised in mock surprise. "Then I've come to the wrong man."

The horse trader frowned, seeing that he'd gone a little too far. "I'll hear what you have to say."

"Not if you're so damned careful."

"Supposin' I ain't so careful?" Jacobs's curiosity was obviously getting the better of him. "I might listen, if you make it worth my while."

"No, you wouldn't do. The man I'm lookin' for has to be blind in one eye and know how to stay three jumps ahead of the law."

Jacobs's thick-lipped mouth took on a down-curving smile. His hand strayed upward toward his belt. "You're makin' tall talk for a man with five hundred on his head." When he saw that this indirect thrust had no visible effect on Bob, he let his hand fall to his side and went on more intently: "See here. Maybe I've done a job or two in my time that wasn't accordin' to the rules. Maybe I haven't a bill of sale for all these lugheads in my string. Maybe we could swing this thing you're talkin' about."

"That's more like it," Bob drawled. "Did you hear what happened up the valley this afternoon?"

Jacobs nodded: "You threw down on Nichols and his understrapper and the sheriff. They came back with a posse and gave those outfits up there two weeks to clear out of the country."

This last was news to Bob, yet it only made a certainty of what he had expected Nichols would do. It didn't alter the thing he had come to see Jacobs about, so he said: "I wanted to make sure you knew about it. We think we've found a way to even things with Nichols."

"That's a big order."

"Not so big, if it's played right. You throw in with us and we'll make that Anchor bunch eat crow."

"Unh-uh, not me. I ain't buckin' the big augur in this country. I've got a livin' to make."

"Wait'll you hear how the cards lay. Tomorrow mornin' the Skull Creek outfits are starting to gather the critters they don't have on graze higher in the hills. There'll be about three hundred head, and it'll take all day tomorrow and the early part of the night to get 'em bunched and into that big pasture below my place. The pasture's fenced, and once they're there, we can forget 'em. Here's. . . ."

"Why you goin' to all that trouble?"

"Because we know we didn't drive off that herd of Nichols's the other night. He did it himself, to give him the excuse for runnin' us out. If he'd do that, he might send men in to make a try at our herds. We aren't takin' chances from here on."

Jacobs nodded, then queried: "Where do I come in?"

"I'll get to that. Tomorrow night we ought to have the herd gathered and in the pasture no later than eight o'clock. It'll be a long day's work, and everyone will be tuckered out. We'll get some sleep and get ready for what's comin' the next night. Nichols won't know what we've done, and we won't even have to throw a guard on the herd."

"What's comin' the next night?" Jacobs's eyes were slitted now as he regarded Bob.

"That's where you come in. Night after next I can give you six men to help gather every last steer in Nichols's east pasture. He won't be expectin' this . . . won't have a man ridin' fence unless it's along his north line where the herd went through the other night. We'll work that east pasture with a dozen men, yours and mine. We'll have the herd halfway to the peaks by sunup. Your outfit can make the drive from there on while my men get back to the valley so they can be seen and have alibis. You'll be across the pass and into the next county before night. There's a sheriff over there who's easy to get on with. He'll put you next to half a dozen quick markets, providin' your price is right. In two days you clean up twice as much as you would workin' a year."

Jacobs queried warily: "What about my chuck wagon and this horse herd?"

"You've got two days to get your outfit across the county line twenty miles west and get back here. Leave one man in charge of the outfit. We'll need all the others."

"What're you gettin' out of this?"

"Not a damned thing but seein' Nichols pay for what he'll steal anyway," Bob drawled. "We're through here, and we know it." He paused briefly, then asked: "Is it a deal?"

Jacobs's answer was long in coming. As he hesitated, there was one fleeting instant when Bob caught the hint of a predatory smile on his face. Then he said affably: "I'd be ten kinds of a fool to turn it down."

Bob reached to his hip pocket and took out a sack of tobacco and built a cigarette, passing across the makings to Jacobs when he'd finished. "There's a big dead cottonwood four miles down along Anchor's east fence," he said. "We'll meet you there night after next, right at dark. Anything else you want to ask about?"

Jacobs shook his head. "We'll be there," he said.

Bob faced halfway about and nodded to his guns lying on the ground. Jacobs caught the gesture, said: "Take 'em. You'll maybe need 'em."

A quarter of a mile east of the horse trader's camp, Bob started a wide swing that put him finally at an equal distance to the north, in the direction of Anchor headquarters. He reined in below the crest of a hogback and came out of the saddle and clamped his hand over the roan's nostrils and stood there, waiting. In less than two minutes the hoof drum of a fast-running pony sounded into the stillness. The rider, forking a paint horse, passed close enough so that Bob could faintly see him. He was out of hearing in less than half a minute, going away fast.

Two hours later, Bob was waiting at the same spot and saw the rider on the paint horse go past on his way back toward the fire. There was only one answer to explain where Jacobs's man had gone during those two hours. Anchor was the only outfit that lay to the north. Jacobs had sent a man across to Anchor, a man who went in a hurry. Bob would have given a lot to know what man Jacobs's rider had passed the word to at Anchor that night.

III

The sun was a huge disk of orange fire hanging above the far, flat horizon when Bob rode in toward the gray, dead cottonwood along Anchor's east fence late the next afternoon, a day earlier than his agreed meeting there with Jacobs. At a hundred yards' distance, he counted eight riders grouped under the tree. He rode in toward the cottonwood, a sober and thoughtful man with a two-day growth of sandy beard stubble on his freckled face. He looked hard-bitten and tough. He reined in a good distance from the group of waiting men and surveyed them for a moment. George Beeson was there, along with Ed Ormsby and his full-grown son, Frank Getchell and Bill Crawford, Tom Oaks and Sam Cherry, and old Nate Dennis—all Skull Creek men. They returned his sober stare with a like gravity, and finally George Beeson said: "We did like you said, Bob. Sims is holdin' the herd up Lost Cañon. We're set to go."

Nate Dennis hunched his stooped shoulders nervously, and qualified Beeson's statement by growling: "We're set, providin' you tell us what you've let us in for. I ain't goin' to cut my own throat for nothin'."

Bob sloped out of the saddle, ground-haltered the roan, and walked over to the group. "Here's the way it shapes up," he said, and squatted down on his heels so that he could look up into the circle of faces. He began talking. Once he picked up a stick, swept the sandy ground smooth before him, and drew a crude diagram in the dust. He looked up at them from time to time to observe any change of expression on their faces. There was little for him to see. Once he answered a snappish question of old Nate Dennis's; a second time he repeated a point, when Ed Ormsby frowned in puzzlement.

Finally he was through talking. He came to his feet and gestured toward the west with a wide sweep of his arm. "There they are," he said, "ready and waitin'. They weren't expectin' this until tomorrow night. If it doesn't work the way I say it will, we'll drive 'em back in here and no one'll be any the wiser."

They all turned to look out across Anchor's four-wire fence and down across a broad, rolling sweep of grass range where dozens of small bunches of shorthorn cattle were grazing. They were four miles to the south of Anchor's north line, seven miles from Anchor headquarters.

George Beeson finally moved his head in a slow nod of conviction. "He's right. We ain't runnin' much risk. Today we seen fence riders workin' that north stretch, but they'll never bother with this now. There's plenty of grass, so we won't be raisin' any dust that could be seen. Sounds like sense to me."

The others were slow in agreeing, but when their consent came, it was definite and final, and no doubts remained with them.

Twenty minutes later, ten rods of Anchor wire was down and the nine riders, Bob included, were far out in the pasture and working the small bunches of cattle in toward the opening in the fence. When the quick dusk had deepened into full darkness an hour and a quarter after the gather had started, a bunch of roughly three hundred Anchor-branded steers were being hazed slowly east from the fence, toward the timbered slopes of the hills that marked the line of Skull Creek Valley.

By nine o'clock the herd was being choused through the wide gate at the upper end of Bob Phelan's pasture. By nine-thirty the steers were spread out across the pasture, grazing, and Bob had sent his neighbors on home, all but George Beeson. He and George were in the loft of the barn, sitting on a mound of hay near the open loft door.

"You may be wrong about this, Bob. You're workin' on nothing but a hunch," Beeson said once, voicing his doubts.

"There's always a chance I'm wrong. But I still think there were men back there in the timber, watching us. The way we came in, they'll think it was our own stuff bein' driven down after the gather today."

They sat listening, waiting, for long minutes. Finally Beeson broke the prolonged silence by saying: "It's turned cloudy. Makes it as dark as the inside of a well out there."

"All the better," Bob replied. "They won't spot the brands."

Five minutes after he had spoken, they were listening to the muffled hoof whisper of a pair of horses being walked in from the pasture gate. Bob peered out into the darkness and thought he saw the shapes of two riders, moving in toward his cabin. In a few more seconds a call echoed down from the cabin: "No one here!"

From then on the many sounds that came to them out of the night were the only things to tell them what was happening in the pasture below. There came the low mutter of many hoofs striking against the soft turf, of cattle on the move. A few low, gruff cries sounded as riders worked the herd down the pasture. Those sounds faded gradually, until at length a complete silence set in once again.

Beeson said: "It'd make me a damn' sight surer, if we followed 'em a ways."

"Can't take the chance, George." Bob stood up. "We'd better be on our way."

They climbed down out of the barn loft. They had left

their horses far back in the timber up the side of the gradual hill slope behind the cabin. Passing the cabin, Bob drawled: "I'm lucky they didn't burn me out." Once in the saddle they came down and passed the cabin and took the trail Bob had ridden yesterday afternoon with Kemp and Nichols and the sheriff. Bob took the lead, alternately running and trotting the roan at a mile-eating, fast pace. At the lower end of the valley they struck another trail that came to right angles with the one they were traveling. Bob turned into it, striking west, and after four miles of steady going he could make out a winking light ahead and knew it to be coming from a window of Anchor's sprawling adobe ranch house.

When he saw the light, he reined in. "Got the story straight, George?" he queried.

"As straight as I'll ever have it. Only Nichols ain't goin' to swallow it."

"We'll make him." Bob touched the roan's flanks with his spurs and went on.

They pulled in to a slow trot as they took the lane that led in between two tall rows of poplars toward the house. They were halfway across the open yard before a call came from far off to the left, in the direction of the bunkhouse. Bob ignored the challenge, swung down out of the saddle, and let his hand fall to the Colt he wore at his thigh. He ran on across the yard, Beeson close behind him, and was in under the wide-roofed portal before the voice called again, sharper this time: "Who's there?"

Long acquaintance with the place told him that the lighted window was the one in John Nichols's small office. He headed for the door that opened into the room, and threw it open without knocking.

As he stepped in, John Nichols wheeled around from his desk in his swivel chair, raising one hand to shield his eyes against the light of an unshaded lamp on the desktop. A bulky ledger was open on the desk before him. Nichols's eyes widened as he recognized Bob and George Beeson. George swung the door shut.

Bob said: "I'm here to collect on that bet, Nichols."

In the two-second silence that hung on after his words, a side door to the room swung forward. Bob wheeled about, his hand streaking to his holster. When he saw Christine Nichols standing in the doorway, his hand dropped, and he drawled: "Come on in, Chris. You might as well hear this."

Nichols's tall frame had gradually gone rigid in the chair. He now snapped bluntly: "How'd you get in here?"

As if in answer to his query, a loud knock sounded at the outside door. It swung open an instant later, with Bob dodging in behind it and drawing his six-gun. The man in the doorway cradled a Winchester in his hands. He saw George Beeson and swung the rifle around on him, rasping: "Want me to throw him out, boss?"

Bob kicked the door shut, and the Anchor crewman whirled to face him, swinging his rifle around. But the blunt snout of Bob's .45 carried its threat, and the Winchester didn't complete the swing. George Beeson reached out and relieved the man of his weapon.

The girl's face was pale, and John Nichols's look was one of mixed rage and bafflement.

Bob said: "We haven't much time, Nichols. I told you I'd get proof. I've got it. Saddle up a horse and come along."

"Come where?" Nichols blazed.

"To see one of your herds headed for the peaks."

Nichols jerked straighter in his chair. His look changed to one of incredulity.

"Better hurry," Bob went on. "Give me your word you'll come along and not lay a hand on me, and you can bring as many men as you want . . . and have them bring guns."

Nichols came up out of the chair. He said tersely to his crewman: "You heard what he said. Get every man and be ready to start in ten minutes." He waited until his crewman had gone out the door and then looked once again at Bob, who had now holstered his .45. "Let's have it straight, Phelan."

"I told you none of our bunch had stolen that herd . . . told you I'd prove it. George and I have taken the trouble to ride your fences. Tonight, less than an hour ago, your east fence was cut and a herd driven off toward the hills." He told the lie flatly, his expression inscrutable. "We're here to take you up there and round up the men who did it."

Nichols's taut expression was slow in relaxing. He breathed a crisp oath and, looking levelly at Bob, said: "If this is a trick, you'll pay for it, Phelan."

Bob's next move surprised George Beeson even more than it did John Nichols and his daughter. He unbuckled his gun belt and tossed it across onto the rancher's desk.

"You're callin' the turn from now on, Nichols. All I want is to come along."

Later, in the bare yard before Anchor's ranch house, Bob surveyed the knot of mounted riders gathered in wait for Nichols. He asked the rancher: "Where's Ed Kemp?"

"At the north line shack with the crew that's ridin' fence up there. We'll pick him up on the way." Nichols turned to his daughter, who had followed them from the office. "You're to stay here, Chris."

The girl nodded, yet Bob thought he saw a flashing smile cross her face as she looked at her father. He and George went across to their horses, climbed into the saddle, and rode in alongside John Nichols as the rancher led his men out the lane toward the trail.

The north line shack was empty when the Anchor men stopped there after half an hour's fast riding. "Never mind," Nichols said. "Kemp's on the job out along the fence. We won't waste time findin' him. If we swing off to the west, we ought to hit the *malpais* beds about sunup. The herd won't have worked any farther than that." His glance came across to Bob. "Maybe I'm takin' back a lot of things I've said about you, Phelan. But I'm keepin' your iron until I'm plenty sure." He was wearing two guns, and, as he spoke, he slapped the holster at his left thigh, Bob's, and then gave the order to go on.

IV

A mile below the V-shaped pass between two high granite peaks, John Nichols and Bob Phelan stood on a rock promontory and looked out across a rocky, uptilted maze of hills. The long line of the herd was crawling upward toward them along the bed of a wide cañon, now plain enough so that they could distinguish individual animals. The sun was an hour high and drove elongated shadows of the land's broken contours toward the west.

Nichols said finally: "We'd better get down before they see us. How many men can you spot, Phelan?"

"Seven."

"I counted eight." He turned and started down the steep side of the barren hill toward his Anchor crewman bunched below. Halfway down the slope he stopped abruptly and unbelted Bob's holster and handed it to him, saying bluntly: "You wouldn't be damn' fool enough to be here, if those were your men drivin' the herd. Take it . . . you may need it."

Nichols took less than three minutes in placing his men, sending half of them across to the opposite side of the steep draw through which the herd must travel to reach the pass. His parting word to them was ominous: "Wait'll they're close. Wait for me to shoot first." He was already holding the .30-30 Winchester that had until now been in the scabbard below his saddle.

George Beeson found an opportunity to talk to Bob alone before he left with the men who were to take the opposite side of the draw. "You thinkin' the same thing I am, Bob?" he queried. "If you are, Nichols is in for one hell of a surprise."

"Keep it to yourself, George," Bob told him, and left him to go with Nichols in behind a high rock outcropping close in to the bottom of the draw, barely out of the path the herd must take when it came through.

Twenty minutes later, the point rider leading the herd came around a shallow bend a hundred yards below and headed into the foot of the draw. He made a squat shape in the saddle, and at sight of his dark-bearded face Nichols let out a muttered oath and asked Bob: "Isn't that Jacobs, the horse trader?"

"Looks like it."

They were silent as the long line of Anchor-branded steers formed in behind Jacobs. Two swing riders came beyond the turning, pivoting their ponies out and in to turn unruly and bolting steers back into the herd. Nichols's glance clung longest to a rider wearing a light-gray Stetson, and he finally caught his breath and exclaimed: "That's Barns, the man I hired from Jacobs to break out some bronc's. What's he doin' here?"

Bob's only answer was a shake of his head. Jacobs was even with them now, a bare thirty yards out from the outcropping. The hoof thunder of the strung-out cattle had mounted to a low roar. Nichols squinted into the dust fog, saw the four drag riders making the bend below, and raised his Winchester.

Bob reached out and pushed the weapon down, saying: "Let the rest get close enough. This time no one gets away."

The rancher's nervousness increased during the next two minutes. At times, the four rustlers riding drag were blotted from sight by the boiling haze of dust kicked up by the herd. But finally those four were close, and Nichols was raising the Winchester once again, when a sudden gust of wind swept the dust cloud from in front of him, and he was staring at a tall man on a sleek black gelding.

"Kemp," he breathed, and jerked his head around at Bob. "You knew?"

"Not for sure," Bob said. His homely, freckled face was taut and there was as much disbelief written in his expression as in the rancher's.

A rising rage lightened Nichols's eyes. He suddenly stood up and in plain sight of Ed Kemp and Jacobs's three riders who were bringing up the drag. Bob tried to reach out and stop him, but the rancher had stepped from behind the protecting rock shoulder before he could prevent it.

Nichols had taken four full strides before one of Jacobs's men saw him and called out sharply to warn Ed Kemp. The Anchor ramrod's glance whipped around. He saw who it was, and suddenly his hand stabbed down to his right thigh.

Nichols caught that gesture of guilt and seemed stunned by it. For a fraction of a second he made no move to swing up the rifle, and then it was too late for him to match Kemp's swift draw.

Bob saw all this and understood it, and lunged from behind the outcropping as Kemp's hand streaked upward. Bob's palm slapped the walnut handle of his six-gun and flicked it from leather in a blur of speed. He wasn't fast enough. A fraction of a second before his weapon tilted into line, Ed Kemp's Colt stabbed powder flame in a burst of sound muffled by the hoof rumble of the herd. John Nichols stumbled back a step as the bullet caught him.

Bob's .45 opened up in a staccato chant of exploding gun thunder. Kemp's tall body stiffened, squared itself, and his weapon swung around on Bob as other guns added to this riot of sound. Once again Kemp's tall frame jerked, and once more he tried to line his Colt. Then a bullet drove him back out of the saddle. He clutched frantically at the horn to stop his fall, but his hand clawed empty air and his horse lunged and he was down.

A dozen rifles were throwing lead at Jacobs and his riders. Two went down and were lost as their horses bolted away and left them to the trampling hoofs of the herd that was milling about and threatening to stampede at the unexpected burst of gunfire. Bob read the signs as the herd slowly turned and started back down the draw. He leathered his .45 and started a run out to where Nichols lay as the fear-crazed animals broke into a dozen separate bunches and came on toward him.

The guns from the rocky sides of the draw quickened their fire. The cattle were at a full run now. Bob reached Nichols and lifted his heavy frame onto his shoulders and staggered back toward the outcropping. A steer plunged madly past him, one long horn ripping the sleeve of his shirt to tatters. Another swung into him, knocking him down. He got up again and barely avoided the rush of another fast-moving bunch. He made the outcropping, lifted the rancher's inert body onto a shoulder-high shelf, and climbed up himself as the main body of the herd came even with the outcropping and came around the foot of it in a solidly packed mass of stampeding animals.

The rifle fire slacked off gradually as the tag ends of the herd raced down the draw and out of sight around the bend. Five riderless horses traveled with the herd. Two others were down. One of Jacobs's riders crawled on hands and knees up the near slope of the draw. Suddenly he paused long enough to raise his six-gun and fire two shots at one of Nichols's crewmen, coming down toward him. The Anchor man's rifle answered with one sharp, exploding shot that flattened the rustler to the ground. That shot was the last.

Bob had been held this past minute in an awe brought on

by seeing men die and trampled beneath the sharp hoofs of the stampeding herd. Now he looked down at John Nichols to see that the rancher's eyes were open and staring up at him. Nichols's right shoulder was matted with blood that crept downward along the sleeve of his shirt.

Bob ripped away the shirt to see the ugly hole in the shoulder. He tore the sleeve into strips and began bandaging to stop the flow of blood. "Bone busted," he said after a moment. "We'll have to get you in to a doctor."

"I'd be coyote bait by now, if it wasn't for you, Phelan," Nichols said in a voice that grated in pain. "Why'd you risk your neck to save a man that's hounded you the way I have?"

Bob didn't answer him, for at that moment a cry came from near at hand: "Dad!"

It was Christine Nichols, reining a palomino horse out from the steep slope of the draw ten yards away. Her eyes were bright in fear as she came down out of the saddle and ran toward the outcropping. When she stood below Bob, she said in a hushed voice: "I had to come. Is he . . . is . . . ?" She could get no further.

"Nothin' much wrong," Bob said in a drawl that immediately erased the fear from her eyes. "He's got a bullet in the shoulder. Bleedin' some. But it's nothin' he won't get over in a hurry."

The girl choked back a sob of gladness and took Bob's hand and let him lift her onto the outcropping. Anchor men were coming down off the hill slopes now. One of them came over to the outcropping. His look sobered as he saw Nichols lying there, but the expression on the rancher's face reassured him.

"We can't make head nor tail o' this, boss," he said. "The boys are saying that that mess out there was Ed Kemp before the herd walked over him." He nodded toward the spot where

Kemp had fallen from his horse.

When Chris's eyes instinctively turned out there, Bob reached out and gently tilted her head aside. "I wouldn't," he said. Then to the Anchor man: "What about the others?"

"Two got away. Three cashed in. They're bringin' another over to see Nichols."

It was Jacobs, the horse trader, who was brought across to the outcropping a minute later. George Beeson and another man were carrying him, for he had a broken leg and a bad flesh wound in his side. Beeson looked up at the rancher, who had pushed himself to a sitting position, and asked bluntly: "Do we take him in to jail or hang him here?"

"What's he got to say?"

"Wants to get his hands on Bob," Beeson said. "Something about bein' double-crossed." His face took on a tight smile. "Supposin' you tell 'em what he's talking about, Bob?"

Bob told Nichols what had happened. When he mentioned his visit to the wrangler's camp and the proposition he had made Jacobs, Nichols asked sharply: "You wanted him to steal my herd?"

Bob nodded: "But it wasn't his fault he did. He thought he was stealing our critters, not yours. Our herd was never in my pasture. It's safe up Lost Cañon. After your men had shot that gray gelding of mine from under that rustler, I had the hunch that Jacobs's men were in on the frame-up but were somehow protected. At first I thought you might be protecting them. Then I wasn't so sure. A good way to find out was by inviting Jacobs and whoever he was working with to steal our herd out of the valley, invitin' him indirectly. I told Jacobs where they'd be last night, told him they wouldn't be guarded. Instead of our herd being in my pasture, it was yours."

Nichols said: "Yet you rode across to Anchor to get me. Why?"

"I had to know for sure. But it was plain from the first that you didn't know about it. Once I'd proved to myself you weren't in it, I didn't know any more than you . . . until we found Kemp missin' at the line shack."

"Then you were sure it was him?"

"It couldn't have been anyone else. It always riled Ed to see how well I got on with Chris. He had the best reason for hating me." Bob glanced down into Jacobs's sneering face. "Kemp hired you to do that first job, didn't he?"

Jacobs breathed an obscene oath that was cut off abruptly by George Beeson's fist striking his mouth. Bob went on: "You don't have to talk, but it'll go a long way toward savin' your hide, Jacobs. How much did Kemp pay you?"

Beeson growled: "You heard what he asked. Spill your guts, Jacobs!" He drew his fist back again for another blow.

Jacobs cringed, then said sullenly: "Not a damned dollar! We was to get what we could in the next county for the critters. That was all the pay he offered us. We'd have been clear that first time, if that fence rider hadn't spotted the break in the wire half a day too early. Kemp wasn't expectin' that. He killed Barney Drew himself. Drew remembered him ridin' across to my horse camp two days before it happened."

Nichols was scowling fiercely now. He shot a question: "Why didn't Kemp turn the herd back this mornin' when it got light enough for him to read the brands?"

"He wanted to see us safe through the pass. Then he was headin' back to frame it on the Skull Creek ranchers. He said he knew how to do it."

Nichols said: "Take him away before I get my hands on a gun." His glance clung to the horse trader until he'd been carried across to a horse and roped into a saddle. Then he looked at Bob and his weathered face broke into a bleak smile, and he said: "I pay off my bets, Phelan."

"What bets?" Chris asked.

Her father turned his glance at her. "Aren't you sorry about Ed?"

"I'm sorry he had to die," she said. Then, with a quick look at Bob, her face took on a riot of confusion, and she added haltingly: "But, Dad, I never wanted to marry him."

Nichols looked at Bob and slowly shook his head. "I never knew a man so all-fired sure of himself. Go on, collect that bet."

Bob did.

About the Author

Peter Dawson is the *nom de plume* used by Jonathan Hurff Glidden. He was born in Kewanee, Illinois, and was graduated from the University of Illinois with a degree in English literature. In his career as a Western writer he published sixteen Western novels and wrote over one hundred and twenty Western short novels and short stories for the magazine market. From the beginning he was a dedicated craftsman who revised and polished his fiction until it shone as a fine gem. His Peter Dawson novels are noted for their adept plotting, interesting and well-developed characters, their authentically researched historical backgrounds, and his stylistic flair. During the Second World War, Glidden served with the U. S. Strategic and Tactical Air Force in the United Kingdom. Later in 1950 he served for a time as Assistant to Chief of Station in Germany. After the war, his novels were frequently serialized in *The Saturday Evening Post*. Peter Dawson titles such as GUNSMOKE GRAZE, ROYAL GORGE, and RULER OF THE RANGE are generally conceded to be among his best titles, although he was an extremely consistent writer, and virtually all his fiction has retained its classic stature among readers of all generations. One of Jon Glidden's finest techniques was his ability, after the fashion of Dickens and Tolstoy, to tell his stories via a series of dramatic vignettes which focus on a wide assortment of different characters, all tending to develop their own lives, situations, and predicaments, while at the same time propelling the general plot of the story toward a suspenseful conclusion. He was no less gifted as a master of the short novel and short story. DARK

RIDERS OF DOOM (Five Star Westerns, 1996) was the first collection of his Western short novels and stories to be published. His next **Five Star title** will be CLAIMING OF THE DEERFOOT: A WESTERN TRIO.